Five Days

Elite Escorts MM 5

Lynn Burke

Five Days

Five drama-free days in paradise.

That was my expectation when I found out I'd been hired as a companion for a vacation on a tropical island off Mexico's shore. I didn't expect to fall in lust at first sight with Callum, but his wary, stoic nature promised pleasuring the client would be an enjoyable task.

But Callum threw a curveball my way in the form of an unexpected guest I just happened to know—and hate.

Landon's arrival brings back the troubling past I attempted to leave behind no matter how much I've pined for him. There's no forgiveness for how he betrayed me, but the men's proximity and persistence toward resolution are breaking down my walls.

I hoped for a relaxing getaway with sand between my toes and sun warming my skin, but I'm tempted to spend more time between the sheets than on the beach.

Those five days in heaven I'd hoped for?

They might end up leaving me in hell if I don't guard my heart.

Prologue - Zack

"I didn't do that," I stated, my guts in knots and forehead dented with a deep frown. Leaning forward in my chair, I picked up one of the pictures Elite's gay branch manager, Sean Fox, had indicated atop his desk between us.

Being falsely accused of sexual assault as a teenager had gotten me kicked out of my foster home, and now having it happen while on the job as an escort riled shit back up. My stomach clenched to the point of nausea.

I remembered the night in the images from a few weeks earlier as clear as though it'd been yesterday. The guy had asked me to make it appear as though I was rough with him. Push him against the wall with faked intent to hurt him. Pretend to choke him out. He'd claimed he had a role-playing kink, and as an EEMM employee, I aimed to fulfill his fantasies in a safe environment.

Causing pain wasn't my thing—but there was *one* little asshole I wouldn't mind choking out until he begged me to let him live.

Whenever I thought of what happened fifteen years ago

with him, my blood sizzled from righteous anger and lust alike. He deserved my rage in spades. But physical hunger? I hated that I still wanted him and that he *still* wouldn't leave me alone, no matter how many times I'd attempted to block him.

Well, fuck the asshole from my past, and fuck my one-time client Jackson Zerig, who was now going to throw me under the bus.

Teeth clenched, I looked at the second image of Jackson that showed a close-up of his neck where I'd supposedly marked him. Bruising appeared on his skin, but there was no way those were my fingerprints. He'd specifically asked me to not hold him too tightly.

So I hadn't.

Please the client—those were words we Elite Escorts lived by, and I tried to always keep the peace and stay out of drama.

"He's demanding two million in cash, or he'll leak these to the press," Sean stated, his voice shaken.

Blood drained from my face, and I jerked my focus off the images to meet my manager's troubled expression. "But I didn't do this! I barely put any pressure on his neck!"

Sean swallowed before assuring me he believed me. Promised I had nothing to worry about.

"Tell me what happened—every detail and word you can remember," Sean said, so same as always, I did as requested. In my book, honesty was the best policy.

Reliving that night *twice* aloud to make sure I didn't remember something wrong only caused my twisted stomach to worsen.

We went over the contract Jackson had signed along with his listed limits. He'd wanted to be wined and dined— his exact words—and seeing as how I was Elite's best at setting clients at ease, Sean had assigned me to him for the evening.

The fucker had set me up. Used me in the hopes of swindling money out of Elite.

"You're booked tonight then again on Friday, right?" Sean asked as I finally got up to leave.

"Yeah." I pulled my car keys from my pocket, half expecting him to suggest I take a few days off until shit got straightened out.

"Are they new or returning clients?"

"Returning."

Lips pursed, he nodded while gathering up the falsified yet damning pictures still strewn over his desk. "I know I don't have to tell you to be careful. Along with Drake, you're one of the best escorts we have. Rave reviews. Weekly requests. You've made quite a name for yourself, so fingers crossed this shit will only end up being a bump in the road."

Swallowing hard, I nodded. How long had it been since someone had my back?

My afternoon had been ruined, and my thoughts jumbled like a riotous mess that wouldn't allow me to consider much else as I exited the building.

Ever since I'd been forced to go off on my own at eighteen, I'd been living by the rules as much as possible. Doing whatever work I could find to keep my head above water. And now, some asshole hoping to make a quick buck had to go and drag me into unwanted drama.

I'd always feared being accused of something else. It was why I didn't trust people and had chosen to only look out for myself.

When the senator's son had done this to me while we'd been teens, I'd moved to another state and started over, heartbroken and aimlessly wandering. I'd recognized I had no one to rely on but myself. No family. No close friends.

But now?

Jaw clenched, I turned my car back toward Boston, the place I'd come to love. The rich suburbs were beautiful and all, but the city was my home. I'd found a quasi-family in EEMM, bound by our work that straddled legal lines. Before I'd left, Sean said he and his brother, who owned Elite Escorts, would take care of the attempts at extortion. I had no choice but to believe him, as neither man had let me down yet.

At least I had no record staining my past should the event end up going to trial. It'd been my foster brother who'd initiated the affair by stripping down and climbing on top of me, dragging me from sleep. He'd intended to gift me his virgin ass as a present for my eighteenth birthday.

He hadn't taken my refusal to break him in too well but hadn't given me time to explain that I *did* want him—once he came of age and I wouldn't get thrown into jail. I'd had no plans to leave our neighborhood once I'd graduated in two months, no thoughts of ever abandoning the kid who'd owned my heart.

And kinda still did no matter how hard I tried taking it back from his selfish grip.

True to himself, he'd thrown a nutty like the spoiled brat he was whenever he didn't get his way, not giving me a chance to assure him that I would claim his hole—eventually. His hollering and crying had drawn attention. His father, the senator, had crashed into my room, getting an eyeful of me trying to restrain his son from punching me for the fifth or sixth time.

It didn't matter blood ran from my broken nose or that I

was innocent. I lay atop my foster brother, my hands wrapped around his forearms and pressing him to the bed.

The little shit's screams of rage that he never wanted to see me again were the icing on the cake for his dad to assume the worst.

The senator had sent his son back to his own room, and the kid continued to rant his hatred of me until his bedroom door slammed closed behind him. Rather than pressing charges and dragging his family into negative drama, the senator had told me to leave. I'd had a single bag of belongings and a grand in cash he'd given me. Probably to make him feel better for tossing me from his home after acting as a parental figure for the previous seven years.

Things hadn't gone well for me after I'd left Rhode Island.

I'd made do on my own, eventually escaping the streets thanks to a real job that allowed me to rent an apartment. It had taken me over a decade, but I'd risen from the ashes, and I prayed like hell some money-hungry asshole didn't fuck up the good life I'd managed to create for myself.

Body still tensed into knots, I pulled into the parking garage for my condo's building off Storrow Drive. A few months after starting at EEMM, I'd been lucky to get a steal of a deal that included a living room view of the Charles River. While not as high-end as Drake or Sean's condos, I loved my place. It seemed like a real home with its comfortable furniture and older appliances.

It was also within walking distance of the shelter I volunteered at, the place that had kept me out of the cold, rain, and snow for longer than I cared to remember. I donated cash too since I had more than enough to live a meager existence while those less fortunate went without. Giving back offered me a sense of satisfaction, and I hoped they saw my actions as proof someone cared. I sure as fuck hadn't felt the sentiment while I'd been homeless.

I trudged through the hallway to my condo, let myself into the dim interior, and went straight for my bathroom. A client had booked me for the evening, one of my regulars, someone I trusted not to call a bullshit foul against my character.

Rarely did I need help in pleasing clients, but after manscaping, showering, and trimming my permanent scruff, I popped a little blue pill. Better to be safe than sorry.

I shouldn't have worried though.

Jamie met me at the hotel's door, his country-boy good looks and muscles hot as fuck. And a white-toothed smile lit his blue eyes, stirring lust that would ease my mind for a time.

Nothing about this night would be a chore.

The soft cushion of Jamie's lips met mine before I even kicked my shoes off, his hands greedy at my groin, making quick work of my button and zipper to get at my cock.

"Oh fuck, yeah," he groaned into my mouth as his hand wrapped around my thick length. "Been too fucking long, man. Need this dick."

"Whatever you want," I assured him as I did every client, but I couldn't have been more pleased to have him after the news I'd gotten earlier. Jamie never failed to meet me with hunger, an equal give and take that left me physically satisfied every time.

With a curse, he pulled away from me and yanked his shirt off, revealing ripples of muscle honed from years of playing football. He'd come down to Boston College on scholarship from some small town in the sticks of New Hampshire.

Other than that? I knew the guy could suck cock like a

pro. Had a tight, hot hole he enjoyed having stuffed full. He also had a nice, thick dick for when the time came to flip.

Jamie's knees hit the floor, his hands pulling down my jeans mid-thigh.

"Jesus," I hissed, head tipping back as his wet mouth closed over my cockhead. "Fuck, did I need this."

He hummed in agreement, his short hair prickling my palms as I clasped his head, allowing myself to get lost in the feel of his slick tongue and suction.

When I'd first sold my body, I'd been the one on my knees. Upon signing with Elite, I'd expected the same but had been thrilled to find those willing to pay for better service than a back-alley blowjob tended to have all sorts of wishes and kinks.

The extortion issue slammed into my brain, and I gritted my teeth, pulling Jamie off my dick when I should have let him have whatever he desired, what he paid for.

"Want your ass, Jamie. Now."

Pupils already blown, he nodded up at me. "I'm not the only one needy tonight, huh?" he asked with a smirk while pushing to his feet. A quick shove sent his jeans to the floor.

He'd gone commando, same as always.

And his cock reached for his belly button, pre-cum welling at the tip.

"Fuck yeah." I moved in close, palming his erection, smearing my thumb through his slickness. "Wet for me already."

"Been too long." He spun before I could take his mouth, bending over the end of the bed, juicy ass on display. "Fuck me clear into tomorrow morning, Zack. Give me all you've got."

"Goddamn." I palmed both cheeks, jiggling them. "Fuck." A quick swat, and I fished a condom and lube from my pocket before kicking my shoes and jeans off. "Want me to eat your ass or get straight to the fucking?" I asked, rolling the rubber over my aching length.

"Just shove it in, Zack. Wreck my hole, then I wanna switch and fill you the fuck up."

Growling my appreciation of his perfect plans for the evening, I quickly prepped him with one then two fingers.

"Hurry," he demanded through clenched teeth, shoulders bunched, hands gripping the sheets.

"So impatient."

"Fuck yeah, I am. Give it to—" The words ripped from his throat as I thrust deep into his ass, sinking over halfway.

He cursed, rising onto his toes, and I clasped his hips to hold him steady.

"You good?" I checked in.

"Fuck yeah. I like when it hurts."

I pulled out and stabbed in again, my balls resting against his cheeks. "You took every inch of me, Jamie."

"Fuck." He gulped, chest collapsing onto the bed, hands fisting the blankets.

"So sexy." I slid my hand up his arched spine, worshiping his gorgeous body he'd honed to perfection.

"Fuck me hard," he begged. "Need to feel you clear into next week when—shit. I can't even. Don't hold back, Zack. Please."

Same as always, I gave the client what he wanted, taking my pleasure then switching places so he could double his.

And obliterating my mind into silence.

Chapter 1

Zack

Seven Months Later

I loved fucking for money, but it'd been months since I'd had a break. The stress had kicked me in the balls when EEMM had almost been taken for two mil, and even though Sean and his brother, along with an ex-client hacker, had fixed the mess, I hadn't been able to set that shit aside as easily as everyone else.

Add in the fact the senator's son had somehow gotten my new cell number, and I'd walked a fine line of going feral on people's asses—and not in a good way—for a couple of weeks.

He texted the same as every time he managed to get in touch with me, asking if we could talk.

I had jack to say to him other than to fuck off, and there was nothing he could spew that would erase the betrayal that had ruined my life. Hadn't he figured that out after the similar responses I'd sent every time?

He'd fucked our friendship and knifed the love I'd had for him when he'd left me to deal with the fallout of his own goddamned selfishness.

What he'd done was unforgivable.

Period.

Automatic block—again.

But the reminder of my past had laid heavily on my mind, making my need of a little help to get it up almost a constant in the previous couple of months. Except for the two other times I'd met up with Jamie again, I'd been hard-pressed to perform. Something about that boy filled the hole inside me and not just my ass. Had I been willing to put my heart on the line again, trust someone other than myself, it would be for someone like him.

EEMM hadn't heard a single complaint from my other clients because I did whatever I had to for the sake of getting the job done—and well. With Drake moving in with his stepbrother Preston a few weeks earlier and no longer being on Elite's menu, I'd become their number one escort. The demand was tiring as fuck.

Easier nights meant merely being eye candy with a ready smile and simple conversation, and while I preferred to withdraw into silence and be on my own, I'd learned how to play a room and bullshit with just about anyone. It helped that people tended to enjoy talking about themselves, and asking questions as though interested in their lives stroked egos and kept them focused on their favorite topic.

I'd gotten even luckier with my latest booking.

I was in-flight—first fucking class with all the perks—for five days in paradise playing a companion for some rich guy on vacation at a secluded island resort somewhere off the coast of Mexico.

Sure, I still had to put out, but a few days of relaxing with only one man's needs to fulfill? Hell, even if he proved insatiable, I didn't have to do anything else but shower, eat, and breathe.

No cooking. No cleaning up after myself. No worrying about the kids I sponsored at Humanity House, the LGBTQ community home I spent time at in Malden. I also didn't have to volunteer or check in with the regulars at the local shelter someone—I expected Drake—had gifted with a hefty donation. The money would outfit the old building with a new roof, rehab the living areas and kitchen, and update bathrooms, thanks to Blake Harper, another ex-Elite, and his construction company. Brand new cots and linens would offer warm, comfortable beds for those in need, and there would be enough left over to cover electric and water bills for the months ahead.

The semi-break couldn't have come at a more perfect time too, since that uneasy, sick feeling over the attempted extortion still stained my mind, casting a shadow over everything and dragging me low.

Blue waters stretched outside my plane's small window, reaching for the western horizon lit in a rainbow of color. Peaceful beauty untouched by the ugliness of the world gave me hope I might find more of the same in the paradise we approached.

I looked forward to soaking in the heat and rays since it hadn't been a warm spring in New England, and I was jonesing to catch up on my sleep. I imagined drinks with little umbrellas. Sand between my toes. Sunlight to reawaken my mind and tan. Refreshing waves breaking cool over my thighs. The scent of the ocean and fresh air in my nose and filling my lungs, rejuvenating my spirit.

And the file I'd gotten from BetsyAnne assured me the guy who'd hired me was easy on the eyes too. Slightly older than my thirty-two years, just shy of six feet, lithe from what I could tell in his picture from the waist up. Not skinny but far from bulky since a hint of pecs had bumped his T-shirt.

Definitely my type with dirty blond hair, blue-green eyes, and a clean shaven, sharp jawline. And he was vers—major points right there.

Fucking Callum or bending over for him would be a pleasure rather than pure work.

The plane touched down on what felt like weightless wheels, as smooth as the flight itself. Grinning at having things go my way for a change, I grabbed my carry-on from the overhead bin and exited the plane, ready to start my vacation.

No responsibilities other than sex on demand ahead for the next few days...sign me the fuck up.

I'd been asked to meet our client in the outdoor restaurant behind the hotel for dinner. Once checked in to a room I would have to myself—another bonus, which promised some privacy if I wanted it—I hopped in the shower for a quick scrub to rid the day-long travel off me. Hoping for some good food and that Callum was just as hot in person as in his file's picture, I made my way back outside into the humid warmth, thankful the sun had set.

I wore shorts, a nice T-shirt, and flip-flops because why the fuck not? There was no dress code in the email from my client, Callum, no suggestion of how I ought to prepare for him either. But I'd cleaned myself out just in case he was in the mood to top.

Actual butterflies played around in my stomach, a sense of expectation and excitement I hadn't felt in years. Sure, meeting new clients tended to be a good time, but something about the ocean breeze caressing my face, the scent of flowers and spice, and even the ruckus of tropical birds in the forest off to my right suggested peacefulness.

Tranquility and rest.

All of which I was in desperate need of.

Tiki torches lined a stone pathway leading toward the outdoor dining area. Palm trees swayed and rustled overhead against a pink-streaked navy sky, and a hint of charcoal and grilling meat teased my nose.

I filled my lungs, expecting I looked like a dork with how wide my grin stretched my face.

A hostess in black shorts and a white button-down greeted me by name as though she'd been supplied with a picture of me.

"Right this way, Mr. Briggs," she murmured with a welcoming smile.

I followed the twenty-something woman through a maze of greenery and flowers, noting the private nooks for intimate dining we passed.

Live music played quietly off to my left, and when we rounded a bend in that direction, I noted a small dance area and a few couples all up in each other's spaces. A sense of romance and love hovered, and even though my jaded heart wasn't interested in either, its allure tingled over my skin and left me hungry for more than seafood or steak.

The hostess led me to an area tucked away from the music and other patrons. The table was narrow enough that my and Callum's knees would touch beneath its surface, and two tiki torches on either side provided plenty of light so our faces wouldn't be cast in shadows and unreadable.

"Your dinner date will be joining you shortly," she assured me, motioning for me to have a seat.

"Thanks." I settled into one of three chairs, noting the bucket of ice and bottle of wine chilling. While I'd rather have a cold beer, I would make do with what had been supplied.

Glass of chilled white in hand, I sat back, lingering flutters in my stomach enticing adrenaline into my bloodstream as I glanced over the menu. A heady, rich scent of some sort of flower sweetened the air, intermingling with the grill, causing my mouth to water. I swallowed it down with a sip of the crisp wine.

The liquid cooled my esophagus, and I made a noise of appreciation for both the wine and the local cuisine listed on the sheet I held. Pasta and steak were available as I'd expected considering the fragrant scents around me, but it was the seafood that drew my eye. No lobster, but I could do without until back in New England.

Could the evening get any better?

I mean, I was all about fucking hot clients, but this guy obviously wanted something more, the type of "date" I enjoyed most and didn't get to experience often. A slow start. Small talk, bullshitting, putting the client at ease prior to rocking their world and making them feel appreciative for having spent their money on an Elite escort.

I would ensure his satisfaction, watch him shuffle aboard his flight home in five days, his ass sore and balls spent. His mind would be at rest too from whatever had caused his need of a vacation with an escort as his guest.

Said client appeared, heading my way without guidance, proving that the night ahead of me would indeed be a good one.

Heart thumping with a strange yet heady cadence, I set aside both my wine and the menu.

Firelight danced over Callum, causing the wavy hair atop his head to glint like spun gold. Wide shoulders tapered down to a trim waist. He was on the slim side, more a swimmer than weightlifter, or perhaps a runner. But it was his fisted hands that piqued my interest the most. Was he nervous? Scared? Or just uptight and in need of a good, hard fuck?

I slid my gaze back up to his face to get a quick read on the sexy man I'd been hired to cater to. Our eyes connected, and instantaneous attraction roused to life like I'd never experienced before, waking every hair follicle on my body.

I'd had some hot-as-hell clients in my day—Jamie included—but this man? Goddamn, he was fine as fuck.

He attempted an easy smile with his full lips but didn't quite pull it off. Arresting blue-green irises framed by excessively long lashes revealed the same unease as his hands, but I had practice at helping men relax when they felt tense from guilt over hiring a sex worker.

Not having to force the visible desire like I did with some clients, I rose to my feet and offered Callum my hand. We stood almost eye to eye, electrical currents teasing all my erogenous zones, balls especially, as a hint of cedar filled my nose.

Time to wine and dine his ass straight into his or my bed so I could sniff and lick every inch of his body.

"Callum?" I asked. His file hadn't done the man justice.

"Yes, and you're obviously Zackary." He greeted me with a low, warm voice, his palm sliding along mine in a firm grip, considering his apprehension.

Zaps of lightning shivered up to my shoulders, raising the hairs on my forearms.

His lips parted on a quick inhale as though feeling the same, and I let him see the need tightening my groin in my bold stare. "Zack. And it's a pleasure to meet you."

"Same," he murmured, swallowing hard before releasing his hand from my hold.

I lightly touched his back while pulling out his chair.

"Wine?" I asked, already reaching for the bottle as he sat.

"Please."

Silence hovered over us until I settled across the small table from him. "Thank you for choosing me," I stated.

His gaze flickered over my face as though searching for...I wasn't sure what. Recognition? Confirmation of some assumption he'd made prior to seeing me in the flesh? Assurance I would live up to his expectations? Fulfill his desires and make sure he got his money's worth?

Whatever went through his mind, I had no fucking clue, but something about the man called to me on a soul-deep level, causing a shift beneath my usually sturdy feet.

For the first time, I found myself unsure of how to set my client at ease. But, I would have no issue bringing him pleasure.

And not because I'd been paid to.

Chapter 2

Callum

My boss hadn't been wrong about Zackary Briggs.

The tall drink of cool water tempted my sex and love-starved body to guzzle him down at first sight. An initial glimpse of him sitting alone at our table before we'd made eye contact had heated my blood. The scent of bergamot and lime filled my nose, causing my mouth to water. And the way he looked at me...

I was in trouble.

His hazel eyes hinted at a wealth of hard-earned wisdom and promised a mystery that wouldn't be easily unraveled. But it was the blatant lust in his steady gaze that suggested hiring him hadn't been the best choice.

Regardless of who he was, how off-limits he was to me, I wanted him with a burning hunger inside I thought only one man would ever be able to fulfill. Fire licked over my skin when Zack and I had touched. Shivers raced down my spine at his palm's tender press against my lower back.

And when his fingertips brushed over mine while he

handed me a glass of wine, a shock blasted through my chest that caused my heart to race.

"Thank you for choosing me," he said, pleasure coating his every word.

I hoped bringing him here hadn't overstepped in some way. All for selfish reasons, of course, but a sense of having been ensnared in an unescapable trap twisted my insides and made me question what I'd done.

Fighting off the need to rub damp palms down my slacks, I sipped my wine, searching for something to say even though I'd planned how the evening would go from beginning to end. I'd never been good with conversation. I tended to keep to myself and immerse myself in work as the world went on without me.

Invisible.

Such a perfect word to describe how I felt most days, and while I didn't trust my instincts, I had to do this for my own peace of mind.

I'd suffered for long enough.

"Tell me about yourself," I said rather than explain to him I didn't really *have* a choice in who I hired when I'd gone onto Elite's website with a mission.

Zack's grin remained even though a question hinted in his eyes.

"I suppose that's not a request you often hear from clients," I rushed to say, not wanting to raise any red flags before I got a feel for the man. "But this is something...new for me, and I'm not really sure how to proceed."

Not one lie in my words, but my reason for bringing Zack to a remote island wasn't exactly honest.

He settled back in his seat, seemingly completely at ease, his eyes flitting over my face as though seeking out my truth.

I fought the need to shift, deciding on another sip of my wine to occupy myself.

"Good evening, gentlemen."

I hadn't heard the waiter approach. Tearing my focus off Zack, I glanced up at the young man who brought hand-made tortilla chips and a few different salsas. One appeared to be the usual tomato-based, another perhaps mango, the third more along the lines of guacamole.

"Are you ready to order?"

I glanced over at my supposed date.

"Would you allow me the honor of choosing for you?" he asked quietly.

Why did his question light up my insides *and* make me want to weep?

I'd been in charge for so long, looked to for answers in every facet of life for years, that bubbles of excitement exploded in my core. Yet another part of the dark-haired man that caused my insides to purr. He was the type who would care for my exhausted soul.

The sudden urge to change what I'd done, my reasons for bringing Zack to the gorgeous, remote location, hit me hard. I'd made a mistake, but there was nothing left to do but go forward and watch how things played out.

Consequences were a bitch. Always had been, and this time would prove no different, I feared.

"Please," I murmured, taking comfort in the momentary respite from his undivided attention. A part of me selfishly yearned for hours—days—of having his focus on me when I knew damn well I couldn't.

Taking advantage of the situation would be the ultimate betrayal to the man I loved, my only grounds for booking this vacation.

Zack rattled off our orders, something about grilled

shrimp with coconut rice and a salmon dish in a leek and saffron cream sauce. Regardless of how delicious the meals sounded, my mouth watered for a taste of the man speaking rather than actual food.

But I needed to get my libido under control. After I'd laid eyes on Zack, nothing about the five days ahead promised me anything but sure heartbreak.

That plan I'd impulsively made was about to backfire in more ways than one. I was doomed—and I couldn't hate the man sitting across from me even though I had thought for sure I did. Would. Well, wanted to.

I jumped into conversation before Zack could lead me astray.

"So back to my question," I said the second the waiter left us alone, sure whatever Zack shared with me would only make my desire for him harder to ignore.

He hesitated before answering, his gaze once more inquisitive. "I get the feeling you aren't looking for a canned response in order to fill the silence."

"You would be correct."

Zack cocked his head to the side and sipped his wine before replying.

Turning from his focus, I helped myself to the chips and salsa—mango, I identified as the sweet tang hit my tongue. Perhaps my churning stomach wouldn't mind an addition to the roiling bile.

"I don't usually offer personal information with clients," Zack stated quietly, also reaching for the chips.

We both crunched in silence, eyeing each other with appreciation and a hint of wariness.

"Why are you asking?" he finally questioned when I didn't speak.

"Because I would like to learn a little more about you before we...become involved."

"Is this your first time hiring an escort, Callum?"

A shiver once more licked at my spine as my name whispered off his lips. "Yes."

"There's nothing to be nervous about—"

I barely withheld my snort. If only he knew.

"—and I promise EEMM is professional. Nothing we say or do will leave this island unless you choose to speak of it."

Being at my wit's end, anxiety having ridden my body since I'd made the decision for a vacation, lended toward a stirring of impatience in my mind.

"If that's the case, then what does it matter if I wish to know more about the man I hired for the next five days?" I shot back with more snip to my tone than I'd planned on.

A slow smirk curled one corner of Zack's lips, and he lifted his wine in a mock toast. "You're going to keep me on my toes, aren't you?"

I'd rather have you on your knees.

My eyelids fluttered closed. I was *not* supposed to feel this way, damnit.

"Callum."

I chose to meet Zack's gaze when I would rather have ignored his inquiry.

He leaned onto the table with both elbows, the intensity of his stare making it impossible for me to hide.

"You're obviously uncomfortable with your decision to bring me here, so if you'd rather return to your room alone for the evening, I won't be offended. I would love to try again tomorrow, or we could just pack up and return home if you prefer. I'm sure I could talk to my manager about getting you some sort of refund."

I licked over my lower lip, feeling as though I drowned when I supposedly had my shit together. I'd been the safe haven, the rock, for so long, that I suddenly floundered at finding myself on shaky ground all because I was desperate for my best friend's love.

"No," I managed, knowing I wouldn't be able to keep my next words from sounding like a desperate plea. "I—need this. Please."

"Then I'll give it to you." A softer smile curved Zack's lips and lightened his gaze as he once more settled back in his chair. "To answer your question, I spend a lot of my spare time in the gym."

Zack's shoulders and prominent pecs bulging against the cotton of his shirt already suggested that truth about him. Add in his clear skin, groomed scruff, and styled hair, and there was no question the man cared about his health and appearance. But nothing about his character thus far, unfortunately, suggested cockiness or an untamed ego that would have been a complete turnoff to me.

"What else?" I asked, my desire for information troubling to my already anxious mind.

"I enjoy reading about places I hope to visit someday," he continued without hesitation. "Italy. Switzerland. Cyprus. Thailand and Japan—I want to see the world. And lucky me," he said with a wink, "I finally got a stamp on my passport that has been sitting unopened atop my bureau for the past ten years."

He crunched on a chip loaded with guacamole, and I allowed my hungry gaze to trail over his strong jawline and the muscle bunching there as he chewed.

"What's your passion?" I asked, focusing on his mouth.

He licked lingering salt from his lower lip as I'd done moments earlier.

The sensual move shot lust through my groin, and I barely managed to contain my groan.

I expected another slow grin, a knowing look, but Zack shifted his gaze from me as though seeking out the live band playing quietly in the warm night off to my left.

"I volunteer at a homeless shelter down the road from my condo."

A slew of questions rose to my mind, but I blocked them out as a shadow passed over Zack's face. Anger, perhaps? Or a sad...fondness, maybe? I opened my mouth to tell him that I too volunteered, but he blinked and straightened, a less genuine smile on his lips.

Our waiter had returned with dinner.

Zack wore a mask, I realized, something he'd allowed to lower slightly with me. The sting of guilt intensified as whispers of happiness swirled in my chest.

The young man took his time refilling our wine glasses, then quietly slipped away when we assured him we didn't need anything further.

A few minutes passed in quietness as we ate, but my mind was far from silent. Regret and desire battled in my brain, keeping me on edge.

"Do you like shrimp?" Zack asked.

"Yes, but you made the right choice for me with the salmon."

"Trade a bite?"

My thoughts quieting at Zack's easygoing nature, I agreed.

He went first, offering me a forkful of the coconut rice and a piece of shrimp.

I should have felt awkward leaning over the table with my mouth open but strangely didn't.

He stared as I chewed, hunger for more than food in his heated gaze. "Delicious, isn't it?"

"Mmm." I hummed and prepared a bite of my dinner for him.

His parted lips held me transfixed. My mouth dried as his tongue flicked over the bottom of my fork before he closed his lips around the salmon.

He smirked.

Face heating, I returned my focus to my plate.

"So, what about you?" Zack asked, and I shook my head.

"This vacation isn't about me."

"The fuck it's not." He huffed a light laugh while I took another bite.

The salmon melted on my tongue like butter.

"My sole reason for living these next couple of days is to make you smile, Callum. Fulfilling your fantasies and just overall creating a vacation you never want to end. So tell me —what do you hope for? How do you see our time here in paradise playing out? Do you simply require a companion to keep loneliness from interfering with your rest, or are you in need of some tender loving care? Because I have to be honest." Zack slid his gaze over my face, my shoulders and chest, stalling out at the table that hindered his perusal from slipping toward the bulge growing in my slacks. "I want nothing more than to give you pleasure however you desire."

Jesus.

Since when did tingles race over my skin from a mere stranger's words? My body had only ever reacted to one man in such a way, and Zack having done as much within minutes of meeting him confused me.

Unsure what to say or do, I returned my attention to my half-empty plate. "I-I'd rather not say just now."

"Fair enough." Zack didn't sound put out or upset.

We finished our meals in silence that once more made me uneasy.

"Dance with me?"

I jerked my focus up while wiping my lips on the linen napkin.

The firelight glinting off his hazel eyes hinted of lust that incited the same inside me. "Let me hold you in my arms close enough that you'll realize I won't bite unless you ask me to. And even then, I'll be sure the graze of my teeth only makes you groan with need for more."

Swallowing hard, I nodded without meaning to.

Zack stood and offered his hand.

I stared at his palm that appeared strong yet soft. Imagining his fingers on my skin roused my desire to an even greater height, and even though my instincts screamed for me to deny him, I found myself reaching for Zack.

Chapter 3

Landon

Callum had claimed we needed a vacation, and since I trusted that man with every aspect of my life after almost eight years of living with him, I'd agreed. He'd seen to the booking of a hotel, the flight, even my baggage.

I rarely went out into public, and the fact Callum had talked me into spending five days at an island resort said a lot about me believing he always had my best interests at heart. He was my comfort place. My Band-Aid, the one I ran toward and clung to when shit got to be too much, which happened more often than I cared to admit.

Especially when my mind overran with longing for the man I loved more than anything in the world, the one who still owned my heart regardless of the fact he'd abandoned me. Zack was my obsession even after fifteen years—and he was also the reason I wrote happily ever afters.

Regardless of the pain in our past, I couldn't help but want him. Dreamed about growing old with him. Tried to manifest that very thing for years on end while living out each good memory we'd shared in childhood.

Unhealthy, yes, but Callum offered me nothing but support in every endeavor. He'd told me countless times he only wanted my happiness, which meant one day making things right with my lost love and planting myself back into his life where fate intended me to be.

Callum had arrived at the island an hour earlier than I did. We'd ended up having to take different planes since our original flight had been cancelled. He had texted before I'd landed that he headed to the restaurant and would bring something to our room for me. His assumption that I would be peopled out from the airport and flight was spot-on.

But.

The warmth after leaving a frigid spring behind in New England, the refreshing scent of the ocean and flowers surrounding the resort made me want to take advantage of every second my hard-earned cash had afforded me in paradise.

I decided to surprise him, focusing on the good tingles of anxiety in my belly rather than the underlying fear of being recognized and stared at. While Callum had assured me over and again that enough time had passed since the event that had all but ruined me, I couldn't get past the festering wounds. The guilt and shame of having made one hell of a wrong choice ten years ago and being found out.

Publicly.

Virally.

The outcome had been self-esteem ruination atop my parent's bitter disappointment.

While I told myself I didn't care about impressing anyone, I didn't rush readying in the two-room suite Callum and I shared—just in case pictures of me once more ended up plastered across social media and the news.

And you know...in case *he* ever happened upon them

and got inspired to miss me enough he took one of my calls and allowed me to apologize for what I'd done.

My light brown hair refused to be tamed, I noted in the bathroom mirror, its longer length brushing over the tops of my ears and forehead. Even though I actually wanted to go outside and join Callum at what must be a lonely dinner, I looked like a timid mess. My shit brown eyes appeared wider than normal, my skin pale from being shut up inside my condo, since I'd been hunched over my keyboard without a break in far too long.

A model, I was not, but at least I had a decent body thanks to good genes and daily sparring matches with Callum in our house's spare bedroom I'd turned into a gym.

My family might see me as lazy, believing that I lived off my grandfather's inheritance, but I was no fool. I also didn't lie around all day taking advantage of my friend who Father approved of because he thought Callum kept me in line.

Ha!

I snorted a laugh.

If Father only knew what I got up to during my work hours, where my mind went and how fantasies padded my bank account rather than just the investments he assumed, he would have that heart attack Mother had been warning him about for years.

Smirking and self-esteem somewhat boosted, I turned away from the unflattering bathroom mirror and exited the suite, following the signs to the outdoor restaurant.

Rarely did I go anywhere without Callum, and the fact I'd stayed put at my gate and boarded a plane after he'd disappeared into the sky spoke volumes about how far I'd come in the eight years he'd worked for me. But my codependency on Callum would never end, nor did I have a wish for it to do so.

Neither did Callum. He took pleasure in doting on me. Caring for my needy ass gave Callum a sense of purpose. His words, not mine. Placating me whenever the embarrassing selfish brat of my childhood reared his ugly head or threw a temper tantrum helped to settle his soul, he'd stated countless times.

We'd discussed our probably toxic friendship. But since we were both content with what we shared, what did it matter that we needed each other's issues to fulfill certain parts of each other? Callum accepted me, messy roommate that I was. He watched after me when the people who should have done so kept me on the fringes of their lives due to the many mistakes I'd made in my early twenties.

Just shy of twenty-nine, I'd learned a few lessons. Some, perhaps, a bit too late, but who gave a shit?

Well, honestly, I still did even though I pretended I didn't.

While following after the hostess who said she would show me to Callum's table, I recounted the good things in my life. I had a kickass job, the one I'd always dreamed of doing since I'd learned about romance, love, and lust. A faithful PA in the form of my best friend—

Who danced with another man.

I stumbled to a stop alongside a flowering bush, blinking a few times in case my eyes betrayed me.

Callum didn't date. Didn't hook up. He'd told me he was gay like I was, but I'd teased him about being ace before assuring him that I would love him forever no matter how he identified. He always flushed—fucking *always* when I claimed that fact—making him look like a teenager rather than a thirty-three year old man who tended toward proper stoicism like no one else I knew, Father included.

And there he swayed, a dark-haired man holding him close.

"Sir?" The hostess returned to my side when she realized I'd stopped dead in my tracks.

I couldn't tear my focus off Callum or find words to excuse my stunned behavior that had drawn me up short.

Callum and the man he danced with were of similar height, a few inches taller than my five-ten. And the wide shoulders on the dark-haired man with his back to me promised he could carry a burden. He took care of himself, that was for damned sure, his fitted T-shirt doing little to hide his thick traps and the muscles in his back.

And his ass.

My dick perked up at the shorts clinging to cheeks that suggested the man spent more spare time at the gym than Callum and I. His thick thighs and calf muscles stated the same.

Swallowing a flood of drool, I slid my gaze upward once more, noting how Callum stared at his...unexpected hookup?

I had never seen naked desire in Callum's gaze before. Never experienced my best friend looking at someone like he wanted to throw them to the ground and fuck until he passed out.

"Sweet baby Jesus," I whispered, needing to adjust myself from the porn playing out in front of my six-month celibate ass. Even though there was no actual fucking going on, Callum and that man together were a fantasy I couldn't imagine cooking up regardless of my well-paid ability to do so.

Callum's dance partner had the body of a god, the kind that used to tempt me toward trouble after the love of my life broke my heart. I'd rebelled against my stubborn feelings that had refused to relent, but at least now, I avoided situations that caused nothing but drama.

They shifted, angling enough I clearly made out the man's profile in the flickering tiki torch's light.

Recognition stole every thought in my brain, and my breath abandoned my lungs like I'd taken an uppercut to the solar plexus.

He had a prominent nose. Strong jawline darkened by scruff. Dark brows overshadowing deep set eyes I knew the color of even though I couldn't make them out from the distance separating us.

Zackary Briggs.

I curled slightly in on myself, whimpering in ecstatic happiness at seeing him in the flesh, for the chance to talk to him, like I'd been desperate to do for too damned long. But a slew of questions jabbed like fists at my brain, stalling out my ability to make my dream come true.

What was he doing here?

Why was Callum dancing with him?

What the ever loving *fuck* alternate reality had my plane entered while flying over the Gulf?

There had to be a reasonable explanation, but I couldn't for the life of me come up with anything that made sense.

Zack's hand lay low on a back that wasn't *mine*. His nose trailed over Callum's ear as he whispered sweet nothings I wanted to swoon over. His thick thigh slid between my best friend's legs when it should have been me trembling in Zack's hold.

They moved together like liquid sex, arousal flushing though my entire body rather than the expected stab of jealousy. Zackary Briggs had always been irresistible, even as a teenager, so I didn't blame Callum for being all up in his space.

As though feeling my stare, Callum glanced my way. He quickly stepped back from Zack as though he'd been caught with his hand in the cookie jar, and I could almost hear the hard swallow that bobbed his Adam's apple.

Zack reached out to touch his arm but dropped his hand to his side as Callum shook his head.

I focused on Zack.

Finally—fucking *finally*—I had the opportunity of a lifetime. He'd denied me for too long, and I wouldn't be set aside again. My feet moved on their own, rushing me toward the man I intended to have forever.

Zack turned, the blood draining from his face as our gazes clashed across the twenty or so feet separating us.

"The fuck?" he muttered, red flushing his face as fast as the blood had fled a second earlier. "What the actual *fuck?*" he repeated harshly, glancing at Callum as I closed the distance between us, my sole aim to reclaim what I'd lost.

Chapter 4

Zack

Callum jumped away from me as though he'd been electrocuted.

Awareness prickled over the back of my neck —and I fucking knew who I would see before I laid eyes on him. He'd had that effect on my body when we'd been kids, and it had only intensified to the point the hair rose on my nape as though desperate to reach for him.

Shifting around, I took in the man I'd hoped to never lay eyes on again.

Landon *fucking* Matthews.

Same as back then, he was like a siren's song entwining around my soul and yet squeezing like a deadly python hell-bent on stealing my breath.

He was quite a bit taller than when I'd last seen him at fifteen, and Landon's body had filled out to perfection. The light brown hair that could never be tamed still topped his head in a rumpled mess I wanted to spear my fingers into. He approached on swift feet, and those amber eyes with the gold around his pupil came into focus, full of stubbornness as they used to be.

I cursed as heat rushed through me over the fact he'd only gotten even better looking and twice as magnetic. Goddamn him to hell for making me feel this way.

"What the actual *fuck?*" I shot a scowl at Callum, who stared at Landon as though he'd seen a ghost.

"Zackary." Landon breathed my full name with a deeper, richer voice than I remembered him having, sending shivers clear from my nape to my tailbone.

Every muscle in my body prepared to throw down, I turned on him, ready to punch his lights out—or shove my tongue down his throat because the conflicting feels were that. Damned. Strong. My five days in paradise had just gone to hell in a handbasket. What that meant for my job and client, I was about to find out.

"Why the fuck are you here?" I growled at Landon.

His gaze darted to Callum. "Was this your doing?" Landon's voice lowered in a soothing tone.

Wait.

I stepped back, glancing between the two men, wanting to flee over the unknown and discomfort racing through me. Curiosity killed the cat though. "What the actual *fuck* is going on here?" I demanded yet again, hands fisted at my sides.

"I-I can explain," Callum said before swallowing hard. He gestured toward our private nook. "Can we please sit down and talk?"

Landon knew from experience the last thing I wanted to do was have a little chat that included him, but Callum didn't.

Or did he?

The way his nervous gaze flitted toward me, his blue-green eyes filled with wariness assured me he was well aware of Landon's and my past.

"Absolutely not," I bit out between my clenched jaw. The shrimp and rice I'd enjoyed for dinner wanted to make an appearance due to the vise squeezing my stomach.

Callum's gaze flitted over my face before his stare hardened slightly with resolve even though a tremor rippled through him. "What happened to pleasing the client?"

Fucker.

"What about goddamn boundaries?" I shot out, heat lacing every word even though the man obviously wasn't aware of mine. Still. I stood off-kilter, a riotous mess in every way imaginable, wanting two different things.

Pink flushed Callum's high cheekbones, and he inhaled slowly as Landon shifted on his feet in my periphery. I became conscious of having every set of eyes in close proximity on us.

"Please," Callum whispered, and fuck me for not being able to say no. His pleading puppy dog eyes I'd enjoyed staring into while dancing, our bodies pressed tight, arousal thick between us, did me in. "Allow me to explain, Zack."

"Goddamnit," I whispered harshly, stomping toward the table we'd vacated a few minutes earlier. So much for a night spent sweaty and sated between the sheets with my new favorite client. Sean would definitely let me out of the contract if I called him, but I found myself flopping onto my chair. Arms crossed, legs spread wide, I glared as the two men approached.

Callum lightly touched Landon's back, brushing his lips over Landon's temple before whispering, "I didn't mean for things to unfold like this."

A strange ache lanced through my chest at their comfortable affection. Perhaps it was nothing more than a bit of jealousy over Callum—definitely not Landon. That kid could go fuck himself with a twelve-inch dildo.

Actually, knowing him, he was probably a size queen.

A fist or baseball bat would be better.

Something big enough to make him cry at the very least and not because it felt good.

Callum pulled out the extra chair, and Landon didn't reply to his quiet words or take his hungry eyes off me as he sat.

My abs tightened as blood once more seeped back into my groin after having fled at the first sight of Landon. I couldn't deny the kid was hot as fuck and still roused my body to life after all these years, but I did *not* want him.

Hard. Fucking. Stop.

Continuing to lie to myself, I pushed against memories of Landon's smile that used to light up my insides. Make me feel wanted. Appreciated. How he'd laughed at every stupid joke I told in the hopes he would forget for a few brief moments how his busy parents ignored him.

How he'd curl up beside me on the couch while we played X-box. The way he'd let me win but claimed he didn't. Landon had always put me first.

Until that fateful night he didn't.

Jaw clenched, I glanced between the two of them, trying to figure shit out. Until Callum started talking, I was in the dark.

He settled uneasily across the table from me.

"Gentlemen?" Our waiter appeared like a wraith, his voice shaky as though he approached shark-infested waters. Guess he'd been privy to our little confrontation on the dance floor.

"Three shots of the strongest alcohol you've got," I muttered without looking at him, my stare solely on the man who'd hired me—and wouldn't meet my gaze. Shady, hot-as-hell fucker.

"Right away, sir." The waiter scurried off, leaving the three of us in silence.

Callum and Landon shared a long moment of eye contact as though having an entire conversation between them without voicing a word. Same as Landon and I had done once upon a time.

I hated surprises, and these two were more than friends, that was for damned sure. Toss in the suspicion I was being used again, and my defenses rose to towering heights, self-preservation ready to boot a body off the ledge. Landon's. Callum's. I didn't care. I just wanted answers about what the fuck was going on.

"Start talking," I demanded, my tone hard.

"It's a long story," Callum finally said, the words hesitant as though he searched for them.

"Callum is the most unselfish man I know," Landon cut in, laying his hand on his friend's or perhaps lover's forearm as though offering comfort, "so I'm assuming his bringing you here was for my benefit."

The teenager turned gorgeous man shifted his amber eyes back on me at Callum's nod, and fuck my dick for liking his attention with no less potency than when we'd been kids.

I ground my teeth over the unwanted lust, my ears expecting what had been texted dozens of times.

"I've been wanting this chance to talk to you. To apologize," Landon murmured.

And there it was.

Luckily for Landon, the waiter reappeared with my drinks. He sat one in front of Callum first, and I shook my head.

"Nope. They're all mine." I tapped the table top with a firm fingertip where the glasses rightfully belonged.

The waiter's hands shook as he placed the first shot in front of me before adding the others alongside.

"Leave," I ordered the second he straightened.

Once more, he scurried off, and I tipped all three drinks back one after the other, losing myself in the burn for a few seconds of relief from my surroundings.

Since there was no blocking Landon with a swipe of my fingertip over my cell phone this time around, I settled in my chair in the same *bring it* pose, arms once more crossed as though confident I could take on the world when I knew damned well a lot of good and bad memories I'd tried to erase from my brain were about to be stirred up.

But first.

I stared Landon down, not about to let him get another word in until I had my say. The little selfish fucker needed to know what his actions had caused.

"It's one thing to be betrayed by an enemy," I all but hissed, "but by your best friend? You have *no* idea the consequences of your choice to turn your back on me, Landon. *None.* Your parents had taken me in. Promised me a college education. I'd hit the jackpot as a foster kid, and I'd done everything to not fuck shit up—and you did it with a temper tantrum that brought your father running to the supposed rescue. You ruined my fucking life, Landon. There's no forgiveness for that shit."

"I was a child." He leaned forward as though sensing I would rather stand up and get the fuck out of there than listen to his excuses. "Selfish and spoiled."

"Damned right you were!" If fire could shoot from my eyes, he'd have burst into flames. The heat inside me rose to the boiling point, and I was about to blow. "You fucked me over, and there's *nothing* you can do to fix that shit. Not a goddamned thing!"

I shoved up from my chair, knocking it over in my haste, but I didn't bother righting it. Stomach a rock, I spun away from the two men and strode away with heavy footsteps, my flip-flops making a stupid clapping sound when I'd rather they portray the harsh, heavy thuds in my chest.

Five days in paradise.

A snort huffed from my nose as I strode into the hotel and smashed the elevator's up button.

More like a sure five days of hell.

How the fuck would I get out of the contract without telling Sean or Micah about the event that led to my demise? I'd attempted to leave that shit buried where it belonged, out of sight, out of mind, even though Landon had always managed to rouse memories.

And he'd done so *again*, only this time in person where the mere sight of him brought all the good, the bad, and the ugly, crashing back down atop me.

The last thing I wanted to do was dredge up more drama. I'd rather be dancing with who I'd thought would've been a sure, exceptionally satisfying fuck.

But he'd orchestrated this whole affair.

So, stay or go?

Allow this useless, latest attempt at resolution while basking in the sun and diving into salt water, or head home to a cold, rainy New England, doubly bitter?

Seeing as how I had a room to myself, a balcony over-looking the Gulf of Mexico, and gorgeous weather, I wasn't going to make a hasty decision that would leave more than just Landon disappointed.

Keeping my bosses happy and pleasing the client were the rules I lived by.

But fuck me, neither sounded appealing at that moment.

I chose to reflect on my options, and the sliding glass door leading outside my suite into the ocean-scented air offered me privacy. A few small shot bottles in hand from the suite's mini bar, and I closed myself off from everyone and everything but that which weighed on my mind: the dredging up of my past and that latest attempt at extortion.

I also had to decide what the hell to do with my client now that he'd fucked up our vacation I'd once upon a time been ready to take advantage of.

Even worse?

My desperation for Landon hadn't eased one fucking bit. I feared what self-preservation I'd built with the distance between us the past fifteen years would crumble at his feet, leaving me vulnerable and on a second crash course for heartache.

Chapter 5

Callum

"Cal."

I ripped my focus off Zack's retreating back, ready to face possible wrath for having caused Landon even more pain.

His soft smile eased the tension riding my shoulders, allowing me to draw an unhindered breath. "You're too good to me," he murmured.

Shaking my head, I turned toward where Zack stalked, but he'd disappeared. I swallowed my disappointment. "I'm sorry he didn't stay to hear you out."

"I'm not surprised, considering his actions whenever I texted him over the years, but you can't force a man to offer forgiveness no matter how much you want it. I'll find a way to wear him down since he's stuck on an island and can't escape me this time."

"I'll talk to him," I declared, once more shifting to face the man I loved.

He studied my face with his beautiful brown eyes framed by long lashes a shade darker than his hair. "Why, Cal? Haven't you already done enough for me?"

"Never enough, and because this part of your life should be settled once and for all. You need to be able to move on. I want—" I snapped my jaw shut to silence my runaway tongue.

Landon continued his steady perusal of my face that heated beneath his stare. "What?" he pushed.

I released a slow, steady exhale, only able to admit to a partial truth. "For you to be free of him."

"You know I wish for the opposite."

My heart stumbled inside my chest even though I was well aware of Landon's deepest desire when it came to Zackary Briggs. "Then it's my hope that he'll eventually listen," I forced myself to say. "That you find peace between you and what you've always longed for."

Even if that meant I would have to live with unrequited love until I breathed my last.

"You hired him." Landon didn't voice a question, but I nodded anyway. He snickered. "Sly dog." He laughed with more lightness than I'd ever heard grace his voice. "Have I ever told you how much I love you?"

All the time, just not in the way I wished for.

"He's under contract and not going anywhere tonight," Landon continued before I could utter a word.

My boss slash best friend slash roommate hadn't hidden any part of his past from me, so I knew what he'd done when they had been kids. How he'd stalked Zack over the years afterward. He'd even shown me Zack's profile on EEMM, which had led to my crazy plan to force them to face each other—and hopefully bring them together, making Landon's dreams come true.

Or, I would be left picking up the pieces of Landon's heart. But that's not what I *truly* wished for. I wanted his happiness more than anything, and that meant having the man he'd been in love with since middle school.

"I say we let him sleep his pissiness off, and I'll try again tomorrow," Landon stated, his mind clearly made up and focused on getting what he'd wanted for the past fifteen years.

Landon's buoyed spirits proved potent enough that I dragged myself from wallowing self-pity enough to see to his needs as I always did. "Are you hungry? I can order you a late dinner."

"No—I'm fine. Let's just go to our suite. I saw a basket of snacks and drinks. They'll be good enough for tonight."

"I'll speak to Zack," I promised as we meandered side by side back to the hotel, our shoulders brushing lightly. "Perhaps he'll meet you for breakfast, and the rest of our vacation won't be a waste of money."

We stopped by the elevator, and I caught Landon nibbling on his lower lip, a promise of his anxiety, an action that made me wish to ease his mind by tasting his mouth. I shoved the desire deep inside where the thoughts wouldn't cause heartache.

"Do you trust me?" I murmured, hands in my pockets so I wouldn't reach for him.

Landon's gaze jerked toward me. "Of course I do! You've never let me down."

He spoke the truth. "So trust me with this, okay?"

"You're too good to me," he stated again.

"I would do anything for you." I'd never meant the words more, even if helping him find the fulfillment of his heart's desire shattered mine in the process. The idea alone of that outcome made me want to curl up and cry.

I put on a brave face, acting confident while we readied for bed, all the while my spirit sagged beneath the weight of selflessness. Had I made the right choice or only set Landon up for even deeper emotional pain?

I'd fucked up with my brother and feared doing the same with Landon.

Surely, if Zack knew the reasoning behind Landon's behavior that night when they'd been innocent kids, he would offer forgiveness. Perhaps that would be enough for Landon to find peace and actually be ready to move on like I hoped for.

The minute Landon finished in the bathroom, he poked his head through my bedroom's doorway I'd left open in invitation—same as I always did at home for whenever he needed me.

I pulled back the blankets, and he scooted forward, tossing himself onto the mattress. Pink flushed his cheeks, making him even more beautiful as he snuggled in, the sheet tucked beneath his chin where he lay on his side facing me.

We didn't touch, nor had we ever crossed the platonic line between us. He'd made his stance against relationships outside his dream man clear at my first hint of flirting when we'd met. I'd kept my body in check along with any discussion beyond platonic love.

The unreturned feelings sucked, even more so when Landon put himself in my bed. But telling him the truth of how much I loved him would only tear us apart.

We also didn't talk about the fact he slept with me more nights than not. And the mornings we woke wrapped up in each other, I reasoned his unconscious action away as seeking out comfort in his sleep.

Landon never argued, simply agreed and slipped from my bed, attempting to hide his morning wood, same as I did.

Fuck.

I rubbed a weary hand over my face, too aware of the

warm body stretched out inches from my own. My instinct to nurture Landon proved a formidable foe along with my desire to touch him with sexual intent. I doubted myself, every decision I made acting as his GPS through life since we'd met. The man was codependent on me, and I was selfish and so far gone on him enough not to care the two of us together might be seen as unsafe from the outside.

I wanted Landon, but I longed for his happiness more than anything, which made me reason away my choices in how I looked out for him.

Martyr syndrome, perhaps, but if Landon got his happily ever after, then I had to believe I would be satisfied no matter how torn I would feel over losing him.

Landon slept long before I did, proving yet again how he trusted me for the days ahead.

But I had no such reassurance, and my mind refused to rest.

I replayed my night with Zack from the initial magnetic draw and lust to the disappointment in watching him walk away, and not just from Landon but from me as well.

While I'd gotten two suites in the event this very thing ended up happening, forced proximity between the three of us in a shared space would have allowed Landon to have his say. He couldn't move on, and neither would I until this shit was taken care of once and for all.

One way or the other, this situation between them needed to be put to rest, and waiting to see what transpired on its own had yet to show fruit. I had to be proactive when it came to dealing with Landon, since he usually wouldn't budge without a cattle prod.

Perhaps Zack was the same.

I snuck from the bed, quietly pulled on my shorts and shirt from earlier, and gently shut our suite door shut behind me. Silence reigned in the hotel's hallway, my slow shuffling feet as loud as the pulse rushing in my ears.

Zack's room was a short walk around the corner from us. Close enough for easy access in the event things had gone well between the two men. I'd even been prepared to switch lodging with Zack if he and Landon wanted to be together.

Blowing out a slow exhale in attempts to slow my thumping heart, I knocked on Zack's door. I stared at the peephole, expecting he wouldn't just pull it open without checking first.

I didn't hear any movement beyond, but the door swung inward a few inches before I had to knock a second time.

Zack stood in low-slung cotton shorts and nothing else, I quickly noted while glancing down over his hairless chest and the obvious outline of his gorgeous dick.

Fuck.

I swallowed hard and jerked my focus upward.

One brow raised, he waited, fingers still clasping the door handle as though unsure if he should open it the rest way or slam it in my face for the uncomfortable position I'd put him in. I deserved to be ignored, the contract broken for what I'd done—but I hoped with all my heart he would hear me out.

"Can I come in?" I asked, my voice raspy from sleepiness and raging lust.

"As long as you're alone."

"It's just me," I assured him.

He stepped back without a word and gestured me forward.

My lungs sucked in the scent of bergamot and lime as I moved past him. Temptation emerged to brush against his skin I imagined was warm from having crawled from bed, but I held steady in keeping space between us.

The door snicked shut.

Turning, I opened my mouth, ready to plead Landon's case, but the heat in his hazel eyes, the sight of tattooed skin covering his god-like body showcased on EEMM's website proved too much of a distraction.

I'm in trouble.

Chapter 6

Zack

Why the fuck did Callum have to be so damned hot? And why the hell did I want to throw him to the floor and fuck him senseless even though he'd put me in this awful predicament? That whole sit on the private deck and figure out my options hadn't given me any clear definition on what I ought to do.

Still pissed, I thought of hopping on a jet to head home where this kind of drama didn't exist. But I was also still horny as fuck for my client. Same as Landon on that dance floor, the proximity of Callum all up in my space made my body crave intimacy. Interaction. A give and take that would leave us both spent and exhausted enough to find oblivion from the thoughts crowding my brain.

From how Callum stared at me, he felt the same regardless of what Landon was to him. It looked like a cat had gotten his salivating tongue, but he was as unsure as I was about what to do.

Going with lust rather than anger, I reached to wipe away make-believe drool from the corner of Callum's lush mouth.

He gulped, and I smirked before crossing my arms and leaning against the door at my back. I would rather have dragged him into my arms and tasted his mouth like I'd planned to do a couple of hours earlier before Landon had interrupted us. But words needed to be exchanged before I gave him what we both desired.

"What are you doing here?" I asked since it was apparent Callum couldn't find his voice to explain his arrival at my door an hour after midnight.

"C-Couldn't sleep."

"Hmm." I glanced down over his form, noting the clothes he'd worn earlier and the hardened dick he sported. "I could help you with that—if you want."

"That's...not why I came."

I could make him *come*, would gladly do so, but he shifted, pushing a hand through his thick hair and showing his unrest.

This wasn't about me but him. My client. I hated that I had to remind myself of that fact. I'd been ready to lower my usual defenses and enjoy my vacation with Callum, but then he had to go and pull a fast one on me.

Couldn't trust a single soul, and I should have known better.

"Where's Landon?" I asked, needing to get this little chat with Callum out of the way so I could go back to my bed and try to shut down my brain. The alcohol hadn't helped do more than put me just over the edge of buzzed.

"He's sleeping."

"So are you canceling and sending me back to Boston or what?" I pushed when Callum still couldn't tell me why the fuck he'd shown up at my door. I could have done both options myself, but something inside me hesitated, made going home without answers as to what was going on inside me impossible.

Pressing his lips together, Callum glanced deeper into my suite. "I don't want to sound mean, but you look like you could use the vacation," he reasoned, not giving me his eyes.

"What I could use is a good hard *fuck*," I muttered the truth of what would shut my brain down. I checked Callum out again, noting the turn of his head toward me in my periphery. He would be even more gorgeous writhing on a bed, begging for my dick. His expressive eyes hazed over with need rather than the unease he hadn't been rid of since I'd first seen him.

Add in the underlying anger over what Callum had done, the fact Landon scraped at the back of my mind like a jagged fingernail on itchy skin, and I was totally down for fucking to relieve the stirred aggravation inside me.

Yeah, that was what I needed.

"You paid for tonight..." Lust bled through my every word.

Callum exhaled loudly, his hands fisting at his sides in a determined stance to not touch me.

So much for a good time. I pressed my lips together and waited for the buttoned-up man to state what he needed to get off his chest.

"He climbed on you that night because you'd turned eighteen—a legal adult who had every right to leave your foster home, which he feared," Callum murmured, his blue-green eyes intent on mine. "You were his anchor, the one person he could trust to have his back."

I didn't give a shit about his excuses. "And he didn't have mine when I needed him most," I snipped, hating that my chest still ached from his betrayal.

"Because he was hurt!"

My arms uncrossed, and I straightened, taking a step to put myself in Callum's face. "He was fucking *fifteen*," I growled as the low-burning anger in my gut flared fully like it had when we'd sat at the table. "If I'd given him what he begged for, I could have gotten put away for twenty-plus years for sexual assault!"

Callum stumbled away from me as though I'd punched him in the chest with my words. The blood drained from his face as he blindly reached for the small couch's arm.

"What?" I asked, following him, my buzzed brain thinking for a half second he was having a heart attack. It was enough to calm my anger to alarm.

He sagged onto the couch rubbing his face, clearly not about to fall over dead, but still.

"What?" I repeated, my brow furrowed, adrenaline still pumping.

"You dragged some stuff to the surface is all," Callum whispered and swallowed hard. "Just...it's nothing. Never mind."

More questions littered my brain as my ingrained need to please people and put them at ease roused again. "You okay?"

"Yeah." He exhaled noisily before lifting his focus to my face. "Landon is my best friend, and I would do anything for him."

Not lovers, then. I'd been in those shoes before. Hopefully, Callum wised up and created his own distance from Landon before his kindness bit him in the ass.

"He's a spoiled brat and always has been," I argued without heat. "Let him fight his own battles."

Callum stiffened but remained seated. "You have no idea what he's faced, the pain he's endured. The secret life he now lives—how fucking fantastic of a man he's become."

I studied the color in Callum's cheeks, the intense passion blazing in his steady gaze. A huffed exhale left me as I realized what was going on, again, so goddamned reminiscent of how I'd felt once upon a time and lied to myself that I no longer did. "You're in love with him."

Callum didn't argue, nor did he look away.

"What's holding you back from claiming him yourself," I asked quietly, even though I already knew the answer.

"He still wants *you!*" Callum bit out the truth with more hurt in his tone than anger. "More than anything. He's obsessed. So far gone on you that he sees nothing else."

Him included, obviously since Callum seemed to be one hell of a catch.

An intense silence fell over us, heavy with strife and underlying desire. We both stared as though trying to sift through the other's thoughts and emotions, but we were nothing more than strangers who'd had a single dinner date. Even though we'd danced close enough to feel how our bodies responded to each other.

Yearning to possess him slithered through my veins at the memory of holding him in my arms, making me itch to take his mouth before bending him over the edge of my bed.

Callum stood before I decided to devour him. He kept his distance even though he had to feel the draw to close the space between us regardless of the massive stumbling block of Landon. "Please...meet him for breakfast at nine."

The last fucking thing I wanted to do was sit and submit my ears to Landon's apologies and excuses for his behavior that had landed me on the streets. There was no reason enough for his actions to make me open to amending what he'd broken.

But I'd signed a contract, and that meant I *had* to please the client. While there was leeway for EEMM employees to call shit off, I didn't feel threatened or uncomfortable enough in a way that warranted the action.

That was what I told myself anyway.

"Fine," I stated, moving toward my door to usher Callum out, since I wasn't going to get a taste of him like my body ached for.

The dude was an absolute martyr, a fucking *faithful* friend Landon didn't deserve as far as I was concerned.

Or...

My hand hesitated as I reached for the door handle.

Did Callum have another angle, and I was just a pawn in whatever game he played? Fucking hell, it was bad enough he might be using me—I did *not* want any part of their drama.

My stomach turned rock-like as I ripped my door open.

Callum followed a little slower, pausing with only a foot or so of distance between us.

Another one of those sparking silences settled, and regardless of that instinctive need to protect myself, every molecule in my body reached desperately for him. To touch. Taste. Possess.

"I'm only doing this for you, Callum. Not because I want reconciliation with the brat."

He dipped his head as though he'd expected as such.

"Goodnight," I bit out, and he turned away without another word.

Fuck.

I watched him amble quietly up the carpeted hallway, my chest hurting a little more with each step he took. He disappeared a second later around a corner.

The door slammed shut as I stalked toward the bathroom with a deep scowl, making the water hot as hell's flames before stepping into the shower.

Surely he had to believe that Landon and I making amends would only strengthen the asshole's feelings for me. So why insist on us speaking? Did he keep his fingers crossed I would go off and rip into Landon in the exact way I wanted to? Was it Callum's hope that I would shatter Landon even further, leaving mere pieces he hoped to glue back together? Was he so desperate for Landon's attention and love that he would break the man's heart in attempts to heal it?

I hardly knew Callum, but he didn't seem the sort to intentionally cause hurt to someone he cared about. He'd been nothing but genuine as far as I could tell, and having escorted for a handful of years, I'd gotten pretty good at reading men.

Regardless of my initial impression of Callum, and thanks to my past, the idea of him setting himself up to be the hero fed off itself. It was a nefarious plan that might serve him the man he was in love with on a platter, but where did that leave me?

Why the fuck do I even care about the outcome?

That question settled in my brain after showering as I lay down in the king-sized bed and stared out the massive window at the pale full moon watching me from high in its lonely sky.

Even though I didn't think myself capable of trusting anyone enough to be in a relationship, I *was* tired of being alone. Had been since as far back as I could remember, having gotten tossed into the system as an infant. Seeing my friends at Elite hooking up, marrying, and some even talking about having kids together sent a pang through my heart every time we all got together.

Part of me yearned for what those couples shared—everything. Thoughts, feelings, struggles, and accomplishments. It took serious balls to lower one's walls and be vulnerable like that, and I wasn't sure I had that capability.

I'd been fine on my own for years and had a lot to show for it. A nice condo with its heavy blanket of silence I told myself I enjoyed. Appreciation at the shelter and community home I volunteered at. Two men I exchanged up-nods with at the gym and occasionally spotted for.

What I didn't have?

A close friend, because I'd learned the hard way how easily betrayal happened and how it shattered dreams and ruined lives.

Huffing an exhausted exhale, I closed my eyes and rolled onto my stomach, punching my pillow before settling in once more.

Blue-green eyes flashed behind my closed lids. Lush lips at a height I wouldn't have to do anything but step forward to taste. A warm palm on my lower back that sent shivers up and down my spine and promised comfort and safety regardless of how well I knew the man.

Floppy light brown hair and amber eyes with their golden ring around the irises rose alongside Callum's face in my mind. Need like a goddamned tractor beam pulled me in same as it had fifteen years earlier when Landon had climbed atop me, making my dick hard. I longed for the familiar warmth of him against my side regardless of the truth between us. The memory of how tears had welled when I'd whispered no to what he'd wanted to gift me tore at my insides.

Groaning, I turned my head to face the other way, but the images and thoughts of both men followed me into the early morning hours. They drifted in and out of my dreams like haunting wraiths intent on wrecking my soul with both sweet memories and beautiful possibilities of what could be.

Chapter 7

Landon

I woke in Callum's bed.

At least this time my sleeping ass hadn't gone all octopus around him from dreams he might leave me and never return. God knew what I would do if he ever walked out on me. Without Callum... Hell, I couldn't begin to imagine how I would survive. Making it through a single day without his assuring presence and guidance seemed impossible.

Nope. I lay on my side, fuzzy memories fighting for clarity in my brain that was slow to power up. He and Zack had been clasped tightly together in an embrace, even more erotic a sight than when they'd been dancing.

Neither wore clothes, I realized as the colors from the fantasy world I'd been inside while asleep became vivid in my consciousness.

They'd been locked in a kiss, hands groping, frotting in desperation for release against each other.

And I'd been turned the fuck on, dick aching.

I blinked myself out of the memory, and Callum came fully into focus.

He still slept on his back, his far arm wrapped up above his head on the pillow, fingers slightly curled, completely relaxed. Lips parted, he exhaled soft puffs of air without much sound.

Callum had a strong brow and prominent nose, classical almost in its appearance as though he had aristocrat blood in him. Even in sleep, he appeared so put together. Calm and collected. Everything I wasn't and needed. I'd been lucky to have my first manuscript land on his desk, even though he'd never learned how it had happened. He'd been in charge of marketing, far from acquisitions and having no say in what authors the publishing house he worked for took on as clients.

Whoever or whatever had made our paths cross that day had blessed me beyond measure.

Sighing, I pulled my knees up to ease my morning wood that raged more than usual thanks to that dream of him and Zack.

What Callum had done for me, the money he'd used to hire Zack for five days, was above and beyond what a normal friend would do. I didn't deserve Callum, and nothing in my past suggested otherwise even though he insisted I was a good man and ought to have whatever my heart desired.

Which would be Zack.

Callum knew that truth of mine—hell, I'd talked the entire affair to death more than once to his kind ear.

My mind focused on the man who owned every piece of me, and a not so sweet ache settled in my chest. He and Callum were a lot alike, or at least the younger Zack had been. Wiser than his years, Zack had been an old man even at eighteen from having grown up in foster care. He'd been nothing but sweet and nurturing, same as Callum.

He was a perfect fit for all the fragmented pieces inside of me that I couldn't glue back together on my own and Callum attempted to. Hell, I didn't even know how to deal with my emotions or the heavy silence while being alone that forced self-reflection.

That's why I lost myself in writing. Focusing on make-believe men and their love lives made dealing with mine easier and escaping reality a simple feat.

A quiet noise left Callum's mouth, one he always made right before waking, thankfully giving me respite from my mind. His soft-looking lips drew my focus. The upper was slightly plumper than the lower. I remembered how beautiful of a smile he had and that dimple I stared at whenever I coaxed laughter from him.

Without thought, I brushed my fingertip over his cheek right where the dent would appear, strange flutters in my stomach.

Callum's eyelids slid open from the slight touch, and he turned his head toward me, his eyes sleepy.

I didn't remember crowding closer while studying him, but I realized my pulled-up knees touched his thighs, my face inches from his shoulder.

He made a low growl-like noise that sounded like a grumpy bear who'd been woken too early.

I grinned, readying to tease him for not being a morning person.

Callum grunted and weaseled his arm around me, pulling me tighter against his side though, erasing all jesting words from my mind.

My legs straightened, and my still hard cock slid along his thigh.

I gulped, my heart suddenly thumping in my chest. He'd never intentionally hugged me like this. "Um..." I cleared my throat, feeling a desperate need to ease the situation. "That's awkward?"

"Don't worry about it," Callum muttered, his eyes still on me and much more alert than seconds earlier. He didn't look bothered by the fact my body pressed against him. His hand remained on my lower back as though he wanted me to stay right the fuck there.

"Morning wood is a real thing in case you haven't figured that shit out by now." His voice sounded ragged, and the fact he reached beneath the blankets to adjust himself...

A tingle raced through my groin.

What the hell was that?

What the *ever* loving hell?

I studied my best friend, trying to make sense of the feelings suddenly stirring inside me. Was it...desire? It was similar to the affection I'd felt for him for years but *more*.

"Do I have a zit on my nose or something?" Callum muttered, rubbing a hand over his face, and I realized I stared a little too hard for much too long.

I shifted my hips back, suddenly antsy to put some space between us even though my body disagreed with my head. I'd gone too long without sex and seriously needed dick. "N-No."

He sighed, sounding almost disappointed I'd pulled away. "I went to see Zack last night," he stated quietly.

My heart stuttered in my chest at the thought of him with the man I wanted back in my life.

But.

Oh, but...

It wasn't out of jealousy or fear Callum would leave me. Nope. That trip in my heartbeat was because of a sudden shot of adrenaline and lust over the memory of the two men entwined in my dream. Saliva and pre-cum between their skin. Heat and panted breaths. Groans and sounds of slap-ping skin, the squelch of lube in an ass being stuffed full.

Blinking a few times, I forced myself to focus on Callum rather than my fanciful imagination that earned me a shit ton of royalties every month.

"I think he'll be more willing to listen to you this morn-ing," Callum said. "He agreed to meet you for breakfast at nine."

All thoughts of anything but having the chance for reconciliation with Zack fled from my brain as hope and warmth rushed through me. I finally had an opportunity to make things right.

And maybe more.

I scrambled off the bed in my haste, shoving at the blan-kets with my feet when they attempted to keep me in place.

Same as always, Callum cared for me, untangling my foot that had somehow gotten wrapped up in the top sheet as I grabbed my cell off the bedside table.

Eight-thirty.

"Shit," I muttered, a burning desire to get my ass ready and out the door taking over my brain.

"I owe you one!" I shot over my shoulder while rushing to the bathroom, my morning wood leading the way.

Not sure how shit would go down between me and Zack, I cleaned myself out rather than empty my balls. You know, just in case. That choice could bite me in the ass. I might end up with a raging hard-on distracting me while talking to Zack, but at least we would be at a table that would hide the proof of the way my body still wanted him after all these years.

How much would I have to share in order to gain forgiveness? Was he aware of what he'd meant to me when we were kids? Had he noticed only he had ever given me the time of day? That he was the one person in my life I could rely on?

Yes, I'd behaved badly the night he'd left our home, but I'd been sure he felt the same about me as I did him.

His rejection had stung, had triggered what I learned later was fear from childhood trauma thanks to parents too busy to give me attention—good or otherwise.

I'd fucked up back then.

But this time I would do everything right, no matter the cost.

Chapter 8

Callum

Wishful thinking had my brain believing Landon had looked at me with something more in his gaze as we'd been tangled up together. An awakening of what I'd felt for him since day one. The possibility of exploration and eventual satisfaction.

I'd been tempted to do more than pull him against my side, but that action had startled him into some revelation. Rather than pushing for more or overcrowding his already filled head with too many new feelings, I focused on our reason for being on a tropical island.

So like an idiot, I'd opened my mouth and given him a bit of information that would light him up. I just hadn't considered the idea of breakfast with Zack would rip Landon from my arms as though I was disposable. That his hard-on against my thigh was exactly what I'd reasoned it away as. With how quickly he'd attempted to escape the bed to get ready to meet Zack, I realized that his body's supposed response to being in close proximity to me *had* meant nothing.

Heart heavy where I lay by myself, I pressed my palms against my face, exhaling slowly until my lungs completely emptied and burned.

Why did love have to hurt so damned badly?

In fairy tales and romance books, his especially, everything was rainbows and rose-colored glasses. Fluttering in the chest and breathless anticipation.

Regardless of the pain, my dick still ached to burrow inside Landon's body and claim him as my own. I longed for everything with Landon that he wanted with Zack.

Fucking Zack.

"Goddamn," I muttered as my dick bucked against my briefs at the memory of the escort.

What situation had I gotten myself into? I loved Landon, but something about Zack called to me and not like a gentle whisper on the breeze. We were talking a shrieking wind with hurricane force, laying waste to my existence.

His words from the night before about sexual assault and going to jail had hit me even harder though.

Memories had slammed into me like a foot to the sternum, breath-stealing and staggering. And even though the trauma from my own past strengthened my resolve to nurture Landon, I couldn't help but feel ashamed over the choices I'd made that had ruined more than one life.

Landon didn't know it, but he was my means of making atonement of sorts even though we hadn't been involved back then. He was my secret second chance to do right after I'd failed my brother all those years ago.

My cell rang, breaking through my thoughts from the troubling memories.

I rolled to grab my phone off the bedside table, aware of the shower running in our suite. Recognizing the number, I answered without hesitation. "Hey, Cyn, what's up?"

Cynthia, Landon's kickass editor, didn't waste any time with small talk. "How set in stone is the release date for this manuscript?"

I pushed upright to sit against the bed's headboard. We were already behind schedule due to some bullshit Landon had to deal with a few weeks earlier, and I'd lined up promotional events across social media, podcasts, newspapers, and magazines—sans pictures of Landon, same as always. He had a pen name for a reason.

"There's not much wiggle room," I replied, unease trickling down my spine like a droplet of sweat.

"Well there's a serious plot issue going back to book three in this series." Cynthia went on to lay out the problem, a massive overlooking of the fact Landon had killed off a secondary character, who showed up in his latest manuscript and held a prominent part in the plot for book eight, which was currently being edited. Not an easy erase or fix.

"How the fuck did I miss that?" I muttered, scrubbing a hand over my face.

"His death in book three was that last minute add-in with the others," Cynthia said, and I cursed again, remembering her suggesting Landon rain down some bad shit on characters who hadn't deserved to live anyway. It had been an unexpected twist, one that had ended up shooting the book to the top of the charts because it'd drawn so much emotion from readers.

Seeing as how Landon was a complete pantser and wrote his stories from the hip, I wasn't surprised by the mistake. He'd made plenty over the years of his publishing career but nothing so substantial that it ruined an entire plotline.

How the fuck had I missed it too?

"We don't have time to fix this," I said, staring at the bathroom door Landon had disappeared behind.

"Maybe if he sits his ass down, figures out how to weave in a new character from scratch to take the dead dude's place, and does nothing but type for the next three days straight, we might."

We're fucked.

The shower had shut off, and I chewed on the inside of my lip.

Did I drop this bomb on him now in the hopes he would have the remainder of our vacation to take care of this mess? Or did I allow him the chance to set right what he'd been desperate for since childhood?

Yeah, given the choice, there was no way would Landon would ever pick his job over Zack.

That man would always come first.

I swallowed hard at that truth, knowing even I, his best friend and rock over the years, took a backseat.

Best to let him get that shit with Zack straightened out over breakfast—hopefully—then spill the news he needed his focus elsewhere for the next couple of days. Maybe he would be able to pull some magic out of his overly active imagination.

"Let me talk to him, but send me your developmental notes in the meantime," I said, about to commit Landon to something that might prove impossible. But what choice did we have when the countdown to release couldn't be stopped without major consequences? "We'll get this taken care of and a manuscript back in your inbox before the end of next week."

"That'll be pushing the ARC schedule."

"Only by a couple days. I'll spread the word that the manuscript is so hot he burned his fingers ensuring everyone's satisfaction. Building up the hype a little more will only ensure his fans are knocking down doors to get their hands on a physical copy."

"If anyone can incite fans' need to buy, it's you," Cynthia said with a snicker.

But I wasn't laughing.

I pressed my lips tight and hung up a second later after bidding the editor a better day than the one ahead of me.

From the first manuscript that had magically appeared on my desk, I'd been smitten with the unknown author. His weaving of words, regardless or perhaps because of their eroticism, had spoken to me and invoked a physical response that had surprised me. I'd felt attraction before but never with consuming focus.

Mere words typed on paper had changed my life.

I'd literally dug up the roots I'd planted deep in the publishing world and left New York behind. Rearranged my entire existence to make myself available to an author who had potential, quiet charisma, and a spirit alluring enough that I couldn't refuse him a single thing.

Add in the fact he needed to be looked after, a firm disposition to keep him in line and on track, and I'd been a goner for the beautiful boy with amber eyes.

It'd been eight years since I'd first spoken to Landon over the phone, and I didn't regret one choice in leaving my job in marketing to work as his PA. Laboring for a secret, breakout indie author proved ten times more fulfilling and lucrative than any desk job at some skyrise in Manhattan where we pushed cookie-cutter books in the hope of making us all a few million.

There were less restrictions, more independence, I had control without anyone higher up the chain breathing down my neck, and I got to watch over Landon. While some probably saw me as more of a babysitter than personal assistant, I loved what we shared as best friends and roommates.

But I want more.

The thought echoed in my head as the bathroom door opened, releasing rolling steam.

Landon exited like a supermodel, freshly shaved and his hair done, a towel wrapped around his waist. His slender yet muscular arms and chest were still damp from his shower, and my tongue salivated to lick the droplets off him.

The man wore sensuality like a second skin in the way he walked, spoke, and thought up raunchy stories. He was a sexual creature, which had almost led to his demise not long before we'd met. While I knew about the hookup apps on his cell, I wasn't aware if he utilized them.

Sure, we didn't spend twenty-four-seven together, so there was a possibility Landon got laid when his hand just wasn't cutting it, but he'd never admitted to doing so. And I would never ask. It wasn't my place, nor did I want to hear about someone having access to his body when I didn't, all thanks to the man who owned his heart.

He shot me a grin, easing my hurt over how quickly he'd left me alone in my bed, but he didn't linger. His fine ass skipped toward his own room to get dressed.

I imagined that his sole focus was on first gaining Zack's forgiveness, then getting his hands on the man or vice versa.

An image bloomed in my mind, one of many secretive sights Landon had brought to life with his words, but this time, the character's bodies intertwined and writhing in need weren't faceless. Zack and Landon lived in vivid color in my mind.

Oh fuck.

A hard swallow bobbed my throat, desperate need sending blood straight to my groin.

The draw to Zack was potent beyond measure, equal although different in feeling than Landon's hold on me. But, I didn't sense being torn in opposite directions or a need to choose or focus on one attraction over the other, exactly as Landon had spelled out in the first book of his I'd read. A gay triad that fulfilled the three men how each needed.

I'd never considered a poly relationship to be sustainable like in some of the erotic stories Landon wrote, but the picture in my head made me pause. I could see myself sitting and watching Landon and Zack together. Imagining the various ways they would fuck and how a third—me— could blend into their passion stole my breath.

I slid from my bed and ambled to the bathroom where the scent of Landon's bodywash flooded my lungs as I filled my fist with a few days' worth of cum.

All while imagining the three of us together.

Chapter 9

Zack

I'd considered skipping out of breakfast. Calling Sean and telling him I would be home early and available to book with another client as soon as possible for that good, hard fuck I still needed.

But somehow—fuck the unchanged desires deep in my soul—I ended up seated at the hotel's first floor restaurant where a breakfast buffet spread over a dozen feet worth of tables with heated trays and iced bins with various foods. Others on vacation ate quietly around me, but I merely sipped black coffee. My stomach knotted, not the least bit interested in true sustenance.

It didn't matter if Landon lobbed more excuses my way. I would exercise restraint and act like a gentleman and hear him out like I'd agreed to—for Callum's sake, even though unrest over his motives still raked at my mind. I'd dreamed about him. Landon too. Their faces and bodies had morphed from one to the other while I'd slept. Beneath me. On top of me. Even a glimpse of being spit roasted had attributed to waking with a raging boner, my balls on the verge of nutting.

Two strokes had shot spunk up over my chest, and the truth Landon would soon be mere feet across the table from me already had me warming up for another round.

I hated but couldn't deny that my body still desired him regardless of the pain he'd caused me when we'd been younger.

Add in my lust for his...whatever Callum was to him, and I considered bashing my head against a wall.

Landon stepped through the arch leading into the restaurant, glancing around and halting all thoughts.

Fuck. Me.

I took the time to catch my breath and soak him in before our eyes met.

He had a gorgeous body and perfectly mussed hair I wanted to yank on while I bruised his mouth with punishing kisses. He licked over his lower lip as though anxious.

While I'd have preferred to feed off his insecurities and make him suffer like I had, that goddamn need to set him at ease slithered through my wish to wreck him.

But Landon wasn't my client, and I owed him no such satisfaction in any way, shape, or form. He'd made his bed. He could fucking sleep in it for eternity for all I cared.

Lie—you do *care.*

Scowling over the whisper of sympathy and love for Landon that had claws dug deep in my soul, I lounged in my chair with feigned indifference. Every muscle in my body became tense as fuck—*ready* to fuck—while waiting for him to spot me.

Landon rubbed at the back of his neck I wanted to hold tight while pounding into his ass until he cried and begged for release I would forever deny him.

My goddamn dick liked that image in my head a little

too much and leaked pre-cum in my shorts. Internally cursing my cock, I glared at the man I'd rather see sunken into the depths of despair. Loneliness. Struggling to survive. Empty and aimless.

The same things he'd put me through.

Landon shifted my way, finally making eye contact.

A bolt of awareness, a sense of ownership I'd felt for him once upon a time, zapped through me, raising the hairs on my nape. I fought to keep from shifting on my chair at the unpleasant yet addictive feeling.

His arm fell to his side, his shoulders hitching up near his ears.

At least the kid wasn't cocky in finally having pinned me down thanks to my goddamn client. Still, he moved with lethal grace like a big cat on the prowl, sleek lines and sexy as hell shifting of muscles that made my groin pulse with the need to bury deep and claim.

Landon was a goddamn treat for my starved, aching body, and I lusted to burrow so far up his ass that I tickled his goddamned tonsils while ripping my teeth into his neck.

A muscle ticked in my jaw as he drew closer, those gorgeous eyes of his ensnaring me, making me want to agree to whatever his selfish little heart desired.

But, once bitten, twice shy and all that shit, so fuck whatever trap his deviousness readied for my soul.

I raised my chin and stared the fucker down regardless that my shield of self-preservation felt like nothing more than a flimsy sheet of foil.

He slid into the seat across from me, our gazes latched tight. "Thank you for agreeing to meet with me."

Fuck, even his low husky voice moved through me like a promising caress, causing tingles to sizzle in my blood.

"Not like I have much choice." I refused to acknowledge the way the sweet scent of him filled my mouth with excess saliva too. "Your friend hired me, and if I want to keep my job, I please the *client*."

I chose to ignore the glimpse of a grimace on Landon's mouth, since I'd intended for my crock-of-shit words to sting. One call, and I could end this mess.

So why hadn't I?

"How long have you been an escort?" he asked rather than apologizing yet again like I'd expected.

"Couple of years." I wasn't up for a reconnection chat, nor did I trust him with my personal shit, but as long as he got what he needed to finally let me go...

I reminded myself I was desperate to be free of his constant resurfacing in my life, that having set eyes on him hadn't changed that fact.

"Do you like it?"

Frowning, I sipped my coffee while eyeing the inquisitive asshole who sat as rigid as I did. I had no fucking clue what game he played, but exhaustion from a near sleepless night swayed my mind to go with whatever the fuck this was.

I'd had enough.

"Cut it with the small talk." I grunted the words and set my mug aside. It was time to end this shit between us so I could attempt to move on—eradicate that piece of my heart he still owned. "I'm not interested. Say what you have to so I can go find your gorgeous assistant-slash-best friend, invite him back to my room, and earn every penny he paid me. Ass, dick, mouth—I'll gladly take whatever he'll give me because he's so damn hot."

Rather than reacting or scowling in jealousy like I'd hoped for, Landon shifted on his chair and bit his lower lip.

Did the idea of me and Callum fucking turn him on?

I raised an eyebrow, not exactly hating the resurgence of lust in my groin by thoughts of dicking Callum down while Landon watched.

His face flushed a rosy pink at my knowing look. He cleared his throat, glancing away. "I won't apologize again."

"Good because words don't mean shit when it comes to broken trust."

He nodded as though agreeing, settling the slightest bit as a slow, steady exhale slumped his shoulders. His gaze latched onto my eyes again. Festering hurt radiated toward me with grasping fingers as though trying to tractor beam me into what we'd once shared. "I didn't want you to leave our home back then."

"Bullshit," I bit out, fighting hard to keep my crumbling walls in place even though Callum had basically said the same thing. Excuses. End of. "You *told* me to go that night. Screamed it, in fact, which brought your father running. In true brat form, you threw a tantrum because I wouldn't give you what you wanted."

Liquid turned Landon's eyes into whiskey rather than glinting amber.

Tears had been my downfall when it came to him. Every. Fucking. Time.

"Don't fucking attempt to manipulate me with emotions," I growled, remembering how he'd done so too often when we'd been kids.

"I'm not," he snapped, the sheen of wetness lingering over his expressive orbs. "I reacted out of fear, not because you denied me. You were the only person in my life who gave me attention and looked out for me. You knew me inside and out—that I was gay. You had my back when I finally told my parents that year too, standing firm by my side. You did nothing but encourage me when I started writing stories to lose myself in. It was *you* who influenced me to follow my dreams."

I couldn't argue anything he'd claimed because he spoke the truth about how I'd bent over backwards to make sure he wasn't alone. But that last bit?

"What dreams?" I asked, hating my interest had been piqued. I did. Not. Care.

Landon waved his hand, frowning. "Doesn't matter. What *does* is that I felt like my world was ripping in two, that the one person I trusted to stay beside me had turned eighteen and was going to go seek out his destiny without me. I thought giving you my virginity would tie you to me, make you stay, and when you rejected me as though I meant nothing to you—"

The words ripped from his heaving chest, and he pressed his lips tight while swallowing hard against the tears threatening to spill down his flushed cheeks.

"You were only fifteen. Fucking *jailbait*, Landon," I said, my voice low as I leaned forward, wondering how the fuck all that emotion lingered inside him after so long.

But didn't anger cling to my mind, desire in my soul no matter how much I denied it, in the same way? His appearance had only intensified the desires too, much to my annoyance.

"I was young, but can't a teenager fall in love?"

"Lust, maybe," I said, "but not long-lasting commitment."

"Bullshit." Fire blazed in his stare regardless of the wetness darkening the base of his blond eyelashes. "My feelings for you haven't changed one bit since that night. I loved you then, and I love you still."

I sat back in my chair, stunned by his adamant reply. "You...you don't even *know* me anymore, Landon. Where

I've been. What I did in order to survive. The man I became after leaving Rhode Island."

"The heart wants what the heart wants. Cliche, but that's how it is."

Fucker hit the nail on the head, and I hated him even more for speaking the truth between us.

Landon leaned forward to occupy the space over the table I'd vacated while I sat in wary uncertainty. "I chased after fulfillment elsewhere for years. Zack, if you knew half the shit I got myself into—"

He pressed his lips tight again, his eyes revealing conflict and even more pain as he shook his head as though disgusted with himself.

"Not that I'm blaming you," he finally continued, his voice broken when I couldn't cook up a goddamned thing to say. "I take full responsibility for sowing my wild oats. But you're the one I always came back to in my mind. It's *always* been you. The only man I've ever wanted."

He sounded sincere, but emotional wounds and too much time lay between us to simply falling into what we'd been, the platonic relationship that had once held potential for so much more.

Besides, there was now another card here at play. And while I wasn't usually impulsive, I found myself in a situation where a risk had to be taken in order to find peace once and for all.

"What about Callum?" I watched Landon closely for micro-expressions that would reveal his thoughts for the other man who loved him in ways I no longer could.

He blinked, his head tipping to the side. Giving up the table's higher ground, he sat back, his shoulders wilted again as his hands landed in his lap. "What about him?" he whispered, uncertainty in his tone I refused to be moved by.

Still, I hesitated crossing over a line I swore I never would.

But Callum and I weren't friends as Landon and I had once been. What did it matter if I betrayed Callum's trust he'd put in me by sharing his feelings for Landon?

He played a game I was ready to participate in to free myself from the enemy I refused to see as anything else no matter how much my heart disagreed.

"That man is madly in love with you and right at your fingertips," I stated quietly, refusing to feel guilt over the truth I spilled. "He's gone above and beyond for you—and you're still stuck on *me*?" I shook my head, holding his unblinking stare. "I'm not the right choice here, Landon. Be smart for once in your life. Grab hold of the one who has the ability to entrust his heart to you—because that will never be me."

Chapter 10

Landon

adly in love with you.

That damned statement hit me like an uppercut to the chin.

The words echoed in the vast chamber of my mind, and I sat stunned. Staring and uncaring that Zack had basically called me stupid for making poor choices. If he only knew the truth of how far I'd actually gone in my need to rid my heart and body of want for him.

But back to Callum...

I remembered how my best friend had looked at me a mere hour or so earlier. Similar warmth as always had filled his sea-like eyes, a swirling of emotion I'd considered to be tenderness, the kind of caring a person felt for loved ones. Like brothers, maybe.

Had there been more intent behind his affection this morning? Every time I'd woken up in his bed after snuggling up to him in my sleep? If I'd shown the slightest indication of wanting Callum, which I totally had experienced in that moment, would he have leaned in to brush his lips over mine?

My heart beat a little faster, a stir of desire rousing inside me again. The feeling excited me, like a door had cracked open, allowing a peek into a whole new world of possibilities.

After Zack had left me, I'd had difficulty trusting anyone. But Callum had come in like a gentle breeze, a soothing balm who had helped ease the hurt I'd caused myself. I'd been empty inside for so long, and he'd filled a part of the void that my writing still hadn't been able to.

Memories raced through my brain, reminding me of how doting Callum had always been with me, how my best friend nurtured me in the same way Zack had done when we'd been kids. I tended to be handsy in response to his tender touches. Did I cling to Callum because his nature reminded me of Zack, the rock I'd hung onto when shit had gotten too real back then?

Or did I grasp onto Callum out of an unconscious yearning for more with *him*? The thought echoed in my head, making me believe it might be true. Or perhaps I held tight to him because I feared he would leave me as Zack had done.

But Zack had taken off because of *my* decision, the words I'd screamed out of fear of abandonment and pain over his rejection. That choice had led to many other wrong ones afterward that had taken my life into a downward spiral.

Callum had been the hero sweeping in to offer my heart shelter from the backlash storm, but he wasn't my replacement for Zack.

Or was he?

Did I love Callum beyond friendship? That morning's moment between us on his bed suggested I very well might.

Warmth continued to rouse inside me, arousal I wasn't sure what to do with.

Looking back, I realized it wasn't the first time Callum had peered at me in such a way, but I'd been too focused on my love for Zack to recognize his feelings. Add in his tender touches to my lower back, the brush of his lips over my temple, his lingering fingertips on my skin...

A shudder rippled through me.

I stared at Zack, working through the thoughts ricocheting through my mind. There was a lot of shit to unpack, thanks to Zack's statement about Callum. He and I shared something more potent than Zack and I ever had. How could that not be love? And even if Zack and I worked things out between us, I would demand Callum remain on my other side since I couldn't bear to live without him.

My throat tightened, eyes once more welling at the thought of losing Callum—even if I were to attempt to make Zack his replacement, which he could never be.

Zack's lips pursed as though he grew annoyed by my troubled silence.

I needed to focus on the *now*, even though underlying fear of Zack walking away again tempted me to push off a discussion we still had to finish. While I didn't deserve his forgiveness and didn't truly believe I would get it, I hoped for it. Maybe if we reached an understanding at least, I could find a way to move on from the hold he had over my heart, since he'd clearly stated I would never have access to his again.

Callum would be enough. He'd been my everything for years, and I'd been a lucky bastard who hadn't realized how good he'd had it until now.

"I've never been known for my smart choices," I admitted quietly, "but I can't help what I want."

Zack's intense stare made me long for Callum's assuring touch on my lower back. "And what's that?"

"Do you…" I glanced at his half-empty mug of coffee that'd sat untouched long enough it'd probably grown cold. "Do you think you would ever be open to at least being my friend again?"

"You're joking, right? After what you did to me?"

I grimaced, closing my eyes. "I really miss having you in my life, Zack. That closeness we shared back then."

"You don't need me. You have Callum."

"I'm greedy," I stated what he was already aware of while meeting his hazel eyes I could still drown in without effort.

He huffed what sounded like a laugh, the corner of his lips giving me a hint of smile that made my pulse race. "You always were." Leaning onto the table, Zack pinned me in place with a glint in his eyes that wasn't exactly friendly but held heat I recognized. He might not like me, but a part of him recognized and appreciated the sexual tension between us. Something I'd felt the stirrings of when we'd been younger but hadn't known the full extent of until now.

"What *exactly* do you want from me, Landon?" His low, suggestive voice trailed over my skin like teasing fingertips. "And don't lie."

"Everything, even if it hurts," I whispered the truth, even though pain of some sort lay around the corner in one form or another.

Zack pursed his lips while considering my words, eventually releasing a heavy sigh that screamed of resignation.

My pulse once more sped up, regardless of the fear attempting to knife at the back of my mind.

"Temporary truce for now," Zack said, his words making my heart soar even though it wasn't exactly what I'd hoped for. "Callum hired me for the next five days, so my dick, mouth, and every other part of me, belongs to him. If he asks me to pleasure you, worship your body, or make you come while I'm buried balls deep in your ass, I will."

Oh, Jesus.

I gulped at the one-eighty topic change that swelled my cock to the point of aching.

Dream fucking come true.

"J-Just to clarify," I whispered, my voice shaking, "you'll agree to do...all that to me *only* because he told you to? Like a one-time thing?"

"No matter the good parts of our past as kids, I don't have space in my life for more than fucking for money, Landon."

I chewed on my lower lip, mollified a bit that he too had fond memories. "So that would mean at the end of these five days, we go our separate ways, kind of like fucking each other from our systems and moving on?"

"Yes. You're both a job. Nothing more."

Ouch.

I tried to not flinch. "So no friendship," I asked slowly, still unsure I understood what *was* on offer. "Just fucking if that's what Callum wants for us."

Zack nodded, a professional sex worker who could shut down emotion in his eyes.

But what if Callum didn't ask Zack to pleasure me? What if my best friend had zero wish to share me and only hoped for Zack and I to make amends? Did Callum cross his fingers I would give him my heart even not knowing both men shared equal parts?

Fucking hell, my mind stewed like a noxious brew, turning me from arousal to anxiety and back again in a blink.

Was it too early for a few shots of tequila?

I glanced around, taking note we were far from the only ones having sat down for breakfast. Couples and even a handful of families dined around us, none of them seeming to pay us any mind.

But what if someone recognized me and saw me on vacation hanging around with two men rather than the more acceptable *one*? I'd been so damn careful with the few hookups I'd allowed myself the previous couple of years since the event that had ruined my father's career as a senator. The last thing I wanted to do was have still shots of me plastered across social media and news outlets again, stirring up even more judgment for my whorish ways.

I'd finally found a quiet life, and while unsocial outside of Callum, I enjoyed a sense of contentment. I couldn't allow five days in paradise to fuck up my inconspicuous existence that had proven to be my safest choice by far.

"Temporary truce," I agreed, my voice low and shaky. "But just a head's up—I'm all for whatever Callum wants from either of us too and will gladly take advantage of his suggestions."

A slow, sensual smirk curled the corner of Zack's lips, sending a rush of blood straight to my groin.

I took a serious chance in agreeing with Zack, but Callum had proven he could be trusted with my everything, body and heart included.

Chapter 11

Callum

I slipped into a chair on the opposite side of where Landon and Zack sat together by the breakfast buffet. Somewhat hidden unless they directly looked my way, I watch them. A deep discussion kept them focused on each other, and even with the distance separating us, I could feel their combined sexual energy radiating clear across the restaurant like a teasing whispered breeze over my skin.

Zack studied Landon as though trying to dissect him. Good luck, without a few weeks' worth of Landon sharing about his seriously messed up past.

Landon stared at Zack with longing in his eyes, the way I dreamed of him looking at me.

My heart sat heavy in my chest at the clear attraction between them. I wanted to do right by my Landon, but it hurt. And while seeing the two of them spread arousal through my blood, the needy ache wasn't entirely pleasant.

I'd failed my brother in making the right choices while he'd been entrusted to my care, and I didn't want to get this wrong. Not speaking up and taking action when my instincts had demanded I do so had landed my only living relative in jail and a young woman broken both emotionally and mentally.

But this time, I'd listened to my gut instincts rather than ignoring them. The urge to give Landon the chance for closure with the man he was still in love with spurred me on. Yes, Zack had been right to deny him and walk away when they'd been kids, but he needed to hear Landon's truth.

So far, it appeared as though the conversation went well between the two men. No angry red faces or heated words rose like from the night before when surprise at seeing each other had caught them both unaware.

Perhaps since they'd calmed enough to think rationally, they were making amends, and my hiring Zack *would* pay off.

But what if the outcome left me along the sidelines, my heart cracked in two?

Landon stared at Zack, his body leaned toward the other man as though drawn by a magnet, and I couldn't deny understanding the feeling. If Zack forgave him and they returned to what they'd had as teenagers—and more —*would* I lose life as I knew it? There would definitely be no more shared home, since the house was in Landon's name. I would have the options of either getting my own place and withering away from a broken heart while continuing as Landon's PA or moving back to New York and trying to pick up where I'd left off in that sad, lonely existence.

Zack sat back in his chair, thick thighs spread wide, hands on his knees. Whatever Landon told him caused a semi-smile on Zack's gorgeous face that made my gut clench. He was so fucking hot with those broad shoulders and all that muscle beneath golden skin.

But so was my best friend with his pale complexion atop a more lithe build.

Pink flushed Landon's cheeks, and I could imagine the sparkle in his eyes that always caused butterflies to erupt in my stomach.

Zack nodded and stood.

Landon pushed up from the table and held out his hand.

Zack hesitated, his focus on Landon's fingers, and what I wouldn't have given to know his mind. Fear? Resigned to burying the hatchet between them? Or did he pause because he recognized things would change once he touched Landon again?

It seemed the three of us teetered on an edge of the unknown.

Their palms finally slid together, fingers clasped, and the electrical current of something potent shivered over me, raising the hairs on my arms. They both seemed caught up in a world of slow motion where every heartbeat throbbed with promise.

Of what exactly, I wasn't sure, but I longed to share in it, for that feeling to go on and on.

As if sensing my stare, Landon glanced my way, shattering the breathless moment hovering over us.

He dropped Zack's hand as though burned, his face flushing. A quick glance at Zack, his lips moving, and they both started toward me.

My gaze flitted between the two men as they drew closer, my inhales too quick. Zack's gaze promised sexual satisfaction if I asked for it. And Landon's held a tenderness I was well acquainted with but also a question that had me shifting on my seat in delicious torment.

The cells in my body vibrated, making me want to shed

the discomfort of my skin. Or better yet cause an eruption from my dick that would empty my tight balls when they'd been taken care of an hour earlier.

I needed answers so I could figure out how to move forward in calming myself one way or the other. "You've made your peace?" I asked as they stopped before me.

Landon glanced up at Zack whose hazel eyes remained fixed on my face as though seeking out my deepest desires and hidden thoughts.

"For now, I suppose," Landon answered, and Zack didn't argue, but the tension, both anger and lust, still lingered around them enough that I could taste it on my tongue. "We've agreed to a truce for the remainder of our stay."

"I came here for you, Callum, so what now?" Zack asked before I could, his question directed at me with sexual expectation in his eyes.

Oh, the ideas flitting through my mind, the images of the three of us—him and Landon while I watched...

I swallowed hard, shoving against any and all thoughts of fucking. "Keep us company," I demanded as his client, my tone ragged from the lust attempting to rule my body. "Enjoy a shared vacation. Snorkeling. Swimming. Air surfing, or whatever it's called when they hook you up with a parachute behind a boat. Let's relax and enjoy ourselves before returning to the real world."

If only I knew what life back home would look like in advance so I could prepare my heart.

"You hired me for more than companionship in paradise," Zack murmured, his voice low and definitely hinting at an agreeable option for some seriously needed physical gratification.

Landon shifted on his feet and placed a not-so-discreet

hand over his groin. My cock throbbed at the evidence he was on board with Zack's unspoken suggestion—but where did I fit into the equation?

I shrugged as though indifferent when I was anything but. "My goal in bringing you here was to make Landon happy. I told you, whatever he wants, he gets." I had to swallow again before forcing myself to continue. "If that's the use of your body, then who am I to deny what he desires?"

"And what do *you* want?" Zack asked, his gaze boring into me, flaying me wide fucking open.

"What I can't have," I whispered my heartbreak, glancing at my best friend.

Landon's lips parted, his eyes darkening as he stared at me.

I fought off the need to move again as I watched ideas go off behind Landon's eyes like fireworks on the Fourth of July.

He licked his lower lip, leaving behind a sheen I longed to taste.

"Lan?" I rasped, my insides clenched up tight as though on the brink of falling off a cliff with no bottom in sight. Fathomless depths. Unknown consequences. Scary as hell. Breath once more held, I waited for his answer that would dictate where I landed.

Tension radiated from Zack too as everything once more stilled around us. But this time, the heartbeats sounded like a countdown to what I feared would be a soul-crushing answer.

Landon blinked, tearing his focus off my eyes for the table between us. He shoved his hands in his pockets and shook his head. It appeared as though he tried to put his thoughts back in order when they'd been focused on the same type of chaos that had been his demise years earlier.

I sagged, my body suddenly exhausted in knowing what he would choose—and why. He'd learned his lesson about messing around with more than one man at a time the hard way and would never push his luck again.

"There's a snorkeling class in an hour," I broke the silence with something that wouldn't bring about questions I expected Landon had no wish to answer. Even he and I didn't talk about his past unless absolutely necessary. "Why don't we take advantage of the buffet then head over there?"

"Sounds good to me," Zack said, lightly elbowing Landon.

"Yeah—okay," Landon agreed, his voice no more than a whisper.

I released a slow exhale, wanting to grab my best friend and hug the hell out of him—and latch onto Zack with my needy mouth.

Chapter 12

Zack

Spending the day beneath the water with only my breaths and thoughts to keep my brain company wasn't exactly relaxing. Neither was watching Callum and Landon in nothing more than swim shorts gliding through the water with graceful undulations of their hips that reminded me of sex.

Sleek movements. Flexing muscle. Firm ass cheeks mere feet in front of me proved a better sight than any coral reef and colorful fish. I imagined stripping both men bare but got caught up in too much possibility to focus on one fantasy. Watching. Directing. Being on the receiving end. In the middle. Owning Callum's ass while he plowed into Landon.

Swimming with a hard-on wasn't exactly comfortable, but at least the group we were a part of seemed intent on the sea life around us rather than a horny man on the verge of nutting.

At the back of the group, it would be easy to rub a quick one out. Just a few strokes over my swim trunks would cause it to happen. Temptation to do so had me reaching for my aching cock, but a fish caught me by surprise and brushed against my leg, making me kick closer to those in front of me.

But the flagging erection quickly returned.

I managed to force the damn thing away by watching a curvy woman in a string bikini take in the sights, since nothing about her soft body turned me on. Sure, her new husband was easy on the eyes, but I kept my focus on her. Jealousy had weaseled in over the newlyweds' public affection while we'd been aboard the boat, that same sense of missing out I experienced with the guys from home.

Until my head broke the water line and sunshine kissed my face, my dick had chilled.

Once back on land, the three of us walked through warm sand, stopping at one of the bars for a drink. The momentary peace we'd agreed to was tenuous at best, a mere means of getting through the next couple of days.

Since Callum had said Landon could have whatever he wanted, if he initiated, I would look at him like a client. That made it easier to avoid thoughts of how much I still lusted after the brat. Pleasuring Landon would be nothing but a good time.

I just had to keep deep-rooted feels on lockdown and stick purely with fucking the asshole from my system like I was desperate to do.

Like I'd told Landon, I didn't do spontaneity, but this situation was beyond my control. I wouldn't overthink, just lock my heart away and enjoy my little vacation. And if that included sex, bring it the fuck on because I needed release by some means other than my own fist.

Things weren't forgiven and forgotten between me and Landon, but the animosity had taken a backseat for now. As long as I didn't focus on the fallout of his actions from back then, we could make it through the days ahead without any heated tension outside the sexual sort.

I'd explained to Landon over the empty breakfast table between us earlier in the morning that I hadn't intended on leaving after I'd turned eighteen. While I didn't go into my reasons for why I'd planned to stick around—*him*—I'd assured him that his distress had been unfounded. And I, in turn, accepted his explanation for his outburst, his fear over being alone in a house void of unconditional love and support.

Neither of his parents had time for Landon back then, both too focused on the campaign trail that would lead to his father eventually running for president. I'd been his everything—big brother, hero, and best friend all wrapped into one. While I still reasoned away his supposed undying love for me, how he looked at me was familiar.

I'd seen too many of my co-workers with the same *something* on their faces when watching their partners.

Yes, it was love as far as the retired Elites went, but I couldn't find it in me to trust what Landon's eyes told me no matter how much my heart longed to. He'd been on the receiving end of my jaded thoughts for too many years for good feels to simply wipe the shit away and take us back to what we used to be.

But fuck, the man was sexy as hell, even more so with mussed, salt-dried hair, his shirtless torso revealing ample muscle, six-pack included. Callum drew my eyes just as often, having the same effect on my body with his similar build. Turned out, the two men enjoyed sparring and also weight trained together to keep in shape.

I allowed myself a moment's fantasy of watching them sweating and swinging at each other. But my libido took over, which ended with them fucking on the floor, panting and groaning.

Then my thoughts shifted—what if they returned home and that exact situation arose...without me?

I clenched my jaw and assured myself I didn't care. Goddamnit, I needed to focus on the now. Hopefully, fucking Landon from my system.

After a few drinks where we discussed the gym, our favorite workouts, and healthy meals, we went to our separate suites to shower with an agreement to meet back up for an early dinner. We hadn't eaten anything substantial since Landon and I had joined Callum earlier that morning after our talk where all three of us had our fill from the breakfast buffet.

I arrived at the outdoor restaurant first and was seated alongside the live band rather than back in one of the private nooks like the night before.

Had it only been twenty-four hours since I'd met Callum? A mere day since Landon had come crashing back into my life totally unexpected—and I told myself unwanted?

He'd been nothing but his usual sweet, pink-cheeked self, constantly checking me out and keeping me on edge all day. Add in Callum's tight ass and the way he looked at the two of us with blatant hunger...

Without knowing what the night held, I'd decided to hold off on giving my balls relief in the shower. Unfortunately, that meant I dealt with a chub of excited expectation that only thickened when the two men headed toward me, their bodies close, shoulders brushing as they walked.

An undercurrent of lust grabbed hold of me, attempting to pull me under into *fuck it* territory, where nothing good would come as a result.

Talk about a flimsy fucking shield to protect my vulner-abilities. I was burnt toast without the hope of sweet butter to fix the mess in my head. I would please them both, then get the fuck out of paradise where there was no threat to my heart's safety. Where I didn't have to rely on anyone but myself for my well-being.

We skirted any serious conversations, choosing to discuss our favorite pastimes, movies, and shows worth binge-watching. Turned out, we all loved those DIY shows, even though not a single one was any good with a hammer or crowbar.

None of us ate a heavy dinner while we chatted, and while I had my reasons, I couldn't say for the two of them. Landon's hands shook pretty much nonstop, possible nerves if I had to guess. Callum? He glanced between the two of us, his expression going from lust to uncertainty. I wondered if the idea of Landon and I fucking turned him on or made him nauseous, considering how badly he was in love with his best friend.

But I didn't ask, nor did I bring up any topic of conver-sation that would lead to some big discussion about what we were actually doing and how fucking around while in paradise might affect their relationship.

I was ready for a good time, and it didn't matter to me what the two of them did once home.

Lies.

Fuck, was I full of them.

Envy weaseled its way through me whenever I imag-ined them returning to Landon's house I'd learned they both lived in. I once more imagined them together, walking hand-in-hand, sharing a bed, loving on each other every night from here on out. They would have what Sean and Matteo did. Drake and Preston.

Shit I wouldn't admit out loud to craving thanks to my suspicious mind and inability to trust another soul.

Once again, I attempted conversation that didn't center around emotions or anything too personal. The snorkeling trip hadn't allowed for much talk, so over dinner we discussed the days ahead of us. Callum shifted a few times as though he had something on his mind beyond the events he'd suggested earlier that morning.

"What's up with you?" Landon asked, pushing his half-empty plate aside.

"I heard from Cyn," Callum said, his focus flitting between the two of us. "I wasn't going to bring it up until later, but...it's bothering me."

I'd already finished my salad, so I sat back, fiddling with my glass of white wine on the table in front of me. Whatever Callum talked about, it had nothing to do with sex like I'd assumed.

"How bad it is?" Landon asked, his tone wary and face a little crestfallen.

Callum pursed his lips together before replying. "Very."

"Fuck," Landon muttered, his shoulders slouching. "Am I looking at hours or days?"

"For a normal guy, days, but I have faith in you."

Landon grimaced. "Shit."

"Yeah," Callum agreed.

I eyed the two men, wondering over their cryptic conversation, a part of me hating I wasn't in the know regardless of my determination to stay out of their lives once we left the island.

"Can it wait until we get home?" Landon asked.

"Not if we're going to keep on schedule."

"Fuuuuuuuuck," Landon grumbled, running his hand through his hair.

Callum reached out to clasp his hand and squeeze—exactly as I yearned to do even though I had no clue what the hell they were talking about. "Don't worry about it tonight, okay? Let's just enjoy our evening with Zack."

Still frowning, Landon nodded.

"Wanna dance?" I tossed out since Landon needed a distraction, and putting him at ease would please Callum.

Landon hesitated like a deer in headlights rather than jumping at the chance to be in my arms again like I'd expected.

"Go ahead," Callum insisted, seeming to settle a bit. "You're safe here."

I didn't get what was going on with *that* statement either, but whatever. I was itching to get my dick inside someone, and Landon was a sure thing.

"Come on." I grabbed his hand, pulling him to his feet, my body vibrating with the need to get the evening moving along in a more pleasurable way than wining and dining.

Our hands slotted together as they'd done dozens of times when we'd been kids, and something shifted inside me, same as it had earlier when we'd shook on our temporary truce before breakfast. I squeezed his fingers a little tighter as we stepped onto the dance floor to join the other couples already swaying to the soft island music. Anticipation prickled my skin, making me feel like a live wire.

I wrapped my hand around Landon's waist and drew him in until our fronts plastered together.

His breath caught, and he stared at me, pink, plump lips slightly parted and tempting as fuck, the same they'd been that night he'd betrayed me. Even though the reminder of that event still knifed anger through me, I couldn't deny how perfectly he felt in my arms.

"Okay?" I murmured, my dick aching.

Swallowing hard, he glanced around before nodding.

"Remember when you taught me how to slow dance for that eighth grade event beneath the stars I had?" I heard myself ask as the memory popped into my mind.

"Y-yeah," Landon breathed, quiet laughter following his answer. "Those ballroom classes Mother made me take as a kid paid off."

I grinned, seeing us spinning around the living room in vivid color. He'd been flushed and laughing while I'd tripped over my two left feet.

I'd never asked a girl to dance that night, but I never told Landon. I let him believe he'd helped me out—and he had, but I never put those lessons to use until years later. Countless times, I'd had to dance at events as an escort, and were it not for Landon's tutoring, I'd have been an embarrassment to my clients.

"I've learned better moves since," I teased, my blood going hot at the thought of how I'd rather dance with Landon.

He arched a brow. "Oh yeah?"

"Mmm." I tucked my thigh between his legs, fitting us together like puzzle pieces, same as I'd done to Callum the night before.

Landon shuddered, gulping at our proximity and my hard dick against his hip. "Jesus, Zack." He bit his lower lip and melted into me, trusting me with his body when that was the last thing he ought to do. I would take—and take some more—and leave behind wreckage exactly as he deserved. A mess of emotion I expected Callum would be too happy to glue together again.

What the fuck ever. I didn't care.

I led him in a dance that mimicked a slow, sensual fuck, both of my hands clasped on his ass to keep his groin against mine. The sweet scent of his shampoo teased my nose, and I lusted to latch onto his neck and mark him the fuck up right there for the world to see.

I hated how easy it was to drown in his amber eyes, to lose myself in the press of his body against mine, the draw of his magnetism that threatened to suck my soul back into a place I couldn't allow.

His hands clasped tight to my shirt, desperation etched in his face. "Kind of feels like a dream—I'm afraid I'm going to wake up."

I refused to acknowledge the *same* whispering in my head.

"Need me to pinch you to prove you're really here in my arms?" I joked, hoping to lighten my heavy, battling thoughts.

A gorgeous flush rose over his cheekbones, the sight causing my cock to buck in my shorts. And how he stared at me, hunger and sexual energy radiating between us, only made my body crave him even more.

We needed to get this party started one way or another before I busted a nut just from holding this stick of dynamite in my arms. Landon was dangerous. I would be smart to include a third wheel, a hot as fuck sexy man I hoped to get my hands on sooner than later.

"What's the deal with you and Callum?" I asked against Landon's ear, and he shivered. "You ever fuck?"

Landon shook his head. "No."

I shifted us in profile to Callum, glancing his way.

He watched us with an unwavering stare filled with yearning and not an ounce of jealousy. Either the man didn't really love Landon or he didn't mind sharing. That definitely boded well for the next few days. At least for me, anyway. A threesome would be safer for my heart behind its fragile shield, but I wasn't so sure for Callum.

"You want to fuck him though, don't you?" I asked Landon, turning to face him once more.

He stared at me, his pupils swelled, but he didn't speak.

There was no need to him to answer. I knew lust when I saw it.

I looked over at Callum again, motioning for him to join us.

Callum stood without hesitation, and when he moved to get all up on my ass, I swung around to put Landon between us.

"Yeah," I murmured, watching him glance at the back of Landon's head as he hesitated to erase the distance between them. "Right fucking there." I grabbed hold of Callum's hips and yanked him closer, creating a three-man meat sandwich with Landon in the middle.

Landon stiffened, but Callum exhaled heavily and pressed his lips to Landon's temple causing him to whimper. "Too much?"

Landon licked over his lower lip before glancing over his shoulder at his best friend. "It's perfection."

Fuck. Yes.

Chapter 13

Landon

Adrenaline sped through my bloodstream over the fear of being seen grinding between two men, but I was in heaven. There was no other word to describe being caged in by hot, hard bodies.

But not just anyone.

Callum and Zack.

Put together, they were the perfect man. Separate? An even better option because there were two sets of arms holding me. Two mouths within reach if I wanted to suck on a tongue. Two dicks to fill and flood me with cum, one after the other.

Oh, Jesus.

My cock throbbed against Zack's thigh, but I was too far gone in my fantasy to be embarrassed about how badly I wanted him.

Callum's news about my manuscript edits had hit hard, but that responsibility also took a backseat to being the sole focus on my lifelong crush and...whatever Callum had become to me.

According to Zack, Callum loved me, and while I'd

avoided any talk about such things while we'd readied for dinner in our suite, a new tension radiated between us. The mutual desire bound tighter with every passing minute, pulling us closer on a possible course I'd been blinded to before. It was only a matter of time before we collided. Combusted into flames. And if I had my way, only good would come of the explosive need rising between us.

Callum had told me we were safe letting loose while on vacation, and I had to put my trust in him like I'd always done, or I wouldn't be able to function. Regardless of his warm hands on my waist, he kept his lower body away from my backside.

I didn't understand why.

Zack's dick dug into my hip, so there was no question about what *he* wanted.

Was Zack wrong, and Callum bookended me because he hoped to get a piece of Zack? Every part of my body yearned to prove that insecure thought to be false.

As though hearing the riot in my head, Zack leaned down, his breath hot against my ear. "Take what you want from Callum, Landon—I promise he won't deny you. And I'm game for whatever you desire. Him owning you for the first time while I watch. My dick wrecking your hole. A fuck fest of three..."

I shuddered, eyelids slamming shut. While I'd only had one drink, barely enough to make me feel buzzed, I was drunk on lust. I'd made bad decisions in my lifetime, and while this might prove the worst one ever, I couldn't stop the train Zack had pulled me onto.

Turning, I faced my best friend, my hands settling atop Zack's on his waist as Callum's fingers slid to my lower back in their usual, comforting press that I realized he'd always done with more than a desire to comfort me.

The sea-color of Callum's eyes were overrun by swelled black pupils, his focus on my face rather than the gorgeous man now behind me. His stare promised desire. Passion. Fulfillment of what I recognized he'd always yearned for with me.

But would moving beyond friendship be an issue outside this paradise where time seemed to have stood still? And how far could I push for what I realized I'd subconsciously always desired with him? Intimacy beyond platonic closeness we'd shared the previous eight years begged for freedom to bloom into something beautiful beyond words.

I ran one hand up along his clean-shaven jaw to his nape, questioning with my eyes, but he didn't make a move.

Do you...

Can I...

"Fuck it," I muttered and pushed up, brushing my mouth over his in a tentative, seeking kiss.

He groaned and pressed in tight, every inch of his hot, *hard* body aligning with mine. Grasping my neck, he held me in place, taking the lead. The cells inside me submitted to his ownership, same as they'd done with Zack.

No thought of reaping what we sowed in public held me back from taking advantage of the situation. I parted my lips, and Callum licked inside my mouth, shuddering when our tongues touched. Slick glides along each other's tender flesh made my groin throb, and I whimpered, clutching at him, desperation to make up for lost time making my blood race.

Callum's dick was granite, and the gyration of his hips had me frotting against him right there on the damn dance floor for all to see.

Wrapped up in the man I trusted more than life, I gave

zero fucks beyond enjoying what had always been on offer —I'd just been too damn blinded to notice.

"Fucking hell," I heard Zack murmur as I lost myself in Callum's kiss. Zack breathed against my ear, his hot exhale ghosting goose bumps down my spine, making me vibrantly aware of his proximity.

Need flooded through my blood, heating me to the point I swore I broke out into hives.

"You two are so fucking hot together. Jesus." Zack's cock bucked against my ass, and I whimpered into Callum's mouth, wanting them both.

Naked.

Now.

Zack slid his hands between me and Callum, rubbing over both of our hard dicks while grinding against my very empty, very *needy* ass. My balls drew up tight, my taint on the verge of spasming.

Oh, fuck—

I tore my mouth from Callum's and wiggled, shoving Zack's talented fingers away and creating some space between the three of us. My best friend blinked, his eyes unfocused and hazy as he peered at me.

"I'm not coming on the damned dance floor," I hissed quietly, hands fisted at my sides, my muscles trembling and skin shivering from the energy rippling among the three of us.

"Then we need to take this elsewhere," Zack suggested exactly what I'd been thinking.

Privacy to partake in a night of debauchery with the man I'd always loved and the other who'd owned the second half of my heart without my having realized it.

"Let's go," I rushed to say, my voice strangled. Shaking, I

grabbed both their hands and pulled them along behind me off the dance floor.

At Callum's assured lacing of our fingers together near the hotel's side entrance, my throat swelled up. "What do you want, Landon?" he asked.

I paused on the darkened pathway, suddenly lacking confidence they would be on board for every idea crowding my brain. "To fulfill a few of my fantasies?" I'd gone for a statement, but it ended up sounding like a question.

Callum knew what I meant. He'd read every single book I'd written, the sex scenes my muse had brought to life through my fingertips. "Are you sure, baby?"

The pet name was new—and I wanted to suck it off his lips and swallow it down, *own* it so he couldn't ever take it back.

Zack had opened my eyes to what had grown between me and my best friend over the years, and with the opportunity to taste Callum, to share in something more with him and the love from my childhood, lit my blood on fire. "Yes—I want this. You. Him."

Callum's gaze softened, and he caressed my cheek before glancing at Zack on my other side. "I'm game if you are."

Oh fuck. I gulped, my gaze swinging toward Zack.

"Anything for you." His words directed at Callum shouldn't have hit me wrong—but they did.

Was he only agreeing to a threesome because he'd been paid to please Callum? Was it more the idea of getting his hands on my best friend that made him hard—not me? He'd claimed it would be as such this morning over breakfast, but the way he looked at and touched me gave me hope his feelings had changed.

I wanted answers, but I also wasn't about to pass up the

opportunity with these two men I had sudden dreams about losing myself between for the rest of my life.

We moved in silence, heavy breaths accompanying us on the elevator ride to our shared floor where we stepped into a silent, empty hallway.

"You two go on ahead," Zack said, bypassing our suite's door and heading toward the bend up ahead. "I'll be there in a few."

"P-Promise?" I hastened to ask, hating how insecurity bled through my tone.

A slow smirk curled one side of his mouth, melting my insides. "Promise." He disappeared around the corner.

Callum rested his hand on my lower back while I attempted to unlock our door. Yeah, that tender press of his palm felt familiar but ten times better finally knowing for sure what prompted it.

Once inside, I stalled out. How did I initiate what I hoped to transpire in the coming hours? I longed for so, so much with Callum and Zack that it scared the hell out of me. We'd all climbed aboard a train barreling down tracks into the unknown.

"Um..." I turned in the entryway and ran a trembling hand through my hair.

Callum stood in front of me, intent on studying my face.

Did he see the insecurity rising up inside me? How growing anxiety over fucking up again might be the final straw to a mental breakdown?

He cupped my cheek in his warm palm, and I sagged at his soothing touch that never ceased to set my soul at ease. "Lan..."

"Don't let this tear us apart," I whispered, pleading with everything inside me. "I won't survive without you."

"Nothing will take me away from you," Callum declared, lowering his head.

Our mouths brushed, gentle and sweet, but I wasn't having this careful, hesitancy between us. The walls had come down. He'd given me the green light, damnit, and I hadn't lied to Zack about being greedy. I was an absolute glutton for dick, and it'd been way too long since I'd been filled the fuck up.

Whimpering, I pressed against Callum, needing to feel how much he desired me. No Zack around, and he was still hard.

Tongues tangling, I shoved him against the entry wall, my fingers fumbling with the button on his shorts, desperate to get at him. "Need," I breathed against his mouth, panting along with him.

"Whatever you want, baby, it's yours. Anything."
Fuck yes.

I dropped to my knees, pulling Callum's shorts down with me. He hissed as I licked up the back of his straining dick to flick my tongue around his glans.

"Landon." He breathed my full name like a prayer, gently cradling my face in his hands while kicking off his shoes.

Taking him to the root earned my nose a close encounter with his trimmed pubes and a lungful of his musk. Thank fuck for my nonexistent gag reflex.

I grabbed hold of his muscular thighs and buried my face fully against his groin, smothering myself in his scent.

"Fuck!" His hips jolted, but I kept in place, twirling my tongue along his base and swallowing around his swollen head. "Your mouth...*God.*"

Humming, I backed off, sucking to the tip where I was rewarded with a bead of creamy bitterness.

So good.

I sank down, soaking in Callum's curses as my saliva dribbled over his tight balls and my chin.

A knock sounded on the door beside us, but I couldn't be bothered to stop feasting on his dick.

Callum must have reached for the handle, because the door swung inward, a body appearing in my periphery.

"Jesus fucking Christ," Zack muttered, dropping a bag beside his feet as the hinges silently shut us once more in where no prying eyes could see us.

Mouth full of Callum's cock, I reached one hand out for Zack.

"You want my dick?" Zack all but growled the question.

I moaned an agreement, sucking up to Callum's tip again.

He hissed and gave me another burst of flavor on my tongue.

I pulled off Callum's cock and peered up at Zack, soaking in the lust and longing in his hazel eyes. Did I want his cock. Ha! I'd dreamed of nothing else for fifteen years. But there'd been more than lust for his body. I'd missed the closeness we'd shared. The comfortable friendship, the connection of two souls searching for love and acceptance.

"Yes—all of it, Zack."

And every other piece of you.

"Then have me."

My throat tightened, wishing I could take his words in more than the way he'd meant them.

I might be greedy, but I'd learned to savor things in life. And Zack's dick? From having his rigid length digging into me while dancing, I expected I was in for a good time. No way would I say no to a taste.

I made quick work of his shorts, shoving them to his

feet. Same as with Callum, I had my lips wrapped around him before he could speak a word.

Finally—fucking *finally*, I had Zack inside my body where he belonged.

My eyes stung over one of my dreams coming true. Let him believe tears slid down my cheeks because of how deeply I'd taken him, because I expected the depth of my feelings for him would have him spinning on his heels and fleeing.

"Goddamn," Zack growled through gritted teeth before grabbing hold of my nape and fucking deep into my throat with a thickness more than Callum's. He filled me to perfection as I'd always known he would, his flavor slightly sweeter than Callum and just as delicious.

As perfect as the moment was, something was missing.

I shifted on my knees, tugging on Callum's hip to bring him closer until they sidled up against each other, thigh to thigh. Backing off, I stroked both of their spit-soaked lengths with my hands while catching my breath, glancing up to find two sets of eyes devouring me.

A shiver rippled through my body, and I swallowed hard, uncaring that saliva smeared over the lower half of my face. "Kiss."

The two men closed the distance without hesitation, their mouths crashing against each other's exactly as I'd asked for.

My cock leaked inside my constricting boxer briefs as I brought their dicks together, shiny heads touching.

Yes—this right here.

I lapped at their slits, one after the other, my tongue swirling and painting their hot skin with pre-cum and more saliva.

Zack groaned into Callum's mouth.

Callum shuddered and grabbed hold of Zack's face.

And me? I stuffed my mouth full of dick, stretching my jaw to the point of aching. Nothing existed in that moment except for the bitter wetness on my tongue, and the little, lustful noises escaping all three of us.

My balls drew up tight, but I didn't slow down or move back for space like I'd done on the dance floor. I didn't care that I was about to spill my load in my pants—completely untouched.

The moment was too perfect to pull away.

Chapter 14

Callum

Landon's hot, wet mouth suckling on my glans caused my toes to curl, and Zack's tongue stroking over mine made my head spin.

While I'd never been with two men at once, I'd watched my fair share of porn and read every word Landon had ever written. He'd spoken of fantasies, not aware that his had since become mine.

I clutched at Landon's hair and Zack's shirt, wanting them closer. On me. Fucking *in* me.

Landon held tight to both of our thighs and garbled a cry around our dicks, gasping and shuddering.

"Oh fuck," Zack rasped, tearing his lips from mine to look down at the beautiful man on his knees who had both of our cockheads stuffed in his mouth. "You like sucking dick that much?"

Backing off, Landon panted, head hanging as another tremor rippled over him like an aftershock of climaxing.

A wet spot seeped over the front of his shorts.

Jesus.

Before Zack could drop a truthful yet degrading comment that might trigger Landon, I bent to pick him up into my arms.

He buried his face in my neck, wrapping his legs around my waist. "That was embarrassing," he muttered exactly as I'd expected, breathing heavily against my skin.

"The hell it was," I argued, the throb in my groin all the evidence I needed.

"Hot as fuck," Zack groaned from behind us in obvious torment as I was.

I set Landon on the end of my bed and pushed his hair off his damp forehead. Saliva still made a mess of his chin and had dripped to his T-shirt.

"Let's get this off." I tugged on the hem, and he lifted his arms, allowing me to bare his smooth chest before wiping his pink face.

He was so damned beautiful.

My heart pounded against my breastbone as I knelt and finished undressing Landon.

Clothes rustled behind me, and something soft landing on the floor, but I couldn't tear my eyes off Landon's flushed dick covered in cum and still hard as nails.

My mouth watered at the sight.

I'd dreamed of this moment for years and didn't hesitate to lean in and take a taste of him—hopefully the first of many.

"Cal." Landon sighed and leaned back on his hands to watch me make a meal of his cock.

I held his base and tongued up his shaft, swirling and licking to swipe up every smear of cum I could. Wrapping my lips around his glans, I suckled the last remnants of saltiness from his slit.

He whimpered when I popped off to rip my shirt overhead.

I surged upward and kissed him, slowly pushing him until he lay down, legs dangling over the bed's edge. My ass was on full display from where I stood between Landon's spread thighs, and Zack didn't waste any time palming my cheeks exactly as I'd hoped for.

He cursed and nosed up my crack, inhaling deeply.

I shuddered, shoving my tongue into Landon's mouth as he wrapped his arms around my torso. My dick strained to rub against his, but I kept my knees locked, since Zack seemed intent on worshiping my taint and hole.

He ate me out like a starved man, growling and groaning, fingers digging into my cheeks to keep me open for him. A quick pause to mutter something about how delicious I was and he went back to it, his tongue spearing past my ring that hadn't been breached in years.

"Oh fuck." I gulped, my forehead tipped against Landon's as a shudder ripped through me. I'd never expected to have this again. "Jesus, that feels incredible."

"What's he doing?" Landon asked, his voice nothing more than whispered lust.

"Sucking on my ass. Tonguing my hole—fuck." I groaned, arching even deeper in a silent beg for more.

Landon whimpered the exact needy sentiment fluttering in my chest.

As quickly as Zack started, he stopped, leaving me bereft. Rustling through his black bag sounded. Gathering supplies, most likely.

I stared down at my best friend, his light brown eyes overblown by black pupils, radiating emotion beyond mere lust of fulfilling one of his dreams.

This was not what I'd had in mind when booking Zack and the hotel.

At. All.

But I wasn't about to complain about where we had ended up. I'd always wanted Landon, what he wrote in his first manuscript about a triad of three men, but I'd never allowed myself to hope for even having him let alone someone else sharing in our physical intimacy.

Our kiss on that dance floor hadn't just opened the floodgates but reassured me of my love for him, my need to keep him close and be his rock until death parted us.

"Zack told me you're in love with me," Landon whispered, stalling out my heart.

I glanced over my shoulder to find Zack once more behind me, a couple of condoms and bottle of lube in hand. He didn't apologize for spilling my secret, simply raised an eyebrow as if to ask, *What of it?*

My jaw clenched as I fought off rising anger. *I* wanted to be the one to declare my feelings to Landon but not until after he'd gotten over his need for Zack and his heart was open for someone else's claiming.

Landon grabbed my chin, and I allowed him to turn my face back around. He leaned up and took my mouth, dissolving my irritation with the sweet flick of his tongue over my lips.

I would be a fool to stop what we'd begun, the fruition of so many of my wishes I'd never expected to come true simply to give Zack a piece of my mind. Hell, for all I knew, it was his oversharing of personal information that had offered Landon the bravery to initiate the kiss that had changed everything between us.

Fingers crossing that shit didn't take a detour down the

road, I gave in to the passion once more flaring inside me, fucking into his mouth with my tongue, bending my knees enough I could grind my aching cock against his. I'd always been in charge and wanted to claim him in every way, but with Zack sharing in the moment, I didn't feel the driving urge to be the caretaker.

Bending toward Zack's dominance came easily, and even though I hardly knew the man and was upset he'd told Landon I loved him, I felt safe in allowing him the lead in our bedroom dynamic.

"On the bed," Zack stated, slapping my ass with a delicious sting I hadn't expected to find arousing.

I climbed onto the mattress, straddling Landon's lap. We continued to feast on each other's mouths, my hands in his hair, his grasping at my back.

Landon pulled up his knees, resting his feet on the edge of the bed, and at his grunt, I wondered—

"Your hole is so damn hot around my finger." Zack's words rumbled, cluing me in on what went down beneath my own empty ass I'd hoped to have filled.

But my needs could wait. Landon had dreamed of this moment longer than he'd owned my heart.

"Oh." Landon gulped, and I lifted my head to watch his face as Zack worked his hole. He frowned. Swallowed hard while writhing beneath me. Head tipping, he moaned.

"Give him more," I told Zack, memorizing every micro-expression flitting over Landon's face so I would know how to open him for myself when given the opportunity. I wanted him to be mine. My lover. I also longed to spin around and see Zack sink his dick into Landon's ass like he'd been yearning for the past fifteen years.

As always, my desire to give Landon everything

directed my actions. I stole a quick kiss and climbed off him, my hand stroking my length smeared by our combined pre-cum as I knelt by his side.

With my body no longer blocking Zack's sight, he stared at Landon as though seeing him for the first time. Wrapped up in past desires rekindled or mere lust in the moment? Either way, Landon seemed lost in Zack's intense gaze as he scissored his fingers, readying Landon's ass to take him.

They were in a world of their own, on the brink of something that had been simmering for far too long. My balls throbbed, desire burning bright to watch Zack own him rather than the jealousy a normal man would have felt at witnessing their undeniable connection.

"Please," Landon begged, his voice hoarse, red flushing his cheeks and chest as he grasped at the sheets.

They were beautiful together, a live-action porn flick playing out right in front of my aching body.

Tugging on my balls kept me off the brink of coming too soon, and I turned my focus on Landon's lithe form, his waxed groin, and already firmed sac. I couldn't stay away, couldn't keep from touching him too. I tweaked his furled nipple, and he squirmed beneath our combined attention.

"Yes, Callum. Oh fuck, that feels good," he whimpered, causing more pre-cum to drip down my length.

"Such a needy boy," Zack murmured, slipping a third finger into his hole with a spine-tingling squelching noise.

"Oh, God." Landon arched his back, whimpering the most decadent sounds from his parted lips.

My cock needed inside his mouth again.

Shuffling forward, I held the base of my dick, guiding it toward his lush lips. "Open up, baby." I whispered what I'd dreamed of calling him, and he rewarded me with another cute-as-fuck whine.

Landon did as told, twisting his torso to better get at my slick length. He tongued at my glans, teasing sucks along my tip, taking me in just far enough my swollen head poked out against his cheek.

"Jesus, you feel so good." I lost myself his lust-blown eyes as Zack moved in closer, sliding his fingers free of Landon's hole.

Landon frowned again, making a noise of disappointment around my dick, and I shifted my focus to my right.

Zack held his sheathed dick by the base and rubbed the tip over Landon's crack. "Ready for me?"

Strings of saliva connected Landon's mouth to my cock as he pulled away to answer. "I've been ready for you for over fifteen years, Zack."

I should have been stark raving mad, raging over the fact Zack would have him first. But my heart had only ever longed for one thing: fulfilling Landon's dreams. And now? I had a front row seat. Getting to see Zack slowly push forward and Landon's body give way to the man he'd always wanted...

Yeah.

Talk about hitting all the good feels in my heart and mind.

My dick jerked, my own hole spasming with the need to be filled up too.

Landon slowly exhaled, and Zack sank in until their groins pressed tightly together. Time paused, our breaths heavy, the scent of sex and sweat thick in the air. My mouth watered as I glanced down at the man I adored more than life who stared at the man he loved.

This was no love triangle.

Something stirred inside my chest, a sense of rightness even though I wasn't physically connected to the two men before me. I settled onto my haunches, idly stroking myself as Zack pulled out until Landon's pucker sucked around his swollen head. Zack groaned, hesitating even though Landon complained.

"Your ass—fuck." Zack shuddered, spreading Landon's thighs wider. "Squeeze around me again. Jesus, yes, just like that. Fuck." He clenched his jaw and slammed in, balls deep as though staking a claim on Landon's body.

"Ung!" Landon arched again, and my entire groin spasmed with need. He grasped at his cock, whimpering.

"Nuh uh," I said, slapping his hand away before I realized I'd moved in on the two of them again. "That's mine."

"That's right, sweetheart." Zack palmed my nape and shoved my face toward Landon's leaking dick. "Sixty-nine with our boy while I wreck his hole."

Our boy.

My heart raced and dick bucked at his unyielding tone, every part of me on board with his command and claim.

"Oh sweet baby Jesus," Landon whispered, and I had to agree with the sentiment. Zackary Briggs, confident escort and lover, knew how to lay down demands, and my body craved to obey in pleasing *our* boy.

Completely trusting Zack with the reins, I straddled Landon's head and shifted my hips downward just enough so he could swallow my dick into his hot, tight throat.

I hissed, wrapping my hand around the base of Landon's dick and bent over, intent on having him in my mouth.

Zack leaned away to make room for me, shallow thrusts bunching his massive thighs inches from my face.

I sank down over Landon's hard length until my lips met my fist. We were connected. Three in one.

And nothing had ever felt so goddamned good.

Landon wiggled beneath me, those sweet noises vibrating his mouth around my cock and rolling my eyes back into my head.

"You're so fucking hot, Callum." Zack ran his strong hands up along my spine as far as he could reach, grinding his groin against Landon's ass and my forehead. "Fuck, yeah." He slammed into Landon's hole, and I shifted higher to give him room, my fist taking over stroking Landon's cock.

Zack met my stare, his hazel eyes hazed over with lust. Sweat dampened his forehead, his lips parted as he panted while thrusting into Landon in a gorgeous display of rippling muscle.

We moved toward each other as of the same mind, our mouths latching, tongues dueling for dominance.

Landon turned his face from my groin, gasping for breath. "Oh, Jesus—you're destroying me." He cried out with every stab of Zack's dick into his guts, and I swallowed down Zack's grunts.

Arousal hovered thick and heady in the air along with the scent of musk and pre-cum.

My balls firmed as I imagined the tongue stroking over mine shoving into my hole again.

As though reading my thoughts, Landon clasped my ass cheeks, spreading me wide. He licked me from balls to pucker, flicking his tip over my pucker.

"Fuck." I tore my lips from Zack's, glancing down.

I watched his thick cock pushing through and pulling against Landon's ring, the wet sounds of fucking ramping up my need to come.

"Suck me," I gasped, desperate for warmth around my shaft.

Landon gave me what I asked for, and I moaned, falling over him to take him back into my mouth. Pre-cum leaked over my tongue, and I buried him as deep as I could lodge him in my throat.

Grunts ripped from Landon's lungs with every thrust of Zack's hips, and his cockhead swelled inside my mouth. Wet bitterness shot from his slit, and I fought the need to cough, swallowing with every spurt of his release.

Landon pulled away from my dick, gasping and cursing, his entire body shuddering beneath me.

"Your ass is squeezing me like a fist—pulsing around my dick." Zack continued to pound into him, chasing his own release. "Ah, fuck...I'm so close."

I released Landon's spent dick and sat up. "Let me have it," I whispered.

Pink highlighted Zack's cheekbones, making freckles I hadn't seen before stand out in stark relief. Hazel-green eyes peered down at me swirling with so many emotions a desperate noise escaped me. "Want my cum, Callum?"

"Yeah."

"God—" He pulled out quickly, and Landon whimpered, but I stared at the gorgeous dick inches from my face.

Zack made quick work of ridding himself of the condom, and he fisted my hair to tip my head back, his other hand stroking his shaft hard and fast. "You've seen my test results?" he asked, his tone low and breathy.

"Yes—I want it." I stuck out my tongue in invitation.

Wet heat closed over my dick again, and I shut my eyes, lost in the sudden climax ripping through me thanks to Landon's throat swallowing around me. Spunk splattered over my cheek, my nose—finally on my lips. My body convulsed as I emptied into Landon's mouth, and I leaned toward Zack.

He slid his pulsing head over my tongue, clear into my throat, gagging me with his final spurt.

I coughed that time but quickly swallowed, sucking, needing another taste.

A shiver slid over my skin in the wake of Zack's hands rubbing over my shoulders

"Goddamn," he murmured with one last shudder, and I couldn't agree more.

Chapter 15

Zack

Callum broke the connection between the three of us. With a groan, he rolled and collapsed onto his back, chest heaving, cheeks a gorgeous shade of pink. My cum striped across his lower face, and he flicked out his tongue as though searching for another little taste.

I'd thought Landon had been done in by how hard I'd plowed into him, intent on ruining him exactly as I'd lusted for. He should have passed the fuck out, but he scrambled atop Callum, going straight for my spunk on his chin. Slurping sounds sent shivers over my heated skin, and I released a long exhale, sinking my knees forward to rest against the bed's edge to hold me upright.

Maybe I'd been the one wrecked by Landon's magical, tight hole and the need in his eyes when I'd finally sunk into his body after years of denied wanting. We'd connected on a soul-level in that moment I would never regret even though the intimacy threatened my shields that protected me from being hurt by him again.

Then came Callum. His passion-hazed eyes while begging for my cum on his tongue, the way his mouth had slotted perfectly against mine. How he'd somehow deeply embedded himself alongside that ache in my chest for what I refused to allow myself no matter how badly I desired it.

I rubbed over my sweaty chest as Landon cleaned up Callum's face with little hums of happiness, pink tongue lapping, mouth sucking him clean of my spunk.

"Next time," Landon breathed against Callum's lips, "I want this inside me—*and* yours. Need you both leaking out of my hole."

I huffed a laugh, loving his insatiable hunger for my spunk. "Little cum slut," I teased.

Landon stilled as though my words had slapped him upside the head.

Callum wrapped his arms around Landon, pulling him down atop him. He made shushing noises, hands soothing his back until Landon melted over his chest and buried his face in Callum's neck.

"Shit," I muttered, slumping even further onto the mattress. "Trigger of some sort?"

"Something like that," Callum murmured an answer for Landon but didn't offer a reason why.

"Fuck. Sorry" I pursed my lips, all sense of ease whisked away from pulling him down seconds after a killer orgasm. All that hurt I'd dreamed of inflicting on Landon over the years? Felt pretty damn shitty when I'd expected elation. My stomach twisted with a complete lack of glee over Landon's apparent distress.

Walls had definitely crumbled between us, and I wasn't sure how to feel about it. Ants of unease skittered over my skin, making me want to flee, but I stood rooted, unable to walk away even though Callum was the one soothing him.

Nose hidden against Callum's skin, Landon held out his

hand toward me as though sensing my apprehension. Another truce?

Pleasing the client meant doing whatever the fuck Landon asked for according to Callum—but I yearned to comfort him too—and cuddle against them both. The second I moved forward, all anxiety melted.

Callum shifted to the side once I was on the bed so Landon settled between us.

Normally, I would suggest a shower with clients before round two, but I felt a desperation I couldn't name or deny. Something inside me reached for them both, a yearning to delve deeper into the connection we'd shared moments earlier before I'd screwed it up with what I'd thought would be a joke. I wanted more of that closeness I'd experienced while we'd fucked, which meant saving my questions about Landon's triggers for later.

I'd had my fair share of threesomes thanks to Elite, and I'd even enjoyed the hell out of a five-guy orgy a couple of years earlier, but nothing had given me any sense of fulfillment outside getting my rocks off.

This?

Closing my eyes, I snuggled in against Landon's back when I should have been running in the opposite direction, his cute ass a perfect home for my spent dick. My arm slid over his side to Callum's hip, and I squeezed them tight, imagining I could keep them both right there.

What we'd done was definitely something...different. *More.*

And unfortunately for my wary self-preservation, I'd liked it. A lot.

I rubbed my face against Landon's hair, breathing in sweetness, a slight fruity remnant rather than cloying sugar.

Weaseling my leg between his, I slid my foot along Callum's shin.

"I gotta be dreaming," Landon murmured, his tone light as though he smiled, my joke's effects seemingly faded from his mind, thank fuck.

Callum kissed his nose. "That's what I'm thinking."

I could imagine he did with how the man loved Landon, but he reached over the body between us, palming my ass cheek. He squeezed and kneaded me while resting his forehead against Landon's.

Attempting to shift closer, to burrow clear through Landon and straight into Callum didn't exactly work, but life stirred south as Landon rubbed his backside against my groin.

"Didn't get enough?" I asked, scooting down so I could latch onto his neck.

He shuddered as I sucked, pulling blood to the surface.

"Oh, fuck—God, no. Never enough. Want more."

Definitely a cum slut. I just couldn't joke about it, no matter how much I wanted to take him bare and fill him up.

"Mmm." I licked over the bruise I'd made before shifting a little to the right and biting into his trap.

He gasped and arched, his lush ass the perfect crack to rub my thickening dick against.

"Jesus, Landon." My pulse picked up pace as I ground against him, my mouth searching his out with urgency I didn't understand or trust.

He reached back and grabbed my hair, turning his head toward mine.

Our tongues fucked between our lips in languid torture, a delicious tango accompanied by Callum's quickening breaths that heightened my need for them both.

Callum released my ass cheek and grabbed Landon's, spreading him open for me.

"Shit." I grabbed my base to keep from blowing my load at the sight of his gorgeous pink pucker.

Condom.

I rolled one on quick as fuck before rutting through his crack. A bit of lube remained around his hole, but it was too sticky for me to just slide into his ass. "You're not too sore to take me again?"

"No. Fill me up while Callum holds me and kisses me senseless."

Shifting my focus, I found Callum watching the two of us with nothing but lust rekindled in his eyes.

"Lube?" I asked, and he patted around the bed behind him until he came up with the bottle.

"Want to do the honors?" I asked, and Callum's gaze darkened with animalistic heat. That was a part of him we definitely needed to explore in the very near future.

He coated his fingers without a word, and I shifted to give him space between Landon's ass and my sheathed cock.

Their eyes met and held as Callum swiped his wet fingertips over Landon's pucker.

"Okay?" he asked with gentleness when I'd expected him to take after pining for eight years.

"Mmm." Landon hummed and nodded, his lower lip between his teeth.

Callum pressed in, and Landon moaned, leaning into him.

Their mouths crashed together, causing my dick to buck.

Jesus, these two men. They were fucking addictive,

potent enough a guy might rearrange his life on a whim just to be with them outside paradise—

No.

I shook the thought clear from my head, reached over Callum, and grabbed the bottle he'd discarded, quickly coating my rigid length.

This was all about fucking and getting my fill of Landon.

Nothing more.

Two of Callum's fingers slid deep into Landon's slack hole, and I rubbed the head of my dick over his knuckles, focused on one thing.

"Let me in," I murmured, poking enough Landon gasped—but he bore down, and the head of my dick popped inside him along with Callum's fingers.

"Oh, fuck—Oh, God that's a lot."

"Too much?" Callum whispered over Landon's parted lips.

"N-No. S-Stay. Want you in me too."

I hissed at the thought of both of us inside Landon's body, our cocks slick and hot, rubbing against each other's. That was an image worth drooling over and a *must* in the coming days.

One hand trapped between Landon's hip and the mattress, the other on Callum's ass cheek, I gyrated my hips in a gentle roll, wishing I had two dicks so I could fuck them both at the same time.

The sounds of their kisses roused my climax before it normally would on a second go-round, and I groaned in frustration.

Not long enough...never enough, just like Landon had claimed.

Callum slid his fingers from Landon's ass and grabbed hold of my hair, yanking my head up from where I'd buried my face against Landon. I didn't care that those fingers had been shoved deep into a hole slick with lube when he shifted forward, his blue-green eyes overrun with lust, his mouth intent on mine.

Our lips crashed together, Landon's whimper spurring us on.

"I'm gonna nut already. Oh, fuck." He moaned, trying to shove his ass harder against my dick.

I took the hint and upped the pace, thrusting in time with how I fucked my tongue into Callum's mouth. Our breaths became pants, sweat once more beading on my back and brow.

"Make him come," Callum whispered against my mouth, and as though he pulled the strings on *my* body's responses, I convulsed, cum shooting up my shaft instead.

"Oh fuck yeah." Landon moaned, his ass clenching around me, my climax triggering his own.

"Jesus," I huffed on an exhale, burying deep, wishing I could mark him with every last drop I had left in my balls.

Landon shuddered, and we came down from our high. I wrapped both of arms around him, squeezing him to me, instinctively keeping him close.

"Callum," he whispered, and I peered over his shoulder.

Landon's best friend stroked his still hard dick in steady rhythm, his gaze flitting between the two of us. "You're beautiful together."

Fuck that.

There three of us were goddamn hot as fuck.

I climbed over Landon, my lower half still atop him and went straight for Callum's cock.

He released himself to my mouth's ownership, and I

took him to the root, groaning over the delicious saltiness of his pre-cum.

"Mmm," Landon hummed as though he could taste Callum too, his hands rubbing over my ass cheeks. "So sexy."

Callum panted, his fingers once more going for my hair.

"Fuck my throat, Callum," I rasped, gathering some saliva to rub over his hole. "I can take it." I swallowed him down, and with a curse, Callum thrust.

Yeah, just like that.

I toyed with his pucker, dipping in just a little—and Callum came with a shout.

I was going to need in that tight ass before our time in paradise ended.

Chapter 16

Landon

Thank God for showers big enough to fit three grown men.

And thank fuck for sudsy hands as greedy for my flesh as I was for their touch.

Both Callum and Zack cared for me after two rounds of the most intense, mind-blowing sex *ever*. That sense of heaven lingered long after penetration, clear through to a three-way make-out session beneath hot spray where I died and went to heaven for a third time in a matter of hours.

Steam surrounded us in a world of our own cocoon where my dreams came true. I couldn't wait to take advantage of the days ahead of us, and even more so, the chance to move forward and navigate a triad in real life because there was no denying our chemistry, how fate had brought the three of us together.

I'd done my research into polyamorous relationships, knew the difficulties from firsthand experiences I'd read about online. But I was also aware of the beautiful gains that could be had if we were on the same page and willing to put in the work.

I was all in, full bore, no holds barred.

Sure, openly dating two men was going to stir up a shit load of issues with my parents and probably bring old news back into the spotlight, but after that moment behind closed doors while being held by both Callum and Zack, I wasn't worried about any negative outcome.

Zack had owned my heart since childhood, and Callum...

Nothing will take me away from you.

His promise had echoed in my ears while the three of us had become one, his sure touch and the hunger in his eyes solidifying that truth in my conscience.

He was my sturdy rock, my safe place. Between the two of them, I would thrive. Find my place. Experience true happiness where nothing could touch me.

Callum had promised me anything, and I was selfish and gluttonous enough to want it all. Add in the fact he hadn't argued when I'd told him Zack had spilled the beans about Callum's love for me, and that collision course I'd imagined us on had raced at breakneck speed toward combustion.

He'd sucked my dick while Zack fucked me, and I swallowed every drop of his cum before licking Zack's off his face. We'd shared a deep kiss, the flavor of Zack on both of our tongues, right where it belonged.

I hoped to have another of my fantasies fulfilled—both of their cum emptied in my ass, dripping out in a combined mess. Double penetration or stuffing me one right after the other, I didn't care. Actually...

I considered both ideas while Zack dried me off and Callum did the same to him.

I wanted to be filled with their spunk from both options. While I'd never had two dicks in my ass at the same time, I'd taken one and two fingers without too much issue earlier.

We could work up to it, yet another thing to look forward to and fantasize about.

Zack caught my eye, his brow rising. "Got something on your mind, greedy boy?"

He had always been good at reading me. I tried to purse my lips to keep my smirk contained and totally failed. "*May*-be." I drew the word out with a flirtatious tone.

He chuckled, laughter I hadn't heard in far too long, a sound that lit me up inside. "Whatever you want."

God, when he made promises like that, I could drop to my knees again and worship his body until I had a belly full of cum.

I glanced at Callum, who toweled Zack's hair from behind.

He peered at my childhood crush like he'd done with me earlier that morning, more than mere physical interest in his gaze.

My spent body really tried to rouse at the sight of the two men moving in seeming ease around each other, but a yawn cracked my jaw instead.

Callum flitted his gaze my way again, a soft smile curving his lips. "Tired?"

"Exhausted." So much so, that any discussions about our future with Zack would have to wait. When I needed my bed, I tended toward grumpy if I didn't get my way. And while I expected Callum and I were totally on the same page about moving forward together, I wasn't so sure about Zack.

He had a job that frankly churned my guts to the point I couldn't think about it in the moment or a shitty attitude would rouse, and I would start making demands I had no right to.

Eventually though, he would have to seek employment elsewhere because I refused to share him with anyone who wasn't Callum.

The truth of my past would need to be dragged into the light of day beforehand too. Zack had the right to know what he would be getting into with hooking up with me, the "Soiled Senator's Son" as the news outlets had called me.

Soiled indeed.

That awesome night's negative backlash wounded parts of my mind therapy had yet to help heal.

Fingers crossed this current situation didn't explode in the same way as the last time I'd partaken of more than a couple dicks in a matter of hours, I held out my arms to Zack, and smirking, he hefted me up against him.

I sighed and snuggled in, sniffing Callum's bodywash on Zack's skin that smelled like the outdoors—cedar and home.

Everything inside me purred at having the two of them morphed inside my nose. God, I wished I wasn't wiped out. I really wanted them both deep inside me, loving me as one before spilling inside my body and marking me as theirs.

Zack deposited me on the freshly cleaned bed, pressing his lips to my forehead before backing away.

I lay on my side, curling up into a ball, but when Zack reached for his clothes, I bolted upright. "No way—you're not leaving," I stated, refusing to hear otherwise. "Tell him, Cal. Remind him that I'm allowed to have whatever I want. And, that's both of you. Right now. In this bed."

Forever, I managed to withhold from spilling. That word would have meant a serious debate, a possible slammed door behind Zack, and no rest for sure.

Zack glanced at Callum, eyebrow raised as he toyed with his shorts' waistband.

"Stay. Please," Callum murmured, and I prayed Zack wouldn't deny the begging in his sea-like eyes I could never say no to. "It's not just Landon who wants you here."

Zack hesitated, glancing between the two of us as though a little off-balance.

What I wouldn't have given to hear his thoughts, to search out the conflicting desires he revealed in his eyes. Either the man was too tired to shield, or he allowed himself a moment of vulnerability.

I mentally pumped my fist over having won that little bit of headway with Zack. Waiting for him to choose, I held my breath. What I'd done to him didn't deserve forgiveness no matter how badly I'd wished for it over the years, but I at least hoped for the chance to prove to him I would love him and be loyal from here on out.

A decision flickered over his hazel orbs—*not* one of resignation, thank God, and he dropped his shorts.

I relaxed again and reached for him, my skin tingling with anxiety to have him pressed against me as proof I wasn't dreaming.

He gave me what I wanted, wrapping me up in his arms so I could bury my nose against his neck again. All sense of insecurity and fear of his abandonment faded into the recesses of my mind.

Callum cradled my backside, sliding his hand between me and Zack to rest against my belly. He kissed my hair while snuggling in right where he belonged with a contented sigh.

"Heaven," I swore I heard him whisper, and I closed my eyes, grinning like a dork even as exhaustion pulled me into sleep.

He and I were *definitely* on the same page.

Chapter 17

Callum

I was too wired to drift off as easily as Landon did.

Zack appeared to feel the same, considering how we stared at one another over Landon's head from where he pressed his face against Zack's neck.

"I'm sorry for betraying your trust," Zack murmured.

While I wanted to still be pissed, I couldn't be, considering how things had turned out. But would Landon be willing to give Zack up at the end of this? I hoped he would be free to love me and yet...

"I forgive you," I offered what Zack hadn't yet gifted to Landon, hoping that while what he'd done to me didn't compare to the pain Landon had caused him, that axe could be buried if both parties were willing.

Zack slid his hand from Landon's back to entwine his fingers with mine where they rested on our boy's stomach.

My heart stuttered, and I swallowed hard, wishing I could read what went on in Zack's head. Specifically what he thought about the three of us and how seamlessly we seem to fit even though

"Tell me about yourself," I whispered something less intrusive.

Zack slowly exhaled. "What do you want to know?"

"Why do you volunteer at that homeless shelter you mentioned the other night?"

Our eyes remained locked, a comfortable steady gaze I had no wish to glance away from. Let him see what I felt. The desires he'd roused to life inside me in less than forty-eight hours.

"It's where I stayed after I left Rhode Island and had run out of money," he admitted quietly.

Considering the surface shit we'd talked about when we first met, I hadn't expected such honesty.

Zack felt safe here with me and Landon, and that truth tightened my throat and made the desire stronger to nurture that feeling in him and draw out more of who he was. But first, I wanted to deepen our connection.

"I spend a few hours every week at a local LGBTQ club for teens," I told him rather than delving into his past, which might shut him down again. "While not a shelter for the homeless ones who often visit, it's a safe place where everyone is accepted and loved."

A hint of a smile curved Zack's mouth, appreciation in his eyes over our shared passion, exactly as I'd hoped for.

"Is Landon aware you lived on the streets?" I asked, hoping I didn't push too hard.

"No." His lips pursed, and I let the matter rest, choosing to prod from a totally different angle.

"On a scale of one to ten, where does what we did tonight rate? I can imagine you've had dozens of threesomes."

"I've had a few, yeah. But this..."

"It feels like something special," I filled in when he trailed off, my fingers crossed in my mind.

"Yeah. Kinda does," he admitted quietly, surprising me once again.

"You'll stay until our contracted time is up?" My heart attempted to stall out while I waited for his reply. He'd already agreed to stick around—but when we'd been discussing vacationing, *not* exploring what the three of us might have found.

"Yes," Zack eventually answered. "Whatever you desire, Callum, it's yours."

More time, I thought to push. *All of your hurts, your hopes, and your dreams.*

Way beyond mere fucking when two days ago, I'd set my mind on freeing Landon from Zack so he might be open to loving me someday.

But there was something about Zack, a connection between us as though our inner selves reached out for the other, innately recognizing another soul we could lean on. Zack was the sort I could share my burdens with, a man with sturdy enough shoulders to prop me up so I didn't always have to be the strong one, like I was for Landon.

Even more, I yearned to give Landon his fantasy, the poly relationship he tended toward when writing happily ever afters.

I'd always thought I wanted my best friend all to myself, but having met Zack?

My focus turned toward taking care of them both, holding them close and protecting their hearts.

I woke Saturday morning still cradling Landon's backside.

He wiggled his cute ass against my morning wood, and I groaned, grabbing his hip.

Blinking my eyes open, I found him peering at me over his shoulder.

"Fuck me."

My stomach clenched in a flash of lust at his blatant demand, but I glanced over at Zack, who still lay slack-jawed and breathing heavily.

"A-Are you sure, Lan?"

"The floodgates have been opened between us," he whispered. "There's no going back to the way things were—at least, I don't want to just be friends anymore."

My throat tightened. "What we have, our companionship up to this point, means the world to me."

Landon reached back and clasped my hip, wiggling his butt again, his smirk the killing stab. "This is the cherry on the top. Fill my needy hole up with your big cock and make me yours forever."

Words fled as I choked back a sob. Everything I'd dreamed of lay at the tips of my fingers—and my aching cock leaking pre-cum over his skin. *Heaven*, I'd whispered before Landon had passed out last night, but to have my unrequited love recognized, accepted, and returned?

There was no place in the cosmos to compare to how fulfilled I felt in that moment. And even though our first time wouldn't be face-to-face with tenderness and him coming apart in my arms, I did. Not. Care. He'd offered himself to me, and I would gladly accept whatever he gave.

We had our whole future ahead of us to create more lovemaking memories.

"I haven't done this in years," I said, my husky tone a reflection of the emotional mess in my chest.

"You're going to rock my world," Landon stated without question, his light brown eyes overflowing with happiness exactly as I'd always hoped to one day see.

But, no pressure.

Landon flipped over to face me, jostling Zack and grabbing my cheeks. He planted a smacking kiss to my lips before pulling away to stare into my eyes. "You're *you*. My Callum Anderson. My best friend. The man who fulfills so many damn parts of me I can't imagine my life without you, so yeah. You're *going* to rock my world even if you blow the second you get your dick inside me."

A chuckle burst from me, and I took my time to kiss him tenderly sans tongue because dragon breath.

The second I released his lips, Landon spun back around.

"Oh, good morning, hot stuff," he murmured, flirty as shit.

I guessed Zack was awake but didn't bother looking with how intent I was on rolling to grab a condom and the lube off the bedside table.

Zack's low voice mumbled something along the lines of a similar greeting as I snapped open the cap and coated my sheathed cock.

"Just slide right into me, Cal," Landon suggested without glancing over his shoulder again. "Fill my ass up like you've probably been fantasizing about ever since you met me."

Cocky little brat.

"Goddamned right I have," I muttered anyway, shuffling in close to the pert backside he kept arched toward me.

Zack's hand rubbed over Landon's side then his hip before dipping into his crack.

Landon tossed his top leg over Zack's thigh, and I

stroked myself, staring as Zack toyed with his waxed, pink pucker.

"Give our boy what he wants."

I cursed at Zack's command.

Those repeated two words hit me in the sternum, but I moved with intent to obey, same as I'd done the night before.

But right now?

I was taking the reins. It was my turn to bring them both pleasure, and it started with letting Zack know he was more than just physically there with us. He would partake, be a part of my loving Landon for the first time.

Same as he'd gifted me when he'd given Landon what he'd always wanted.

Grabbing the base of my dick, I tapped Zack's fingers with the back of my cock. "Hold him open for me."

He did as told, and Landon's hole winked at me, sexy as hell and just as much of a flirt as his mouth.

"Let me in, baby," I couldn't help the pet name while pressing against his pucker.

Landon bore down, and the head of my dick slipped into his sucking heat.

"Fuck." I gritted my teeth, afraid of blowing my load before I burrowed inside his body.

"Give me more," he demanded, pushing toward me.

"When I'm ready, greedy boy."

Landon shuddered as though he loved that nickname too. As long as we kept cum slut out of the air—even if he admitted to being one in his wild days—we wouldn't trigger any negative responses.

But his hot hole proved voracious for dick, and I forced my way in with controlled thrusts until I pressed against him from chest to hips.

I paused, needing to gain control, but Landon moved himself on my throbbing length, grinding away and panting.

"Zack," he begged, more of a gasp really, as though needing our lover too.

"Kiss him," I told Zack. "Help me work a climax out of him."

Both men froze, and I realized they'd fucked but hadn't kissed. I knew from Landon they hadn't as teens either.

"Y-You don't have to," Landon started, but Zack grasped his face and took his mouth in a bruising clasp of lips and teeth.

Fuck.

I swallowed hard, my groin aching as Landon's hole clenched around me, the whimpers spilling past his lips the most delicious sounds to ever caress my ears. How often had he dreamed of tasting Zack's mouth? With the desperation rolling off Zack, I wondered if he'd always longed for the same regardless of the bitterness he'd clung to for years.

Emotion welled up inside me, happiness over bringing them together, elation at having found what I'd always hoped for with Landon. And the bright possibility of so much more than I could have imagined.

Zack ground against Landon's front, and I attempted to burrow deeper into Landon's guts.

I closed my eyes and gave over to lust, grunting over every slick glide in and out of his tight hole. He fit me like a glove, warm and comfortable as though he'd been made for me.

"Put your hands on me, Zack," I demanded, quickly growing winded, ready to voice the same ownership Zack had declared earlier. "Help me fuck our boy."

"Jesus fucking Christ," he muttered but grabbed my ass.

"Yeah—just like that," I praised his firm hold, getting off

on how he yanked me forward into Landon's tight grip. Decadent heat sucked me in regardless of my dragging pulls to the head, and his clench on me and the amount of lube I'd coated myself with made for one delicious-to-the-ears wet fuck.

Making love would happen eventually, but I was too far gone in my lust. I needed to own Landon from the inside out.

Same as Zack had done last night, I latched onto Landon's neck, giving him a mirrored hickey on the opposite side from Zack's.

Eyes clenched shut, I released the suction and breathed against his neck, my hips stuttering regardless of how Zack's hold spurred me on.

"Going to fill you up, baby," I promised what I hoped to truly do some day.

"Mmm," Landon hummed his want.

"Fuck." My taint convulsed, my abs tightening.

And I finally flooded the condom with the evidence of my desire and love I'd held for Landon since day one.

Chapter 18

Landon

I'd kissed Zackary Briggs.

While having my hole filled by a man I loved in equal measure.

Stretching, I let out a sigh of pure elation. I'd thought having Callum's mouth on mine had been a culmination of pent-up desire, but years of unquenched need for Zack had proven just as sweet. Everything I'd dreamed of—but I still wasn't sated.

I eyed Zack's weeping slit as Callum left us to get a wet towel to clean me up.

"My hole is nice and relaxed. It's all slick up there too..." I trailed off, begging with my eyes. Shit would have been even better if it'd been Callum's cum leaking out of me instead of copious amounts of lube, but beggars couldn't be choosers. We would get there eventually.

Zack kissed the tip of my nose. "I'm saving my load for later." His gaze shifted toward Callum, who'd returned, a towel in hand.

Heat flushed through me. "I'm going to need a front row seat for that, please."

Both men chuckled, but the sexual tension was thick in the air, promising one hell of a delicious evening to look forward to.

A short while later, we sat down for the buffet breakfast again, and I hated how my skin crawled from my brain's instinct to assume people watched us. Judged *me* especially. Even worse, the few times I couldn't help but peer around, I made eye contact with two people who glanced away quickly as though they *had* been curious about who I was and what I was up to sitting between two gorgeous men.

Twice, Callum had touched my lower back as though sensing my unease, causing me to cringe, which I wouldn't have done had we been in private. Thank fuck he hadn't seemed to notice my unintended reaction since Zack had held his attention during both instances.

We took a walk on the beach to allow breakfast to settle, me stationed once more between the two of them, enough shoulder brushes to suggest we were together to anyone who happened to glance our way. At least the open air allowed me a sense of safety in thinking those around us were too occupied with the outdoors to give us a second glance.

While I was no celebrity, nor was my father, my mistake had been plastered across US headlines and social media, and I didn't bullshit myself into believing everyone had forgotten how badly I'd soiled the Matthews name.

Parasailing sat on our to-do list for the day, so we spent the rest of the morning and early afternoon taking turns being dragged through the wind high above the ocean waves. I'd always been one for adrenaline rushes, and considering it'd been years since I'd let go and just had some fun, that event didn't disappoint. Add in the amount of sunlight I'd gotten when not used to it, and I ended up crashing on our suite's couch for an hour before dinner.

After sharing three different types of seafood, we sat on a blanket by a small fire pit on the beach, tucked away in a corner lit mostly by moonlight. I snuggled on Callum's lap with my feet on Zack, who sat beside him.

We hadn't kissed again, but I expected it was because he'd only allowed that intimacy in the heat of passion. But we still had a few days left, which I was thankful for.

Even though I'd had a nap, my full stomach and the long day dragged me toward dreamland. Breathing in the scent of cedar and the ocean, I closed my eyes. Callum's heartbeat created a beautiful harmony with the gentle crashing of waves on the shore to my right.

It was the perfect cadence with two sets of hands on me. Callum's in my hair, Zack's on my lower legs, both petting me in a comforting, non-sensual way. Good thing, because I was too exhausted to get it up until I had a solid eight hours of sleep clocked.

"So how did the two of you meet?" Zack's question brought my fading mind back to life and made my heart stutter.

While he didn't have the greatest job according to society, I didn't either. *And* while I expected he wouldn't ever judge me considering what he did for a living, I'd hidden the truth for so long that sense of needing to protect myself from losing him again made me to hold my cards close.

"Remember how you always encouraged me to tell stories?" I spoke since Callum wouldn't ever spill the tea.

"Yeah."

"Well, I decided to write a book and actually grew the balls to send it off to some big publishing house in New York."

Zack squeezed my calf muscle where he'd been absently trailing his fingers as though proud of me for putting myself out there like that.

"I received a rejection form from one of their acquisitions editors, but somehow, my manuscript ended up on Callum's desk."

"He told me he worked in the marketing department at Walters & Whether's Publishing before moving to Rhode Island to be your PA," Zack said.

I nodded, blinking my eyes open.

Zack studied Callum's face with tenderness and a whole lot of interest that boosted my hope. "You saw his potential for greatness when others didn't."

My heart squeezed at Zack's assured words, stated as though he'd never once considered I was anything *but* talented.

"I did," Callum agreed. "So much so, that within a matter of weeks, I uprooted from my lonely existence to make sure he followed his passion—and thrived in it."

"So you've been living together for what...eight years?" Zack asked.

"Close to it, yes."

"And you've never crossed the line of friendship before this?"

Callum squeezed me.

"I never knew he wanted me," I said, "but thanks to you, I now get to have his dick along with all of his attention and time." I considered preening like a cat in sunlight, and I was sure my face revealed my satisfaction.

Zack snorted. "You're a greedy brat."

"He doesn't mind, do you, Cal?" I made a statement rather than a real question directed at my roommate-turned-lover. But I suddenly realized Callum didn't have a life outside the one we shared. I'd never noticed he had already given me everything and had been utterly devoted to me for years.

Shit.

I dragged my weary body upright, turned and straddled Callum's thighs. "How long has it been?" I whispered, searching his face for any hint of weariness from having waited for me.

Callum's gaze touched me as tenderly as his fingertips did my cheek, his blue-green eyes overflowing with adoration that made my chest ache. "From the first day I saw you."

"Why..." I swallowed hard, grabbing hold of his shirt. "Why didn't you ever say anything?"

Callum glanced at Zack. "Because your heart belongs to him."

"*Belonged,*" I corrected quickly.

Zack's soothing fingertips still mapping out my lower leg paused.

Callum shifted beneath me.

"Fuck, that came out wrong," I rushed to add. "I-I mean, he did back then *too* as *well* as now. He'll always own a part of my heart, but it's big enough for the both of you."

The fire popped in the sudden quiet among us. My pulse raced and not in the good way. More like a sixth sense of foreboding. A red flag on the rise.

"This is a vacation," Zack stated quietly. "I'm a hired escort here to please you for the next couple of days. You return to Rhode Island with Callum, and I head to Boston when we leave here."

A solid jab punched my chest, and I blinked against the sting in my eyes. I'd been so caught up in the perfection of us over the span of our day together that I didn't actually think about what Zack wanted or that he might not be on board with Callum and I.

Same as the night I'd betrayed him, I hadn't considered or asked what his plans had been—and look how that shit had ended up.

Zack made it clear he had a life to return to, and while we might be fucking, he'd been *paid* to do it. Why the hell would he dive into a relationship with a guy I doubted he would ever trust again?

Mentally done in, I heaved a sigh and pushed off Callum. A yawn caught me before I could offer an excuse. The involuntary action of my body added to the truth of my tiredness, making my eyelids heavy.

"I'm beat, and seeing as how I'm going to be spending all of tomorrow in front of a computer working on edits, I better get some sleep. That won't happen with the two of you in a bed with me so..." I shrugged, hoping I appeared uncaring and nonchalant. "Enjoy the rest of the night together." I squeezed Callum's shoulder and winked. "Get your money's worth out of this fine man. I'll see you in the morning."

Either I left the two men speechless, or they looked forward to some alone time they hadn't expected to get with how *greedy* my ass was because neither argued my ambling off into the night.

Disappointment lay heavy on my chest, and I might have allowed a few tears to slide down my cheeks while enroute to our suite, but I *wanted* the two of them to connect purely for selfish reasons.

If Zack fell for Callum, that boosted the chance he might consider being with the two of us after we left the island.

Yes, Callum and I would be more than friends going

forward, but I felt sure we would move with a sense of loss, a missing piece, if Zack chose to return to the life he'd had before meeting us here.

There would be no one to fit our triad but him.

Love him good, Cal. Show him what he'll be missing if he goes back to Boston.

I smothered myself in my bed's blankets, lonely as fuck and praying for all I was worth that the happily ever after I'd written about dozens of times would come true for me too.

Chapter 19

Zack

I stared after Landon as he walked away from us, his footsteps dragging. With how many hours he'd spent in the outdoors today which he'd claimed to never do, I wasn't surprised he retired early.

But he'd had that nap in the afternoon, so I'd been sure he'd be ready to fool around again tonight. Although I shouldn't have kissed him—that was one sure way to rip clear through the foil around my heart—I'd given in.

That intimate moment had wrecked me almost as much as fucking into his body the night before. We'd shared breath, our hearts beating in time as we frotted together while Callum filled his needy hole.

Even though Callum's mouth hadn't been involved in the equation, I'd felt his presence as real as Landon's dick rubbing against mine.

I glanced at the man beside me to find his eyes remained on Landon, his brow slightly furrowed.

"Everything okay?" While I'd gotten the sense Landon wasn't pleased by the truth bomb I'd dropped about us going our separate ways, what else could I have said? Reality existed regardless of his fantasies.

"Yeah." Callum sighed and turned toward the fire once Landon disappeared from sight.

I shifted closer to him, suddenly feeling chilled even though the temperature hadn't dropped. Our shoulders brushed, and whatever unease I'd experienced over Landon's slight off-ness in leaving settled. Part of me wanted to rest my head on Callum and close my eyes while breathing in the scent of the campfire and ocean beyond.

A few tropical animals chatted in the growing darkness, joining in the peaceful snapping of embers, waves on the shore, and the restaurant's band still playing live music in the far distance.

We shared a peaceful existence in the silence between us, and although I was ready to get busy loving on Callum's body, I enjoyed the quietness of our spirits simply resting together beside the fire.

I'd never had that sense of comfort with anyone. Not since I'd been a teenager snuggling with my best friend on his parent's couch.

"Landon realized this fantasy truly expires in three days," Callum stated quietly.

I almost said it didn't have to, but I'd been burned and knew better than to set my sights on lofty dreams that included trusting people with my heart. What we had been enjoying was wild and hot as fuck, but three guys together wasn't sustainable. Wasn't more than anything but a good time.

And right now?

Callum was too delicious smelling and gorgeous to let go without a taste. While what I shared with Callum was not as intimate a mental and heart connection as that with

Landon due to our past, the physical draw couldn't be ignored.

The potential, though...

I stared at Callum's profile as he watched the fire flickering. Shadows and flashes of light danced over his skin, and I wanted nothing more than to strip him bare. Kiss him until we were both breathless with the need to lose ourselves in each other.

This man was just as deadly as Landon, but I wasn't about to deny myself partaking while I had the chance.

"The forms you filled out said you're vers," I stated quietly, watching him closely.

A frown flitted briefly over his brow before the corner of his mouth closest to me kicked up slightly. "I am."

I leaned a little closer, running my fingertips along his forearm. "How can I please you tonight, Callum? Hmm? Want my ass or mouth? My dick?"

Callum shivered but didn't answer right away. Was he conflicted about taking advantage of the escort he'd hired out of loyalty to his...whatever Landon now was to him?

"This is sex, plain and simple," I reminded him, set on having him one way or another. "I aim to please the man who paid for the use of my body. So, tell me, Callum, and it's yours."

He swallowed hard, glancing down at his hands resting atop his thighs. "It's never about what I want."

"It is tonight," I pushed. "Unless..."

He glanced at me, searching my face.

"Are the two of you are officially dating and set boundaries that would require exclusivity unless the other is present?"

"We haven't discussed anything."

Exactly as I'd assumed, considering Landon's parting words to him.

"Then explain what you need from me," I pleaded. "I wasn't lying when I said I would give you anything—I *want* to, Callum, and not just because of the exchange of money."

A shudder rippled through him at my blatant honesty, and he closed his eyes, head tipping back slightly as though hoping the moon would absolve him of whatever guilt I sensed he might be experiencing.

"Take care of me," he whispered, the words barely reaching my ears. "No one has ever made me feel safe enough to let go and just be in the moment, but somehow I can with you."

Fuck, did I get that. Empathy kicked in along with a swell of desire, doubling my need to do exactly as he'd asked of me even if it shook the foundation of my flimsy walls.

I pushed to my feet, body starting to vibrate with antici-pation. "My room or yours?"

A heavy exhale left his shoulders sagged. "I'm sharing the suite with Landon."

I didn't need the reminder. Had kind of been hoping maybe Landon would wake up enough for that front row seat I knew he lusted for of Callum's and my first time together.

But after hearing how Callum wanted to connect with me?

"We're going to my room." I held out a hand, and Callum lifted his focus from my palm to my face.

"Do you think he'll be upset if we do this?" he asked. "He's loved you for so long—still does—and I have no wish to hurt him."

Call me a selfish bitch, but freedom remained for all parties until otherwise agreed upon, and I wasn't going to waste a minute in paradise. "Same *but*. Did he or did he not tell you a few minutes ago to get your money's worth out of me?"

"He did."

"Then?" I wiggled my fingers.

Callum slid his palm along mine, our fingers twining, energy zapping straight up my arm to my chest where my heartbeat fluttered.

We didn't speak on the way to my room, nor did Callum hesitate in front of his and Landon's door. I rounded the hallway's corner, Callum in tow, his footsteps just as eager as mine.

I shut us away in semi-darkness, leaving the curtains wide open so the moonlight could pour in and create a pale, magical glow around us.

"Come here," I murmured, drawing him into my arms rather than ravaging him. He wanted to be taken care of, and that meant tenderness.

This time around.

Callum willingly buried his face in my neck, and I tucked him in close to me, soothing my hands down his back to cradle his ass.

We were both hard, our groins pressed tightly together, but we didn't grind or start tearing off clothing. A hug of silence offered us both comfort in that moment, and I could feel his strength even though he wanted me to be his rock in that moment.

"Will you shower with me? Let me wash and prep you?" I asked, pulling away so I could see his face.

A slight haze of wetness covered his eyes, making them appear more a grayish blue than sea-like in the moon's light.

"Yes," he whispered, his tone almost broken.

I pressed a chaste kiss to his lips before leading him into the bathroom.

Callum stood still while I undressed him, the shower warming behind me. I lingered after baring his body, gently touching and caressing his skin with open-mouthed kisses. Regardless of an instinctive desire, I didn't mark him to show ownership. This wasn't anything personal. Simply a transaction.

I quickly shucked off my clothes while the lies echoed in my head and ushered him beneath the spray.

Steam rose around us, creating a dreamy fog bubble where the outside world couldn't touch us. Quietness lay over us like a weighted blanket, offering comfort and a sense of safety I wished I could believe in as much as he did.

Would it kill me to be vulnerable for once in my adult life? To test steps toward maybe trusting someone someday?

I didn't know much about Callum, but something inside me urged me to speak.

My mouth opened before I overthought what I was about to spill. "I've always felt the need to nurture because I grew up in foster care and never experienced the love of a mother and father." I ran soapy hands over his shoulders and back, proud of myself for voicing my self-reflection for the first time ever to a mere stranger.

Callum turned, smoothing dripping hair off my forehead. "Thank you for sharing that part of you with me."

My gaze dropped to his chest, and I mapped out his pecs with what remained of the soap. "That's why once Landon had weaseled his way beneath my skin and straight into my heart when we were kids, I did everything in my power to make sure he knew he was loved. Appreciated and wanted."

I was pretty sure with how close he and Landon were,

Callum had learned his best friend had received none of those things from the two who should have put him first.

The spray beat down on us as I retrieved more shower gel and dropped to my knees.

Callum's semi hung directly in front of my face, but I didn't linger in fondling or attempting to arouse him. Keeping my touch more along the lines of worship, I gave him all my physical attention from navel to toes, turning him by the hip to clean his backside.

My own dick stood at full mast, not yet leaking but ready to claim the pucker I ran a slick finger over.

A sigh left Callum as he leaned forward, forearms against the shower wall, offering his ass to me on a goddamn platter.

I slipped my soapy finger inside him, gently working him.

He shuddered and whimpered when I eased from his hole to retrieve the removable shower head.

"Okay?" I murmured, rinsing off his shoulders, watching the water and suds sluice past muscle and through his crack.

"Yes."

I spent a few minutes cleaning him out, and he sagged against the tile in complete submission to my tenderness. The walls he hid the vulnerable parts of himself behind had crumbled to dust beneath my touch.

Leaning in, I kissed his shoulder, wishing I could be as open with him. "Thank you for trusting me take care of you."

"No one..." He swallowed audibly as though his throat had swelled. "I need you, Zack—please."

I replaced the shower head and pressed against his back, running my hands down his chest, past tensed abs, finding his cock fully engorged, the slit slippery with pre-cum.

He hissed as I pulled down on his tight sac while thumbing over his glans.

"Zack..." His pleading tone made my dick buck where it rested against his crack.

"How long has it been, Callum?" I asked against his ear while slowly jacking him with just enough friction to drive him out of his mind.

"Too many years to count."

"Hmm." I once more went to my knees, going straight for the ass I hadn't gotten nearly enough of a taste of our first night together. I nosed up through his wet cheeks, and he widened his stance with a groan.

"Yes." He choked on the word, and I spread him open, taking a moment to admire the blond hairs around his pucker.

That devotion I'd been hellbent on showing stuttered to a halt at the thought of breaching his body with my dick, and I swallowed hard.

Growling, I buried my nose against him, only able to draw a hint of his musk in thanks to the thorough cleaning I'd given him. Still, he smelled delicious, like herbal soap and earth.

I licked and probed without pushing past his ring, tugging his dick downward so I could tongue his length, sac, and taint. Suckling on his swollen head earned me a few curses, and moaning, I lapped clear up to his hole, finally dipping my tip inside him.

"Oh Jesus—Zack." Callum pressed back against my face, and I licked inside his hole as far as I could reach. "Fuck yes. God, I could come from your tongue alone."

Not happening. My need had taken control.

A few more slurping kisses, and I stood, grabbing the lube I always kept on hand in the shower. I hadn't expected to slicken up someone other than myself, but wasn't about to complain about using my personal stock on a client.

The term for him didn't echo gently in my head, but I shoved against the uncomfortable feeling and set my focus on readying him for my dick. He had asked for it after all.

I gave him one finger while kissing along his shoulders but quickly added a second.

He grunted as I worked them both in deep and jolted when I rubbed over his prostate.

"Goddamn." He gasped the curse, shuddering as I stroked his sweet spot again.

"Close?" I asked against his ear, earning a half-manic nod. "Want to come like this or on my cock, sweetheart?"

"Oh God." Callum tipped his head back, and I licked up his neck while slipping a third finger past his ring. "I need you inside me, right fucking now."

"Condoms are on the bedside table."

"Shit." He growled, pushing against my fingers buried in his hole.

I bit my tongue to keep from asking him if he trusted me. Going without sheathing up wasn't an option with my job, no matter how badly I might want it.

"Come on," I whispered against his ear before kissing his lobe.

The time for slow and comforting gave way to our rekindled lust.

I took care in drying him off but got him quickly onto my bed.

Callum crawled onto the mattress on his hands and knees, but I swatted his flank while retrieving a condom from beside the bedside lamp.

"On your back, sweetheart."

He rolled and watched me with passion-hazed eyes while I tossed the condom and bottle of lube beside him. "Zack."

I climbed atop him, straddling his thighs. "Hmm?"

His soft caress of knuckles along my cheek sent a strange shudder down through clear to my soul. "I need you inside me."

Chapter 20

Callum

Having heard Zack's reminder that what we shared wouldn't be following us into the future, I wanted nothing more than for him to push into my body. Fill me up with his cock. Rock into me until he coaxed every drop of cum from my aching balls.

This was my last chance to bottom because I expected once Landon and I returned home, I wouldn't be getting dick while moving forward in our relationship—because our transition from friends to lovers would stick for the long run. While we hadn't discussed our sexual preferences, if I had to bet money, I would take a chance on every cent in my bank account that Landon would never top me.

Society had all but painted him as a voracious bottom with enough evidence to condemn and shame. But he was perfect in my eyes, and I would never ask for him to be more than he was.

I had needs though, ones Zack longed to fulfill if his leaking tip and tight balls were any indication.

He'd agreed to care for me and had set me completely at

ease, but I would partake rather than just lay there and get fucked.

"Can I?" I asked, reaching for the condom and lube he'd set on the mattress beside me.

"You can have and do whatever you want," he assured me while settling onto his haunches atop my thighs.

What I want *is to own half of your heart and to take you home with us.*

Feeling a little weepy over the fact neither was possible, I sat up and grabbed the condom, ripping the foil packet open with my teeth.

His dick strained toward his navel, his groin area neatly trimmed and his balls smooth. Maybe I would get to suckle on them while fingering his ass open for me in the next couple of days, but right now...

I rolled the condom down his length and took my time making sure his shaft was soaked with lube from base to tip because he would need it to fit his thick cock into my body.

"Fuck, your hands feel so good." He watched me work his length in slow pulls, my palm swirling over his swollen head. A hiss left him as I stroked downward to tug on his sac like he'd done to mine. He dug his fingertips into his thighs, trying to fuck up into my fist. "Shit—fuck, Callum. Gotta get inside you."

"Mmm," I hummed an agreement and lay down, quickly wiping my hand clean on the sheets.

We shifted until he rested between my thighs rather than atop me. I grabbed the backs of my knees, lifting them toward my chest so I could wink my pucker at him.

"Jesus, look at you." Zack stared at my bared asshole before running a fingertip over me and causing me to clench. "I could toy with this hole all night long."

"I'm up for it if you are," I said with a small smirk, my

chest fluttery even though an underlying sadness lingered in the recesses of my mind.

Zack gave me his eyes and shifted closer to plank on one hand, the other hand holding his base. Our gazes once more locked, he smeared his lubed tip around my pucker before tapping it a few times. "Ready for me, sweetheart?"

I had been since the moment our eyes had met. Had it only been two nights ago? "Fill me up," I begged, my voice a ragged whisper. *Make it so I won't ever forget you.*

He pushed forward, and I bore down, allowing him to breach my ring.

I swallowed a curse at the immediate burn, shifting in a natural response to escape the sting of penetration.

"Jesus." Zack clenched his jaw and paused, eyes rolling back in his head. "So fucking tight—god*damn*, Callum."

I bit my tongue to keep from creating any noises that would cause Zack to stop.

"Fuck." Zack planked on his elbows, giving my flagging dick something to rub against. Eyes closed, he rested his forehead against mine. "Tell me you're okay—that I can have more."

"Take it."

Along with the other half of my heart.

I gasped as he shoved in a couple of inches.

"Jesus." Zack blinked open his eyes and cradled my face in his hands. "Still alright?"

His carefulness made my heart ache.

"Mmm." I tried to nod in his hold, praying he could see the submission of my body in my eyes as I clung to his shoulders.

Gazes once more locked, he backed out and pushed in again, almost to the root.

"You're taking me so well," he murmured, pupils blown wide enough to swallow his hazel irises.

"More," I begged, bearing down as he pulled out.

He sank in fully with one last thrust, stuffing me full.

Our mouths crashed together, and I clung to his shoulders, my heels wrapping around his ass to hold him close while I acclimated to being speared in half by his hard dick.

I'd been fucked plenty of times in my thirty-three years, but not once had I felt an intimate connection beyond physical attachment. Our tongues tangled as we shared panted breaths. He angled my head, eating at my mouth as he had my ass.

The man was voracious, and I would sate whatever hunger owned him.

"I gotta move—need to fuck you," he growled around his teeth's hold on my lower lip.

"Do it." I garbled the words from how he bit me, but he gentled his kisses, licking over my lips before suckling on them while gyrating his hips to fuck in and out of my ass.

With every slow, long stroke, I swore Zack reached into my soul, familiarizing himself with my innermost being, the places no one could experience without being laid bare.

I wanted him to delve deeper. Explore every hidden part of me.

Because he seemed the sort who wouldn't judge, who would remain loyal, a rock for me to lean on when past trauma rose to choke out my self-worth as it often did.

"Zack," I whimpered against his mouth, not sure how to ask for what I needed but knowing with every cell in my body that it was him—*only* him in that moment.

"I've got you," he promised. His fingers tightened in my hair as his hips picked up speed, thrusting harder at a different angle, steadily enough he forced grunts from my lungs with every stroke over my prostate.

My dick leaked between us, making a mess between our stomachs, the perfect slickness to rut against.

"You gonna come for me, Callum?"

"Mmm hmm," I agreed, unable to speak with how he railed me.

"Shoot that spunk all over us."

"Y-Yes." He ripped the agreement from me with a harsh jab between my thighs.

"Give it to me, baby. Every. Fucking. Drop." He dropped his demands between each steady stab hitting me just right.

I cried out, my back arching as cum rocketed up my cock to spurt between our bellies.

"Fuck yeah. Your ass is strangling my dick—fuck. So good." Zack drew out my climax with steady, ball-slapping stabs into my guts until I emptied and gasped for breath. He slowed then stilled—without coming.

I clung to him, sucked on his tongue, and swallowed his panted curses as he ate at my mouth. Both of us shuddered, the slick sweat and cum between us a mess I lusted to see painted and dried on my skin.

"Zack," I murmured, unable to catch my breath as he wrapped his arms completely around me, squeezing me tight.

"Wish I could empty inside you," he choked out before his dick began to throb in my hole. A low groan rumbled from his chest pressed against mine. He climaxed into the condom without a single thrust, gasping and whimpering as though I'd taken his soul and shattered it like a ship against rocks.

I clung to him for all I was worth in the same way he did

to me. As though neither of us wanted to let go, well beyond the five days I'd paid for.

But he'd made it clear that would never be, no matter how badly I wished otherwise.

Landon would be enough. Finally having him in every way *had* to be.

Or my pining had only just begun.

Chapter 21

Landon

I woke up alone without a trace of warmth on either side of me. Coolness settled in my chest even though my eyes heated and stung.

Had Callum...

Hopping up, I grabbed my boxer briefs off the floor and hopped around bleary-eyed while pulling them on as fast as possible.

His room's door propped open, his bed still freshly made by the staff from the day before.

He'd spent the night with Zack.

While jealousy riled up inside me, the feeling only stemmed from not being between them. I hoped Callum had made a dent in Zack's defenses. It wasn't exactly early in the morning, so perhaps their night alone had been so damn fantastic that neither was yet ready to leave the bed.

Fine by me—kind of.

I had work to do, which left Callum time to build a bond with Zack that he wouldn't want to break in three days.

Snagging a bottle of water from the mini fridge, I checked my cell.

Mother had left a voicemail, and internally cringing, I hit play.

She'd heard I'd run off to some tropical island, so of course she had to remind me to be careful. Her tone suggested I not forget what I'd done before.

As if I could. That shit haunted me to this day, dictated my choices while in public and otherwise.

Father's current goal was to get back into politics, and he didn't need any more fuckups from his only son.

How had she found out? Who all knew that Callum and I had gone on vacation?

It was bad enough my parents hated two single gay men living together, and while they claimed to be LGBTQ supporters, I wasn't even sure they would feel any better even if we were in a committed relationship or married.

My mind paused on that word as I stared out the slider windows to the rising sun glinting gold over the deep blue ocean.

Was marriage something that Callum wanted? Would he agree if I got on my knees and begged him to stay with me for the rest of our lives? He'd already promised he would never leave me. Putting a ring on it might help to ensure he stuck to his word.

But he would only own half of me. There would be an empty spot on my other side, one Zack owned. A space, last I'd been aware, he wasn't interested in occupying.

My mind began a spiral, which would lead to depression and an inability to focus on anything other than feeling sorry for myself, but I had shit to do.

Me: **Hey, Cal, when you're done with Zack, would you mind grabbing me some breakfast?**

I'm going to start tackling those edits this morning.

Without waiting for a reply, I hopped in the shower, needing more than just bright sunlight to get my gears fully turning in my head. I'd taken a peek at Cyn's email, so I'd gone to bed knowing the task ahead of me.

My muse had simmered while I'd slept, and I had a somewhat clear idea of how to fix the mess of my latest manuscript.

A shiver slid over my body, raising the hairs on my arms.

Callum's shadow darkened the curtain a mere heartbeat after I'd felt him in close proximity. "Mind if I join you?"

Butterflies leapt into flight in my chest, which also enticed my dick to plump back up since Mother's message had killed my morning wood. "Please do."

Callum stepped in behind me, all warm skin and soft hands wrapping me up. He'd come to me alone, which I was surprisingly fine with. A soft kiss beneath my right ear made me sag against him. "Are you okay? he whispered, his breath hot on my skin.

I clasped my hands atop his over my belly. "Why wouldn't I be?"

"Because I didn't come back to you last night." Thankfully, he didn't sound as though guilt ate at him or like he'd been sent away from Zack's bed unsatisfied.

"Did you fuck?"

"Yes." He didn't hesitate in answering.

"Did you like it?"

"God, yes."

Elation swept through me, even more so since his cock thickened against my ass.

"Good. Get your fill, because there's going to be a

serious lack of dick in your future unless Zack comes home with us. I'm a total bottom, Cal."

He snickered while trailing his lips over my neck. "I expected as such, but you're enough, Lan. I don't need anything but you if Zack sticks to his guns."

Talk about a swoon moment. I turned to goo, a smile curving my lips.

Callum and I hadn't discussed our return to Rhode Island or what it would look like. We needed to in greater detail, but I didn't want to potentially ruin the sweet moment between us. In comfortable quietness, we washed each other before once more embracing, but this time, face-to-face.

I'd been abandoned once before by a man I loved, but Callum wasn't the type to run. He'd stuck by my side countless times throughout our friendship, proving I could trust him with every aspect of my life.

"Can I touch you?" Callum asked, his tone low and as arousing as his hard length against mine.

I rutted just enough to make him groan while wrapping my arms around his neck. "Touch, taste, fuck—I want everything with you."

His huffed exhale against my mouth hinted of mint and underlying sweetness. "I want everything with you too."

Tears flooded my eyes, and I whimpered, pulling his face toward mine as elation rushed through my blood.

We kissed and frotted beneath the spray, our mouths quickly turning ravenous. Eight years of bottled up longing seemed to vibrate beneath Callum's thin control, but he kept himself in check rather than pushing me against the wall and shoving his dick up my ass without lube.

I'd have taken him that way if he'd been too far gone in his need, but in usual Callum fashion, he kept his focus on me. My comfort and safety. He wrapped his hand around our straining dicks, working our foreskin with short strokes to jerk us off.

He breathed against my parted lips, our foreheads together in a moment of intimacy with steam swirling around us in the type of tender moment found only in fairytales.

"I've told you lots of times that I love you," I whispered the words, my lower lip brushing over his, "but this...Cal, it's so much more than I ever imagined. I'm realizing now how deeply you're embedded in my soul, how integral you are to my life, not just my work."

"I've loved you for what feels like forever." Callum backed away from me, cradling my cheek in his free hand while gently stroking us. "And I'll love you long after we're both gone from this earth."

I swallowed hard, tears spilling down my cheeks regardless of the joy bubbling up inside me. "What about Zack?"

Callum's eyes flitted from one of mine to the other as though trying to get a read on my thoughts before answering. "You need me." He didn't ask a question, but I had to answer.

"Yes. Now and always."

"But you also want him."

Unable to speak, I nodded, pleading with my eyes that he not make me choose. I would rather die first.

"So do I."

"Oh, thank fuck." I sagged against him, clinging like the greedy boy I'd been nicknamed. "We have to make him fall for us, Cal. We only have a few days, and I have all these edits to get done—"

"Hey."

I clamped my lips shut, trusting Callum to set my mind

back on a straight path rather than that damn spiral, which would lead nowhere good.

"Zack isn't going to be manipulated, Lan. He's too jaded, too crafty to be pushed into something more, no matter how much the two of us desire it. We have to love on him, and while yes, we can continue to show him how perfect the three of us are together, he's going to have to make that decision on his own. There will be no rushing, no pushing our agenda, okay?"

I wanted to pout but chose to nod instead because my best friend knew best.

Callum smiled, popping that damn dimple that had used to make my belly feel strange. I now understood why. "That's my good boy," he murmured, and fuck me, did my stomach dip and roll in the best way possible.

I planted my mouth against his, suddenly horny as fuck and twice as greedy.

He groaned, shoving his tongue between my lips, and enough pre-cum soon oozed due to our face fucking that he released our dicks, grabbed my ass cheeks, and the frotting intensified by ten thanks to natural lubrication. We chased completion, sharing gasps and breaths, an occasional curse breaking the peace around us.

"Are you going to come for me, baby?"

I swallowed his words, whimpering in agreement.

Cum erupted between us a heartbeat later, both of us shooting off at the same time. Our arms tightened around each other, every inch of us melded as we'd always been meant to be.

Being with him, having his gentle hands clean me once we'd returned to earth, took me to an even higher level of euphoria.

If only Zack were there with us.

"Just be you today," I murmured before pressing my lips to Callum's, "and Zack will have no choice but to fall head over heels. I have a good feeling about this—and it's not just my needy heart and hole doing the talking here. We are a three-piece puzzle, I'm sure of it."

He squeezed me tight. "So am I."

Chapter 22

Zack

"How was he this morning?" I asked Callum, who lay on the sand beside me.

The sun shone down on us, and even though it was a couple hours before noon, we both held fruity drinks with little umbrellas. He'd slathered sunscreen on me, and I'd returned the favor, lingering and teasing with my touch until he'd gotten hard, high cheekbones pink and fucking gorgeous.

I'd almost suggested heading to my room again, but I'd yet to just sit and relax on the beach.

"He's focused on his MacBook, typing like mad. Usually, issues with work set him back emotionally, but he's...recharged, I guess you could say."

Work. Typing. Following his dreams.

How they'd met made a little more sense.

"And did your return to the suite have anything to do with said recharging?" I teased, turned on a little by the thought of them together.

That alluring flush returned to Callum's face.

"Mmm," I hummed in appreciation, shifting to adjust

my junk that perked up yet again. While I wasn't one to poke into a client's personal life, I got off on the sex talk that always ramped them up. Made them lust for my dick or hole.

And Callum?

He'd been putty in my hands the night before, and I couldn't deny wanting to play some more regardless of how badly I'd been tempted to tear down my walls and let him in.

We'd shared blow jobs before he'd left my bed that morning, since he'd declined my dick up his very sore ass. Mutual climaxes via each other's mouths hadn't been nearly enough to ease my insatiable desire for him. It was too bad Landon couldn't join us too. At least then I'd have another hole at my disposal.

I refused to think about him in any other way that didn't prove dangerous to my emotions. Bad enough just the presence of his best friend made me want to toss caution to the wind.

"What did you do to him?" I pushed for information, simply for something to fantasize about while being lazy beneath the sun's warmth. "Finally have a taste of his pink pucker? Spill your cum in him like you've been dreaming about doing for the past eight years?"

"Not exactly."

"Get on your knees to suck his brains out of his dick?"

"Jesus, Zack." Callum laughed, glancing my way—with a goddamned dimple in his cheek.

"Fuck. Me."

One of his eyebrows hitched up. "I mean, that could be arranged..."

Groaning, I squeezed the base of my officially granite-like dick. While my thoughts had been quick to go there upon first meeting Callum, with how he'd let himself go with me the night before, I feared inadvertently doing the same should I be on the receiving end of his devoted attention.

The man was hard to resist, and I didn't trust myself not to lay my lonely heart bare at his feet, especially after seeing that little dent of kryptonite in his cheek. I wanted to keep Callum smiling day and night.

"You said you volunteer at a LGBTQ club for teens," I stated, doing a one-eighty that caused him to blink because fucking boundaries, goddamnit. I could *not* allow myself to be tempted more than I already was when it came to him.

"You remembered."

"Of course I did. It's something else we have in common besides binging DIY shows." I turned my focus skyward, eyes closing. "I spend a lot of my free time at the homeless shelter but twice a month hang out at Humanity House, an LGBTQ community for teens, in Malden."

I had no wish to flay my heart wide open, but that didn't mean I couldn't connect with another caretaker, a nurturer who understood that part of me. We talked about the different programs available to the kids and how they seemed much more accepting of all identities.

Fuck knew those before us had fought hard to be recognized. The least we could do was put in the work for future generations.

"You're a good man, Zack." Callum's quiet statement had me squinting his way.

"So are you."

Callum sat and stared out over the water, arms wrapped around upturned knees. I wondered what went through his thoughts that left zero trace of his dimple behind.

The gentle waves on shore acted as a soothing rhythm

that set me at completely ease. Somewhat vulnerable too, same as I'd been in the shower with Callum the night before.

Rather than pushing, I waited, giving Callum time to work through his thoughts. While I wouldn't have minded his sharing, I wouldn't ask for more than I was willing to give in return.

"I fucked up," he whispered, eyes closing briefly.

My initial thought at his confession was that he'd made a mistake in hiring me and forcing a showdown between me and Landon, but something deeper lay behind his words. A festering guilt I'd gotten a glimpse of before.

"Being an escort means I oftentimes get to play therapist." I tried for a light tone. "I'm available if you need to get shit off your chest, and since we both signed NDAs, you can be sure I won't repeat a word."

He glanced at me, studying my eyes as though seeking my true intentions.

Yeah, I cared, even though I wouldn't admit to it.

A soft smile curved his lips as though he'd figured me out, not enough to entice that dick-stiffening dent to appear in his smooth cheek, but my chest ached all the same.

Releasing a slow exhale, he turned his attention toward the swells beyond shore again. "Not even Landon is aware of the full extent of my greatest shame, but it's the driving force behind every choice I've made since meeting him."

The fact Callum shared with me something only his best friend knew hit me hard. Fucking baffled me.

I waited with bated breath, longing to connect with his past trauma that had created my same need to shelter others. Why hadn't he shared the whole story with Landon? Maybe because he'd always needed to be the strong one and couldn't allow himself to appear weak?

If that was the case, fuck my life because that meant he felt safe with me. Trusted me, even after I'd told Landon he loved him. I didn't deserve that kind of forgiveness or a second chance. How could he entrust me with something that important?

"Someone very close to me made terrible decisions when we were kids and ended up in jail," he finally said, his tone low and full of the grief I'd expected. "I had plenty of opportunities to step in but didn't. To this day, I regret not doing more or saying something to prevent what had happened."

My words about sexual assault and how Callum had reacted with what I'd thought had been a heart attack suddenly made a little more sense. Empathy swelled inside me, and I wanted to dive deeper, uproot all of his hurts, and help him find a way to eradicate them from his life.

Still, I wasn't one to pry, especially about something that had obviously caused him a great deal of emotional pain.

"We can lead others to water, but they've got to drink on their own. Whatever went down, it wasn't your fault." I offered what I could. "They made their choice and reaped what they sowed."

"Same as Landon did with you," Callum mused quietly.

I wasn't going to touch that with a ten-foot pole. I refused to take on any blame for what Landon's actions had brought onto himself. From what Callum had told me that first night he'd come to my room, begging me to at least hear Landon out, I expected the messes Landon had gotten himself into hadn't been pretty.

"That's another reason for my volunteering," Callum said, digging his toes into the sand at the edge of our blanket. "For the longest time, I thought I was a bad person, that

I couldn't follow my own instincts. That I wasn't trustworthy. I believed those three lies for years before I realized I could do better. *Be* better. It's originally why I attached myself to Landon, why I've come to care for him so deeply. Nurturing him fulfills a part of me left empty from my inaction all those years ago."

"And you soothe his neediness as well as give his emotions a safe place to land."

"Yes." Callum shot me another small smile.

"It's nice to be on the receiving end sometimes though, isn't it?" I asked, speaking about the night before and what he'd allowed me to do for him.

Longing flooded Callum's eyes.

"You let me take care of you," I reminded him.

"And it was one of the best nights of my life. I'd like to do the same for you. I can't imagine you get that very often considering your job demands that you place other's needs above our own."

Fuck, did he nail that truth with accuracy.

"Getting others off *is* a kink of mine, so I'm always satisfied, but yeah, I'll admit I wouldn't mind being worshiped. Adored. Loved on without having to expend any mental energy."

"I can do that for you, Zack."

The offer made me want to crawl toward him on hands and knees, beg him to satisfy me in the ways no one ever had. Make me feel as though I belonged—for *real*. But these five days weren't about me and the deepest desires I'd never shared with anyone. How he pulled the truth from me so damn easily, I had no fucking clue.

"You can trust me," he pushed gently.

And therein lay the problem. My heart refused to emerge from behind the shredded foil attempting to hide it from view. I'd been set aside, forced away from what I'd hoped to call home one too many times.

It was my turn to escape into inner thoughts while staring over the ocean. Regardless of the character Callum portrayed, of what I'd taken note of with how he cared for Landon's wellbeing, what I *longed* for, I refused to be swayed.

"Vulnerability isn't an option," I stated, my tone quiet but firm. "My biological parents left me to the state rather than raising what I'm assuming they saw as a mistake. Countless foster families only cared about the monthly checks they received. Landon pushed me away too, which regardless of his reasons, only toughened me up even more. My entire childhood lacked in love or affection of any kind, and I've spent almost thirty-three years emotionally on my own. I'm not capable of lowering my walls."

"I could demand as your client that you let me have you however I wish."

I brushed off his words since they were as far from a threat as possible. "You wouldn't."

"So you *do* trust me."

Heaving a weary exhale, I closed my eyes so I wouldn't have to look at his gorgeous face when his voice held a hint of a smile. "Elite contracts allow for personal boundaries, Callum, and bottoming for you after what we've gone through the past couple of days wouldn't be me just offering up my hole as if you were simply another client."

Again, I'd said more than I'd planned on, but Callum deserved my honesty at the very least.

"Zack," he whispered, and I forced myself to meet his gaze.

I might have hard limits, but he'd somehow blasted

through them all. Even without having full access to my body, he'd found a way to pry me open and burrow inside.

Pain and desire filled his green-blue irises, and I fought the need to reach for him. Lose myself in his body as I'd done the night before.

"Please, Callum—don't ask for more than I'm willing to give," I rasped my request, barely hanging onto my self-preservation.

"You have my word."

As much as I didn't want to allow myself to, I believed him.

Chapter 23

Landon

I'd finished.

The edits had left me with a migraine from hell—my reason for begging off having dinner with Callum and Zack after their time on the beach, but I just couldn't join them. Between the throb in my temples and my mental exhaustion, I didn't have it in me to be out in public.

Callum, always the sweetheart, had returned from their late dinner with a boxed one for me, insisting I eat since I'd done nothing but drink coffee all day. Rather than escaping my grumpy ass for Zack's, Callum had stayed in with me, putting me first as usual.

He'd seemed preoccupied, perhaps even a little bit down after spending hours with Zack, but I didn't bug him to tell me what was going on with him. Recognizing he needed me—and vice versa—I'd asked him to take care of me instead.

Callum joined me in the bath he'd drawn for me, and I lounged between his thighs, eyes closed as he washed me. We both had grown hard, but neither of us pressed for more, not even after we'd dried and crawled into his bed.

I'd fallen asleep with my head on his chest, his palm possessively holding my ass cheek.

When I'd woken, he'd already been dressed and had a cup of coffee in his hand. He planned to remain in the suite, reading over my manuscript, while Zack and I got dropped by boat into a secluded cove where a canopied outdoor bed and a picnic basket full of food and wine awaited us.

I would have a chance to get away from any prying eyes with one of the loves of my life. The only way it could have been better would be if Callum accompanied us.

I'd kissed him for the thoughtful gift before hightailing my ass to the shower to prepare for a day with Zack, since I had Callum's blessing to thoroughly enjoy myself while he rested.

That included some dick.

Hopefully.

Relief over having gotten my edits done allowed me to feel the freedom to enjoy my afternoon beneath a blue sky with a gorgeous companion.

"Did you have fun with Callum?" I asked Zack.

He sat beside me on the massive bed, picking at pieces of some tropical fruit that was a little too bland for my liking. I preferred the cheese that paired well with the wine we sipped.

"I did." Proof he'd spent too long outside the day before. The sun had kissed his face with perhaps a bit too much pink, one of the reasons I'd insisted we picnic beneath the canopy.

"Did you miss me?" I teased, telling myself I didn't *really* ask out of insecurity.

"Of course we did." Zack placated me with a smirk, the knowing bastard.

"I always pine for Callum when he's not around, but I'm actually kind of glad to have you all to myself today."

I hoped to hear Zack agree with the sentiment, but he simply popped another bite of fruit between his lips.

"It was nice reminiscing about our childhood this morning," he stated quietly after swallowing, sending a zing through my system. "We had some good times, didn't we?"

"We really did," I agreed before sipping my chilled wine. "But being invited to ride on the elephant at the circus a few months after you came to live with us—that's one of my most treasured memories."

"Really?" Zack gave me the undivided attention I'd been craving since we'd sat down to snack. His gaze roamed over my face like a physical touch, making me hungry for more. "Of everything we did, every vacation your parents dragged us on, *that* stands out in your memory?"

"It was the first time you held my hand."

A soft smile made his eyes twinkle. "You were scared shitless."

"I thought I was going to topple off and get trampled by those huge feet."

Zack chuckled. "You'd have been squashed for sure. You were such a pipsqueak back then."

"Hey." I tossed a piece of that disgusting fruit at his head.

Of course, he shied away, and I missed him by a mile, which made him laugh.

I damn near swooned at the lines at the corners of his eyes. "I've missed that."

"What?" he asked while righting himself, still chuckling.

"The sound of your happiness."

His smile faded. "Can't say that happens too often."

"Same," I whispered what I hated about my life.

We stared at one another for a long moment, and I realized the connection I hoped to find with him again required that I tell him all the shit of my life. I had to be completely honest. With how Zack and I were secluded where there was no escape except for the boat offshore and around the bend waiting on our walkie-talkie request to return to the hotel, Zack had no choice but to hear me out.

And if it made him pack his bags and take off early, then at least I could say I'd been completely honest with him.

"After I told you to leave..." I started, my heart racing badly enough I didn't know how to go on. Showing vulnerability had to be the key, right?

Fuck.

I swallowed hard and set the glass of wine aside before I snapped the stem.

"I'm not going to judge you, Landon." Zack's quiet words assured me as gently and easily as Callum always did. "Get whatever you need off your chest. I promise to listen and attempt to see things from your point of view."

Tears welled in my eyes, and I blinked rapidly to keep from getting overly emotional. I didn't need him thinking I was trying to manipulate him again.

"After you left, I grew resentful. Gave up my virginity to the first guy who showed interest. And once I learned what a high I got from bottoming and making men lose their ability to do anything but nut up my ass, I became addicted." I glanced at Zack, but he didn't appear fazed by my admission.

"So anyway." I inhaled until it hurt. "An asshole ex-boyfriend unknowingly recorded and then leaked a cum dump sex tape across social media. The names I'd been called during the filming used to get me off—which was why he'd agreed to share me so often—but the backlash of that video proved to be disastrous. It even hit the major news networks.

"Father's hopes of running for president got tossed into the sewer along with my reputation. Overnight, I became the 'Soiled Senator's Son', confined to the shadows. They called me a cock-hungry whore, so I sought isolation. I was labeled a cum slut, who had shown my asshole to anyone in order to be filled, since I didn't get any attention at home."

Fuck, did stating that shit aloud *still* hurt.

"You blamed me."

I huffed a sarcastic un-funny laugh, hating that he saw past all the surface to what bothered me the most. "How well you know me, but it wasn't your fault. I made those choices then looked for someone else to hold liable. I'm sorry for that too."

"What happened, Landon?" Zack asked, choosing as always to ignore my apologies.

"More viciousness spread across social media atop the truth the newscasters broadcasted, causing shame and embarrassment. It didn't matter that I was innocent of the accusations in most of the rumors that stirred up to bash my name along with my parents. People will always judge me based on what happened. They'll always wonder about me. I'll never be understood, my supposed addiction to sex when I simply love dick. Being filled with cum.

"But of course, I couldn't deny myself and took on that identity of being an addict. It wasn't healthy, but I continued on in secret. A health scare got my ass supposedly *sober*. And once free from that STD, I vowed to keep my hole to myself, regardless of how starved I was for love and affection. I've broken down a handful of times for quick one-on-one hookups, but that's it. The fear of being taped or even photographed again makes me sick. Literally."

Zack didn't even shift as I spilled my truth, just listened, his focus intent on my face.

"I started to write about the fantasies I could no longer experience in reality."

A slow smile curled his lips. "I'm proud of you."

Goddamn him. My throat swelled, and I had to blink back more tears. "My family thinks I'm living off my grandmother's inheritance."

"And I'm guessing you're writing romance that would have them clutching their pearls."

I actually chuckled. "Taboo and forbidden gay smut," I clarified, my chin lifting a little because I was proud of myself too, damnit. "And I'm making bank, especially with my polyamorous stories."

"You use a pen name, I'm guessing."

I nodded. "Father believes Callum is only my friend and approves of him being my housemate since he 'keeps me in line'." I huffed another laugh at that one. "If Father read the naughty nugget of smut that led to him being my PA, he would be horrified. So you can understand why I don't trust just anyone with this information."

"I do."

"While I'm not ashamed of how I've come to be rich on my own, I can't stand the thought of any more humiliation. It's bad enough being in the spotlight as a politician's son, but with the choices I'd made back then..." I trailed off, shrugging. "I'd rather live without the drama."

"That, I can understand," Zack agreed. "I'm not one for that shit myself. Is that why you were hesitant to dance with me when Callum promised you would be safe?"

"Yeah." I blew out a huge exhale, the burden of secrecy

I'd been carrying on my shoulders for so long a little bit lighter. "I avoid social events whenever possible, keep images of the real me off social media. I cling to the only loyal person I have. And even though Callum tries to talk me into going out more often, it's tough to be vulnerable with anyone else."

I expected Zack got that part of my thinking too. He'd been buttoned up tight when he'd first come to live with my family, but I hadn't realized at the time because I'd been a little kid. Recognition came later, not long before I figured out I was in love with him. I'd been fourteen and had heard him crying during the night.

Instead of being on the receiving end of his comfort, I'd offered my arms to the boy who'd always held me.

Zack had soaked my sleep shirt with his tears, and I'd decided in my heart that I wanted to be there for him until we both grew old and gray.

From that moment until the day he'd left, we'd pretty much shared a bed every night without my parent's knowledge. It'd been purely platonic between us, and that one afternoon I heard my parents discussing Zack's eighteenth birthday on the horizon and what I expected that meant for his freedom to live his own life, well.

I'd been scared shitless then too. Anxiety had made me sick to my stomach for days on end, and every time I ate, I ended up either hugging the toilet or bent over it groaning with the pains knifing my guts.

But all of *that* I didn't share with Zack.

A man could only bare his heart so much before he felt completely eviscerated. And I wanted to enjoy my day alone with him, not wallow in regrets.

Chapter 24

Zack

I packed up our snacks, set the basket off the bed, and lay back, holding my arms out wide in invitation.

Landon scrambled to attach himself to my side like a koala, same as he'd done when we were kids. Still a perfect fit after all these years, I realized while settling my hand on his lower back and atop the forearm he flung over my stomach. Perhaps, even better now that his legs could intertwine with mine, his groin resting against my hip while he snuggled his face against my chest.

"Even better than I remembered," he murmured, his hot breath inches from my nipple that pebbled with desire to be tugged and bitten.

Kissing his hair, I closed my eyes and released a shit ton of tension from my body with one heavy sigh over how right he felt pressed against me. I wanted nothing more than to live without drama, but I couldn't be upset that Landon was tucked not just along my entire side but into the corners of my mind as well.

But I wasn't ready to dissect or discuss my feelings.

My five days in paradise were supposed to be stress and

angst-free, and while I'd had some good moments, it hadn't exactly been a restful vacation for the mind or heart let alone my emotions I couldn't categorize never mind accept.

"So how are we going to spend our final day on the island tomorrow?" I asked, needing lighter conversation, something to occupy my brain with.

"Callum said whatever I want, I get."

I snickered at the reminder, expecting I knew where his thoughts traveled, considering his lust for dick and the opportunity to get as much as he could handle in the time allotted to us. "Let's it hear, then."

"You're still up for anything?"

"Pretty much, yeah." Just no getting caught up in feels or admitting aloud how much I fucking loved having Landon in my arms again. That shit needed to stay buried beneath the surface of knowledge to anyone but me.

"We'll spend the day in my bed. All *three* of us. I want to be cum drunk, my ass aching and dripping, and my heart full to overflowing with memories of my fantasy come to life."

Sounded like a fucking fantastic plan to me except for that bit about going without a condom. If he and Callum wanted to fuck without them though, I didn't care. As for me, I would take the opportunity to get my fill of these two men before heading back home to chilly, wet Boston where I belonged.

But those plans for tomorrow didn't mean we had to keep our hands to ourselves today. I'd been instructed by my client to please Landon, and that gave me the green light for whatever I wanted too since there was no way in hell my old enemy-turned-lover would deny my touch.

"So what do you think?" Landon asked, a hint of insecurity in his tone that I hated to hear and couldn't allow.

In a flash, I rolled him beneath me and nestled my thickening dick against his. "Why wait? Callum's not here, but that doesn't mean we can't put *this* bed to good use."

He released an oomph noise as I took his mouth in a bruising kiss, and he set aside whatever he'd planned to say, wrapping his arms and legs around me like an octopus and clinging to me for dear life. He tasted of the weird cheese and wine, but beneath lay his natural sweetness I'd only gotten one taste of and could easily become addicted to.

We shared panted breaths when coming up briefly for oxygen but dove back in as though of the same mind, making up for thousands of lost kisses thanks to a moment in time that had changed the course of our futures.

I swallowed his whimpers, rutting against his hard length with my aching one until we both nutted. We panted, shuddering and making a mess in our shorts.

Eventually, we came down from our euphoric high, and I released his swollen, red lips.

Landon peered up at me, all that same love like when we'd been innocent kids shining at me like the rising sun.

I pushed up to plank on my elbows, sifting my fingers through his soft hair and wishing I had the strength to let go and drown in his amber gaze. "I shouldn't have left," I murmured the regret I'd carried with me for fifteen years.

His smile faded, the light in his eyes dimming.

"I never should have listened to your dad," I continued quietly.

"Wait." Landon's brow furrowed. "What about Father?"

"He offered me a thousand bucks and told me to get lost rather than have me hauled to jail for sexual assault. And I'd been hurt enough by your words that I took off without argument. I should have stayed in town though. Talked to you the next day and explained that I wanted you too but had only denied your gift because of your age."

"Fucking *hell*." Landon's eyes glinted, shooting off sparks as he tensed beneath me. "That's seriously what went down after I locked myself in my room like he'd demanded?"

I didn't shift away or stop stroking his hair, the need to set him at ease stronger than I'd ever felt. "I never would have gone otherwise. He gave me the means for a new start, and I thought I was making the right choice. I didn't—and I'm sorry."

"I forgive you."

I blinked down at him, my heart cracking wide open at his immediate and adamant reply. "Just like that?"

He shrugged a shoulder and relaxed into the bed beneath us again. "Yeah, because if you'd stayed, I wouldn't have sown my wild oats that led me to Callum or landed me on this deserted stretch of beach with one of the two hottest men on the face of the earth."

I didn't preen over his compliment. Nope. My mind focused on and was blown by the fact he could have zero regrets when earlier he'd seemed bogged down by guilt for his choices. Was changing your mind that simple? A plowing forward into a new truth with the intention of owning your thoughts on a situation?

"Kind of sounds like a story worth writing," I suggested rather than starting up a serious conversation that might tempt me toward switching my stance on relationships.

Landon leaned up to kiss me again rather than agreeing, his tongue flicking over my lips and seeking entry to my mouth.

Knowing him, he only wrote happily ever afters, and I didn't trust that for our future. Couldn't. Landon might be able to shift his patterns of thinking on a whim, but I wasn't capable of that superpower.

Still, I explored his tongue with my own, soaking in his affection, the little noises of enjoyment he made in his throat. I'd picked up on the fact he loved being kissed senseless, and spoiling him had always given me a sense of purpose and satisfaction. Yet something else Callum and I had in common.

I missed Landon's mouth on mine the second I pulled back but shoved that feeling into the recesses of my mind where they would hopefully get lost. "Let's swim. Clean the sticky messes in our shorts."

"You might have to carry me," Landon grumbled as I slid off the low bed, my feet hitting warm sand and sinking into its softness enough that the grains covered my toes.

"Gladly." I swung him up and over my shoulder, making him shriek with laughter that brought a grin to my face.

"Put me down!" He play-smacked my back, same as when he'd been a kid, and I went all Big Foot on his ass. He'd grown quite a bit taller, but I could still manhandle his lithe form.

"Nope." I took off across the burning white sand, his giggles pure music to my ears that trickled straight into my chest.

Fucking hell, these feels were dangerous red flags I had to shy away from.

Knee-deep in warm swells, I tossed him ahead of me, needing yet hating to have him gone from my arms.

"Fucker!" he cried out with flailing limbs before disappearing beneath the water in a splash of water droplets glinting in the sun.

I dove into the next wave to clear my head, breaking not far from him.

Hair plastered to his head, he grinned at me, sunlight making his eyes appear more gold than brown. He was too beautiful for his own good, a greedy yet sweet soul who only wanted acceptance and love.

Thinking back over our time together in paradise, I realized my bitterness had faded.

And as simple as that, I'd forgiven him without conscious effort.

Perhaps healing *could* be found for past trauma. But making the choice to trust a man with what remained of my heart wasn't something that could be done.

Chapter 25

Callum

I struggled to ignore the gorgeous day beyond the suite's windows and the fact Zack and Landon were relaxing in the sun while I read my way through the edited manuscript.

Did they enjoy themselves in their own little corner of the world? Had Zack allowed himself to be vulnerable with Landon?

He and I had walked along the shoreline together in the most romantic setting imaginable, but something had settled firmly between us, far from in a good way. Whatever wall I'd noticed coming down while in his bed the night prior had been firmly erected, keeping me out.

We'd had dinner together then danced, but that underlying fire, that need to possess, simmered rather than boiled over like I'd hoped for.

Being in the sun all day had left us both exhausted, and I'd returned to our suite with nothing more than a kiss goodnight from Zack, Landon's boxed dinner in my hand.

Zack hadn't asked for nor initiated anything further, and I wasn't going to push. He tried to hide, but I saw his desires, the things he'd said he longed for. And how I wanted to give them to him, make him smile and relax in assurance that someone in this world appreciated who he was as a man and lover.

That need to fulfill, the same draw I felt for Landon, bothered the fuck out of me while I spent hours cooped up in the hotel room. I had trouble focusing on the story, but I managed to finish with a couple of tweaks and sent it back to Cyn with hopes we could continue the usual edits without too much difficulty.

I set aside work after having a salad through room service and stripped, readying for a shower to help clear my head of Landon's latest fantasy come to life in black and white.

He'd nailed the story's heart-wrenching ending that had the triad riding off together in the sunset. I could admit to jealousy stirring over their happily ever after. It was what Landon had always dreamed about, what he'd introduced to my thoughts, and meeting Zack had solidified in my heart.

But this was reality, not some romance novel where everything was rainbows and kiss emojis.

The suite's door opened and snicked shut before I stepped beneath the spray.

"Oh, perfect timing." I heard Landon's suggestive tone from outside the bathroom, but even better on its heels was Zack's murmur of agreement.

They'd returned from their private getaway on a secluded beach—and had obviously come to our suite with intent.

Blood rushed to my dick, and I stepped into the shower big enough to easily fit three grown men, hand going straight for my thickening shaft.

The two of them entered the bathroom, and I stroked

myself as they stripped off their T-shirts and swim trunks. They were my newest reasons for living, the desires of my body, and I wouldn't waste a single minute gifted to me in the time we had left.

"Get your asses in here," I ordered.

Landon hit me first, plastering his warm body along my front, his mouth attacking mine. He smelled like ozone and the ocean but tasted sweet as honey. Zack pressed against my back rather than Landon's, his lips and tongue on my nape.

A swell of emotion rose up inside at their combined onslaught of hunger, choking me with happiness and grief at once. I wanted to weep tears of joy tinged with sadness over the sure loss to come.

I grabbed hold of one of Landon's ass cheeks to better frot against him, my other angling behind me to grasp Zack's backside, keeping his hard cock snug against my crack.

Without words, we created magic, their wandering mouths and fingers desperate for me as though they'd felt my absence as deeply as I had theirs throughout the day. I hadn't been envious of their being alone but definitely wished I could have spent every waking hour with them.

Landon came first, gasping into my mouth, shuddering against me. The heat of his spunk over my throbbing dick and balls set me off. Zack followed immediately after, coating my lower back with his release.

We panted and clung to each other for long moments, none of us seemingly wanting to pull away from the steam-filled world we'd escaped to.

Eventually, I moved because my men needed to be cared for, and I wanted to hear about their time on the beach and maybe some progress they'd made in healing and reconnecting.

"Tell me all about your day, baby." I retrieved the soap and began washing the sand and spunk from Landon's body while Zack did the same for my backside.

Landon humored me, and I smiled over his story of the whole caveman act of getting tossed into the ocean. To hear him speak with such lightness and absence of stress made every penny spent and agonizing thoughts over our vacation thus far worthwhile.

The hatchet had been buried between them, thank fuck, but nothing was said about moving forward once we left the island. That would be up to them, and my heart lay at their mercy.

The sun hadn't yet fully set, but we climbed into my bed.

And in the following hours, we were a tangle of limbs, dicks, tongues, and fingers leaving each other satisfied and exhausted before midnight. At Landon's insistence, Zack stayed the night, once more taking up on his opposite side, right where he belonged.

The following morning, we sprawled on the beach after blow jobs and breakfast, allowing an hour to digest our food before returning to our suite like Landon had stated he wanted. He received zero complaints from Zack or me over his wishes to spend the day in bed. Nor did we attempt to talk him out of his demand to be penetrated by both of us at the same time.

Keeping my hands to myself while we lounged on a blanket together beneath the sun proved damn near impossible.

Zack rested on his opposite side, a slightly wider distance between their bodies than mine and Landon's. He too took care to ensure there wasn't any outward appearance of being physically involved, which made me wonder if Landon had told him about the sex tape. His remaining on his side of our large beach blanket didn't match up with the constant heated looks he shot our way though, that was for damned sure. The blatant lust that radiated from his hazel eyes stroked over our bodies like invisible starving fingers, keeping me on edge and Landon on his belly to "hide how horny he was."

There hadn't been any penetration the night before, but we'd all gotten off countless times in our voracious appetite to please each other and fill Landon's belly with cum.

And while today promised more, I would self-sacrifice my own empty hole to make sure Landon wouldn't go home unsatisfied. Because even though Zack didn't hold back with sharing in anything sexual or gazing at us with similar intent, he remained closed off emotionally.

I'd spilled my greatest regret with him, even if a bit vague on details, and how my actions had shaped me into the man I'd become. We'd bonded over our shared passions for volunteering, how nurturing others fulfilled parts of our souls, but it hadn't been enough to break down the barriers still holding strong between us. That would only come with time, which we didn't have much of.

The brief reminiscing over the night he'd cared for me had led to Zack declining my offer to do the same for him.

Not for a lack of want but from insecurities he'd bled verbally when I'd expected him to remain hidden behind his shields. He hadn't realized that his sharing only lowered them further, allowing me a peek into his mind, giving me a better understanding of his stance on relationships.

The night before, I'd kept my hands and mouth away from his backside, allowing him to lead our time together.

No matter how badly I wanted him beneath me, allowing me to fill him physically and emotionally, it wouldn't happen.

But we could be inside Landon together, the three of us becoming one. I would stroke my length over Zack's while inside our lover's embrace. Show him with my eyes and hands that he could trust me with his happiness if only he would allow himself to try.

Landon lit him up.

I could quiet his mind since I too was a switch like him. Zack and I might not dabble in the BDSM lifestyle, but our sexual preferences aligned when it came to being able to both lead and submit. Add in the perfect needy bottom with a voracious appetite for both cock and cum, and the three of us were a match made in heaven.

Silence zapping with physical arousal hovered like a heavy blanket atop us on the beach, eventually stifling enough I couldn't lay peacefully beneath the warm sun any longer. I didn't want to waste another minute in paradise getting lost in my thoughts, the dreams of a future Zack wasn't willing to open himself up to.

I would focus on what I could have for the next however many hours before we once more passed out from sated bliss.

Pushing to my feet, I stretched the kinks from my back, gazing out over the blue ocean and rising sun glinting off its surface.

One last day. An ache traveled through my chest with the reminder.

We needed to make it count.

Chapter 26

Landon

Callum decided he'd had enough time for his breakfast to settle, and I hopped up to join him, the sweetest most delicious anxiety fluttering in my belly.

I glanced down at Zack, who simply smirked up at us, and I huffed, hands on my hips.

He shaded his eyes while peering up at me. "Someone's needy," he said with a chuckle.

"Always," I hissed, keeping my voice low since other beach loungers enjoyed the atmosphere as well.

"I'm kind of comfy out here. Think I might take a nap."

I growled—literally rumbled my chest in displeasure even though I felt sure Zack teased.

He snickered. Damn him and that yummy curl of his lips leaking the beautiful sound of his happiness.

I glanced around, thankful that those in close proximity didn't pay us any mind enough to note the semi-tent in my swim trunks.

Zack stood as though sensing my unease. "Sorry," he

murmured, all trace of joking gone from his tone. "I love riling you up, but this isn't really the place for that."

Nodding, I glanced at Callum, who watched Zack closely. Whether he didn't trust the man with my past and how it affected me whenever in public, I wasn't sure. Callum loved me, would protect me no matter what, even if it meant denying us the man we both lusted after.

Feeling selfish as fuck, I wasn't going to allow anyone to deny me *anything*.

I grabbed hold of both of their hands and started toward the hotel, hellbent on getting what I wanted while I could. If I had my way, Zack would fly into Rhode Island rather than Boston. He would never leave us, sell off his condo, and have a moving company pack up his stuff and ship it to my house.

He belonged with us, and I wasn't sure how to make him see that fact.

We'd made peace between us on that private beach, but I was determined for him to recognize on his own that we belonged together.

Hopefully, spending the rest of the day in bed together would open his eyes to everything that we could be, the three of us having our own happy ending. And to start things off, I was going to have my number one fantasy fulfilled, exactly as I'd requested not long after sprawling on the warm sand.

My ass ached to be filled by both of them. Zack refused to fuck without a condom regardless of proof we were all negative, so Callum's cum would have to be enough to sate my desire to leak evidence of my being loved.

Perhaps it was Zack's stubbornness to keep a final barrier between us since the others had seemed to weaken with each passing day, but I would honor his boundary. It would be for the best since technically we were still nothing more than client and client's lover to him.

I admired how he cared for himself, protected his health, but that didn't lessen my disappointment.

Callum had told me Zack wouldn't bottom for him and the reasons he'd expected held Zack back from the intimacy of being penetrated. The best I could do? Demand Zack lay on our bed where he would have to let Callum control our dynamic.

Zack stroked his thick cock, his hazel eyes hazed over with the lust I'd felt coming off him in waves throughout the morning. He wanted us as badly as I did two dicks stretching my hole. "Come up here, baby."

I clambered atop him, but he spun me around in a sixty-nine position, hands on my ass cheeks.

"Gotta get you ready for us." He dove in without further ado, and I cursed as he shoved his stiff tongue right past my ring.

"Oh fuck." I hung my head, already panting, and we'd only just begun.

Callum moved around the room—bedside table drawer opened. Something hit the mattress beside where I planked over Zack.

"Give me your dick to suck on," I begged, dragging my eyes open to find my best friend watching Zack eat my ass, his cock in hand.

Callum crawled over Zack's legs, straddling his knees, offering me his dripping slit.

"Sit. Scoot closer," I demanded, dropping down atop Zack's body. "Want to suck you both at the same time."

Zack squeezed my cheeks, likely bruising my skin.

Good. A visual reminder of the best day of my life.

I held the base of their dicks together the best I could,

and Callum sank his fingers into my hair. "Fuck yeah," I whispered and went to town lapping at their slits, suckling their swollen cockheads, and stuffing my mouth full like my loosening hole soon would be.

"Jesus fucking Christ, Landon." Zack groaned. He pushed a finger into my ass but immediately gave me two with how relaxed I was. "You're so hot inside, baby. Silky soft. A perfect sleeve for our dicks to fuck."

A shiver slid down my spine, and I whimpered around my mouthful of cock.

We couldn't hurry stretching me out to accommodate the both of them, but fuck me, I wanted to get to the good stuff.

Zack worked in a third finger alongside his lapping tongue but demanded the lube for the fourth. He wet me up good, shoving enough slickness past my pucker to take a fist if I wanted.

Pre-cum leaked from my cock like a faucet, smearing over his neck and upper chest, and I had to focus on my next novel's outline so I didn't blow before having them inside me.

"Think you're ready, baby?" Zack asked, and I couldn't even find my voice through the haze of lust attempting to control my body and brain.

I nodded, and as quickly as he'd spun me earlier, he did so again, trapping our hard dicks together. "Oh..." I ground against him, head thrown back, swallowing hard.

"Easy," he crooned, holding my hips still. "Callum, use your dick to open him up some more."

"Please—yes. That."

Callum, all-wise and privy to my thoughts, pulled me toward him, sliding my groin down past Zack's balls.

I whimpered.

"Hush, Lan. Trust me."

My head dropped to Zack's sternum as the blunt head of Callum's bare dick slid up through my crack. "Empty," I moaned, rocking my head side to side against hot skin and muscle. "Need you."

He sank into me, one torturously slow inch at a time, his harsh grip on my hips keeping me from slamming back until our balls kissed.

"Callum!" I whined, making Zack chuckle. "Shut up, asshole." I shoved up to plank on my hands and glared at him. Why did he have to be so damn gorgeous, his half-mast eyelids promising he wanted to fuck as badly as I needed him in me? "Sheath that dick up and get ready for me."

Heat blazed in his gaze, and I held his stare as Callum began to rock in and out of me, the lack of a condom covering his shaft making me shiver again. It'd been years since I'd gone bare, and I'd paid the price, but Callum would never put me at risk if he wasn't absolutely sure.

Lube dripped off my sac, the squelching noises music to my ears.

"Hurry, Zack. Please," I begged, my voice breaking. "Need you too."

He rolled on a condom and stroked lube over himself.

The second Callum's grip loosened enough I could pull away, I yanked off his dick, ignoring the sudden emptiness that made me want to cry. I scooted forward, whimpering the whole damn time, and slammed down onto Zack's cock.

"Yes," I hissed, eyes closing over the perfection of being filled again. A few gyrations of my hips, and I sprawled over him, holding his face in my hands. "Stuff me full, Callum."

Zack wound his arms around my back, strong hands soothing up and down my spine as Callum worked one then two fingers in alongside Zack's dick. "Okay?" Zack asked, still holding my gaze.

"Mmm hmm," I agreed, easily taking what Callum offered.

"He's good, Callum—give our boy what he's desperate for."

Our boy.

I closed my eyes to keep tears from falling and shoved my face into Zack's neck so he wouldn't see how his words affected me.

A blunt head pushed against my already stretched ass.

"Bear down, Lan."

I did as Callum ordered, and his swollen cockhead slipped inside me.

"Oh, Jesus." I gasped and fought off the instinct to clench.

"Breathe, baby," Zack murmured, his chest rumbling against mine.

I inhaled, held it a second, and released it slowly as Callum pushed forward.

"Fucking hell." Zack let out a few more curses matching the ones screaming in my mind.

The stretch went beyond pain, a thought-stealing sting that once more caught my breath. My erection long gone, I simply melted atop Zack, waiting for the discomfort to give way to pleasure.

"Come here." Zack grasped my head and lifted me from where I hid. He peppered my face with kisses in attempts to erase the deep furrow in my brow, eventually finding my parted lips. His tongue delved in, stroking along mine, enticing me to partake.

I sank into his kiss, and eventually, the morph began

until I realized my cock had thickened again, and I was ready. "I'm good, Cal. Give me the rest."

He pulled my cheeks apart, his thumbs gently caressing along my aching hole. "Please tell me if it's too much."

"I will." I whispered what I had no intention of doing. I was taking them both to the root. Hard. Stop.

Bearing down, I exhaled, forcing the rest of my body to relax against Zack's sweaty skin. I focused on the heat simmering between us, the heavy thump of his heart against mine as Callum slowly pushed into my aching hole.

Zack cursed under his breath, trembling beneath me.

Callum groaned, coming to a rest against my ass before I'd expected. I hadn't realized he'd already buried half his length inside me. "Lan..." He choked on my name, shaking hands running up the muscles along my spine.

They were both balls deep inside me.

Right where they belonged.

Chapter 27

Callum

None of us moved for a pregnant pause, allowing me a moment to gather myself.

Landon once more buried his face in Zack's neck. Pupils blown, stark need reigned Zack's features as he stared up at me. I felt his desperation as vividly as the back of his dick against mine wrapped in slick tightness that threatened to be my undoing.

We owned Landon together in that moment, his muscled body pinned between us.

Soon to be marked by my seed.

I backed out, and Landon groaned the sweetest sound, trying to arch.

The pain had obviously faded.

My shoulders relaxed, and I focused on giving him more pleasure than he'd ever known. "You're doing so well," I praised, tearing my focus off Zack's stare for Landon's hole stretched thin around our combined girth. "My God." I choked again and pushed in on instinct, needing to be buried deep inside him forever.

Zack pulled out partway, and I cursed at the stroke of his length against mine.

"Fuck. So good. So tight," I moaned the words and followed in Zack's footsteps, retreating from my new favorite place as he sank back in.

"Okay, baby?" He checked in with Landon, who whimpered an affirmative.

"More," he whispered, trying to shift his hips between us.

"You're sure?" Zack asked.

"Mmm."

Zack nodded at me, and I gritted my teeth and gave our boy what he wanted. Longer, slower strokes became shorter. Faster.

Landon grunted between us, and Zack wrapped his arms around him, holding him still for our plundering. Curses spilled from all of our lips, but I barely heard them for how harshly my pulse thrummed in my ears. The whooshing of blood dictated my rhythm, and I thrust into heaven with a knuckled grip on Landon's cheeks and my restraint.

I wouldn't let go until Landon did.

"So. Good." He gasped, one hand ripping at the sheet beside Zack's head, the other yanking on the man's hair.

At least Zack had finally closed his eyes, lost in a haze of lust rather than making me drown in desire to gain access to his heart.

"Gonna come for us, Lan?" I rasped, still thrusting with every intent to fill him up with my cum when I wanted to do the same with the man beneath us too.

"Yes—fuck yes."

Zack groaned. "Soak my skin, baby. Shoot that spunk all

the fuck over us. Make a mess on me." His words tipped Landon over, and his asshole clenched around us as he cried out.

"Fuck yeah. Just like that." Zack stabbed deep, his dick pulsing against mine.

I cursed and let loose. Shots of my seed flowed through my shaft, painting Landon's insides and the condom covering Zack's dick. I'd rather have him bare and marked as well, but it was still the most satisfying climax of my entire life.

My hips stuttered, and I managed a few short strokes while emptying myself completely, peace flooding my soul.

We panted, and my ears rang.

"Oh. My. God." Landon shuddered hard, and I made shushing noises while soothing every inch of his skin I could reach. He would be overwhelmed in body and spirit, hopefully in a good way, and I wished to prolong his enjoyment for as long as possible.

Zack lay quietly, his lips pressed to Landon's mussed, sweaty hair. Eyes closed, he appeared more relaxed than I'd seen him in our days together. Completely sated. Perhaps even as peaceful as me.

Fingers crossed.

We were all in desperate need of a shower, but I didn't see Landon moving anytime soon, nor did I want to leave him alone while he came back down from our intense fucking.

Zack's cock slipped free first, and I sighed at the loss. Our time as one had come to an end, taking with it the tranquility I'd experienced while being wrapped up with my two lovers.

I backed out slowly, hating to cause Landon discomfort,

but the sight of his gaping hole and the ooze of my cum was beautiful, stilling my unrest. Groaning, I spread his hole wide with my thumbs.

"Push it back in," Landon whispered, and I gave him what he demanded, reaching deep inside his sopping hole with two fingers to hopefully ease the ache of his emptiness. "Keep them there for just a little longer?"

I bent down and kissed along his spine, scooting away until I could check to make sure we hadn't torn him. His hole appeared well used, red and puffy, but no damage had been done.

Cum oozed out around my fingers, sliding down his taint, dripping onto Zack's flaccid cock beneath.

Landon shivered, and I kissed both ass cheeks.

"Okay?" I asked, caressing his left globe while studying the back of his head where he still burrowed his face against Zack.

"I'm good," Landon promised with a muffled voice, and I slid my fingers free from his ass.

Zack's hands took up the soothing motion of stroking over his skin from his shoulders to his waist. He kissed Landon's hair again, swallowing hard, a pained expression etched on his face where moments ago he'd seemed at rest. There was no way that man didn't love Landon. Zack clung to him as though he never wanted to let go.

The urge to do the same sank its claws into me, and I had difficulty not wrapping my arms around them both as though I could make Zack stay.

Our eyes met, and I bit my tongue to keep pleading words from spilling past my lips. I wouldn't force, nor would I beg. He had to decide about our shared future without prompting.

"Can I take care of you?" I asked instead, my heart still racing. One step at a time. Perhaps that would be enough to sway him toward what both Landon and I hoped for.

Zack hesitated but nodded, submitting at least a part of himself to me. His wary eyes assured me he wasn't yet willing to allow complete vulnerability.

Releasing a slow, steady exhale of disappointment, I climbed off the bed. After cleaning myself, I wet two towels with warm water and returned to find both men unmoved. At my reappearance, Zack gently rolled a limp Landon off his chest.

Pink flushed Landon's face, his hair damp and sticking to his forehead and cheeks. But his eyes... God, he was beautiful. Exhaustion and pure elation peered at me from his golden brown orbs, the kind of emotion that made men write sonnets and love songs.

Throat tight, I first wiped his belly free of his release then between his legs. Once finished, I moved onto Zack, who'd watched me the entire time, unmoving.

Waiting for me to be fulfilled by the level of submission he allowed himself.

Tears stung my eyes, and I refused to meet his while ridding his now semi of the full condom. I wiped his dick rather than sucking it clean like I'd have preferred, then his taint and balls where excess lube had dripped down.

A wet spot lay between his spread thighs, and I dabbed that up as best I could.

Once finished, I bent down and kissed Zack's belly, my lips lingering, my chest aching. "Thank you," I whispered and turned away before he saw my tears.

I carried the soiled towels back to the bathroom, needing a moment to collect myself. Assurances whispered in my mind that Landon was now mine forever didn't ease the ache over thoughts of Zack not being with us when we returned home. My best friend would never be able to fill part of that emptiness inside me where my soul needed nurturing as much as he did.

Perhaps my longing for Zack would eventually fade, and even though I expected Landon's never would, he might eventually be interested in finding another switch to join us in Zack's place.

Because one thing I knew for sure—Landon would never be entirely satisfied by my dick alone. The man was made for a triad, evident by the stories he wrote, the fantasies cooked up from his own inner desires.

We had a few hours until our time together ended, so we couldn't waste a single minute.

Landon rested against Zack's side when I returned to the bedroom, and I cradled against his backside, understanding the urge that had him clinging to the man he'd loved since childhood.

But even the strongest arms wouldn't hold Zack in place. Too much trauma littered his soul, wounds that no man's touch could heal.

Landon's breaths grew shallow, his body twitching as he slipped into sleep.

Zack and I eyed each other like we'd done that first night Landon slept cocooned between us, but unlike then, there were no whispered words. Nothing rested over us but a heavy silence full of emotion I wasn't sure what do with.

He closed his eyes first, and I wondered if it was out of fear or due to weakening walls.

Having no wish to ruin our final hours together, I allowed him his space and nuzzled against Landon's head, breathing in the sweet scent of his hair. Reminders to stay in the moment whispered through my head, helping to keep me grounded.

Landon woke a short time later, stretching and immediately stilling with a gasp. "Goddamn," he muttered.

"Sore, baby?" Zack asked, his stroking hand along Landon's waist bumping into mine resting on his hip. I considered twining my fingers with his but didn't allow myself that act of intimacy I expected would be too much for him in the moment.

"Yes," Landon hissed then whimpered. "Guess my ass is done for the night." Grimacing, he attempted to move, so I gave him some space in order for him to roll onto his back.

He shot me a smirk regardless of his discomfort, his sleepy eyes so damn full of love, my heartbeat stumbled. "I want to watch Zack fuck you."

My pulse rushed, and regardless of how that would only cause a deeper connection between Zack and I, I couldn't deny Landon.

I glanced at Zack, ready and willing to fall harder even though he would hold me emotionally at arm's length.

Heat kindled in his eyes but not anything more than the fulfillment of lust. "On your knees."

Not face-to-face. No deep connection outside the physical allowed this time around.

Got it.

Throat tight, I did as told, arching my back, chest on the mattress, ass on display. I would soak in what I could even though it wasn't what I'd have preferred to be my last memory of penetration for who knew how long.

Zack put on a show for Landon, lubing up my hole for his dick with a slow progression of fingers. He kept his tongue out of the mix, and I wondered if that too was another way he avoided the intimacy he seemed closed off to.

Still, the feel of his fingers in me, his hands worshiping my body, lit a fire inside me. Made my balls ache for release and my cock drip with need.

Landon panted beside us, and I gave him my full focus, watching how his lips parted on quick exhales, his amber eyes almost fully eaten by swollen pupils as he stared at Zack opening me up.

I bit my inner lip when Zack's cockhead pushed against my pucker, soaking in Landon's whimper instead of moaning my own enjoyment of being breached. Every gyration of Zack's hips burrowed him into my soul. Etched his name where no one else had ever managed to caress.

I barely knew the man, but he'd attached himself to the innermost parts of my body's cells alongside Landon's.

Although Zack played out a fantasy come to life for Landon, I appreciated the lack of cringe words and cliche sayings, as though performing porn rather than actually enjoying the moment. Perhaps I read into the act as more than it was, but I couldn't help my wishful thinking.

"Please," I whispered, nearing my end, wanting to be put from my misery of not knowing and overthinking.

Zack leaned over me, his hot, hard chest pressing into my back. He reached beneath me to stroke my cock.

I grunted, eyes clenched shut as he smeared pre-cum to my firmed balls.

"Come for me, sweetheart," Zack murmured.

Something inside me broke open like a dam, cracking my heart. A sob ripped from my chest as I gifted him what he'd asked for, and euphoria swept me up in bittersweet rapture.

Zack's cock bucked inside me as he found his release,

his deep groan against my ear pebbling my skin and sending shivers clear to my toes.

I focused on Landon's soft curse, then his gasped cry I'd recognized as his finding satisfaction.

He'd orgasmed because of my submission, and although more hurt than elation settled into my soul as we finished, I couldn't regret what we'd done.

Chapter 28

Zack

Boston welcomed me home with warmer weather than when I'd left for my little vacation but not nearly as pleasant as the tropics. Spring flowers lay like a rainbow around my condo's short walkway, but they appeared dim compared to what I'd left behind. They also did little to bring hope for more pleasant days ahead.

Emptiness owned my chest, a numbness rather than the ache I'd expected. At least I had that to be thankful for.

The other thing I appreciated was only being booked with EEMM once for the upcoming weekend. I attended an event Saturday night as arm candy that seemed to drag on amidst attempted banter at the table of nine my date and I sat at.

I bullshitted with the two on either side of me, envisioning being bookmarked by Callum and Landon to make the time pass quicker. While I could admit to missing them like two limbs had been torn off my body, I had to stay focused on getting back into the groove of my drama-free, mundane—*safe*—life.

At the end of the evening, I bid my client a good

evening without having to lay lips or hands on him in a way that would have felt wrong. I also attempted to set aside the constant recalling of the two lovers that had seemed the opposite. Absolutely right and scarily so.

Sunday afternoon, some of the EEMM guys got together at Sean's condo overlooking the wharf. We were a smaller group that month, which I tended to enjoy. Regardless of our meager number, evidence of found and appreciated love radiated like blinding light to my dimmed soul.

Preston draped over Drake's lap in one recliner. Pain stabbed my chest over their open affection. Even worse was Sean sitting on the floor beside the other chair occupied by his Teach. Matteo's fingers stroked through his hair, and he preened like a lazy cat at being doted on in his not-so-subtle display of submission.

Their fulfillment in each other slowly weighed down on me, heightening the barrenness in my heart. Jealousy nagged at me like some of the foster mothers I'd lived with, a constant poke of awareness of what I didn't have that made me want to rip my hair out.

"What's up with you?" Jimmy asked from his seat on the couch beside me.

I rubbed a hand over my face, wishing I could scrub my inner self clean of want for what I'd left behind. Regardless of my determination to keep both Callum and Landon from haunting my thoughts after returning from paradise, they'd embedded themselves deep in my psyche. I could admit now that there was no escaping them.

"Just tired," I lied, not about to get into shit with Elite's biggest mouth. Jimmy gossiped like a teenage girl, and even though he wasn't mean, he couldn't be trusted with my personal shit.

As though sensing my unease, Sean kissed Matteo's

knee and pushed up to his feet. "Want to help me out for a minute?" he asked me, nodding toward the kitchen.

"Sure." I followed him through the archway that allowed us a bit of privacy.

The TV droned from the living room, but still, he walked to the farthest end of the kitchen before propping himself against the counter, arms and ankles crossed.

"What's going on, Zack?" While not usually a shrewd guy, Sean's blue-eyed gaze pierced through my armor, and since he was someone who'd proven himself trustworthy, I decided to lay shit on the line because I couldn't deal on my own anymore.

Maybe he could help me get back on track with my quiet lifestyle that used to be peaceful once upon a time.

"So those five days that were supposed to be heaven kind of turned into hell," I muttered.

His brow furrowed, concern filling his gaze. "Did something bad happen?"

"No. The opposite, really." Without going into too much detail about my past, I explained the addition Callum had brought along with him for our little vacation of what was supposed to have been two. While what he'd done hadn't gone against the contract he'd signed with EEMM, the act of manipulation didn't sit well with Sean.

"You should have called me and cancelled," he stated quietly, his frown still fixed firmly in place.

"I wasn't unsafe, just knocked off-kilter, and I can't regret what went down because I feel as though my past has been put to rest."

Sean huffed a snort. "Bullshit. It's obviously stirred up even more trouble."

"Am I that transparent?"

"You are today," he didn't hesitate to say.

"Shit." I rubbed a hand over my face again. Maybe the dreams of my two lovers *weren't* allowing me proper rest, and I was simply exhausted and in need of a real vacation.

"How are you doing?"

I wanted to snort, considering Sean hadn't been one for feels and the discussion of them outside of wanting dick before Matteo turned his life upside down.

Sean cared about all of his employee's wellbeing, and not just because we made him a shit ton of money.

"I don't really know," I admitted. "Like a part of me is missing, envious as fuck over what it seems like my co-workers are finding and scared as hell about what both of those facts might mean."

"Falling happens quickly for some people. When you know, when you experience that draw, you can't ignore it. Matteo fought his need for me and shouldn't have. I'm the most wonderful thing that's ever happened for him."

I chuckled, shaking my head at his usual arrogance. "I think you've got shit backward."

Sean cursed at me, his eyes alight with laughter. "Matteo and I both hit the jackpot." He conceded. "He's the best decision I've ever made."

Nodding, I glanced toward the living room, thinking of the men sitting in there. They'd become my family, had filled part of the void inside me and influenced my contentment in Boston. I couldn't fucking leave them—they were all I had. And the drama the two couples had to endured to be together was cringeworthy. They'd shared their stories filled with the type of angst that could tear a heart in two.

I didn't have that kind of fight in me.

But goddamnit, I missed Callum and Landon badly enough I questioned my stance on trusting others with my heart.

"Take some time off."

I jerked my focus back toward Sean. He still smiled, but a softer curve of his lips showed acceptance rather than disappointment. "Figure out who needs to be first in your life. I'll be sad to see you missing from Elite's menu, but if these two guys are the ones for you, go for it. I just want you happy, Zack. If that means you're as fulfilled as I am and no longer lining my pockets, then so be it, but you'll always be a part of the Elite family."

I swallowed hard, nodding again.

Sean straightened, closed the few feet between us, and grasped my shoulder, squeezing tightly. "If shit doesn't work out, I promise I'll keep you in ass and on dick until you die."

A huffed snort of laughter left me, making his smile morph into a boyish grin.

"Seriously, though, what's holding you back? It's obvious you're pining for them."

"I can't trust people." I answered with the honest to fuck truth.

He settled against the counter again, his gaze unwavering. "Want to talk about it?"

I didn't, but fuck, I needed help. "It started with my parents, who'd abandoned me into foster care when I was like two weeks old." I wasn't sure where to go from there with the story of my childhood that had shaped me into the closed-off man standing here.

"Maybe locating and confronting them would help heal you," Sean suggested. "Trust me, taking steps toward working through the shit in your head and heart can lead to a much more fulfilling life." Sean would know—he'd been open about going to therapy for months, and while he was still his usual pain-in-the-ass self, he had a peacefulness about him that he'd lacked before.

I'd always told myself I didn't give two shits about the people who'd left me to the state since they'd obviously felt nothing for me. So, fuck them and whatever excuses they'd cooked up to make themselves feel okay with discarding their own flesh and blood.

"Preston would help you." Sean pushed when I didn't respond.

I heaved a heavy exhale, assured in the deepest parts of me that the boys of EEMM would go above and beyond for me if it meant me finding healing and contentment. We didn't discuss deep shit, but a bond held us all together far beyond the ties of selling our bodies.

While I still wasn't ready to dissect the desires troubling me, perhaps laying a better foundation for my path going forward would offer me some clarity and bravery.

"Okay," I agreed, and Sean squeezed my shoulder again before releasing me.

"Come on. Let's go finish watching the game."

Jimmy headed out, and once he left, I asked Sean to turn off the TV. For the first time ever, I unloaded the entirety of my shitty past to some of the few men I considered friends. From my early memories of foster care to climbing aboard the flight that returned me home from paradise, I spilled what I could recall. I had expected to feel soiled, dirty in a way that getting on my knees for cash had never made me experience, from uncovering my secrets.

Instead, relief settled in. An unburdening of emotion I hadn't realized pushed me beneath water.

"So here I am with kettlebells attached to my arms and holding me under," I murmured, studying my empty hands hanging loosely between my spread thighs from where I leaned, elbows on my knees. "I'm not one to ask for help, but you all are the closest thing I have to family—and I could use some direction."

"Give me three days, and I'll find your birth parents," Preston stated with absolute assurance, causing my throat to swell up.

"Thanks," I whispered, finally lifting my head since starting the story of my life.

"No need for it," he insisted, his own emerald-like eyes welling along with mine. "It's what family does."

Shit moved fast as fuck after that.

Drake's computer whiz found the information I needed less than thirty-six hours later, blowing my misconceptions about my beginning to bits. I had the name of my mother— and the truth my sperm donor had been unknown.

I'd never missed having a real father, so a lack of his identity didn't hit me nearly as hard as that of my mother. Facts echoed through my head throughout the rest of the day and late into the night as I struggled to accept the truth of my beginning.

Lauren Briggs had passed away at the age of seventeen, less than two weeks after giving birth to me. While learning of her death lessened my sense of abandonment, I didn't know her story or even how she had died. Other questions needed put to rest as well, namely why her surviving family listed in the papers didn't want or keep me.

What had I done as an infant to deserve their backs when I'd needed their arms?

The following afternoon after a near sleepless night, I stood on my grandparents' front stoop, the whirlwind of events leaving me hesitant as reality caught up to me. One thing for certain, Lauren came from a higher society than most. The mansion looming three stories above me promised that truth as much as the printouts from Preston that revealed old money filled the Briggs family's bank.

One slow inhale and exhale, and I raised my shaking hand.

A middle-aged man dressed in black-and-white drab garb answered. His short stature, dark eyes, and thinning blond hair suggested we didn't share DNA.

Regardless of his lack of height, he stood in the doorway as though a brick wall barring entry. Lips in a thin line, he glanced down over my tight Henley and faded jeans before lifting his focus to my face. When our eyes met, he blinked, his already pale complexion turning gray.

From the images Preston had shown to me, I knew I was a spitting image of Lauren's father, Malcom Briggs, the man I hoped to have a little chat with. And while I had zero expectations of being accepted or acknowledged as family, I at least wanted to see him in person.

"Can I help you?" the man before me asked with an uncertain tone, his voice hinting at a Scottish accent.

"I'm looking for Malcom and Iona Briggs."

He straightened slightly, chin lifting as though he attempted to peer down his nose at me. "And *you* are?"

"Zackary Briggs." I watched him closely, noting the flash of disquiet in his eyes and how the paleness around his mouth intensified.

"One moment, please," he finally snipped as though thoroughly put out by my appearance and request.

The door shut in my face with a resounding click.

I stared at the dark, wooden grain, shifting on my feet. Would I be ordered to vacate the premises? Completely ignored as I'd been as a baby?

If the latter, I planned on pounding on the thick oaken

panel until Malcom himself answered or the cops showed up and forced me to leave. I'd taken a huge fucking leap in driving to Rhode Island to seek them out, one I'd never even considered until reconnecting with Landon had inspired change in my soul.

The door pulled inward once more, and I stared at a picture of the man I would someday become—if I had one foot in the grave, the other clinging to the edge of the living.

I just hoped the pursed lips and arrogant lift of his chin didn't afflict me as it did the stooped man who could only be my grandfather.

"What are you doing here?" he demanded in the same accent as his...butler? Manservant? Did those titles even exist anymore?

"I'm looking for answers," I replied somewhat coolly, refusing to cower down as I was sure plenty of people had done over the years of this man's life.

Malcom Briggs took me in from head to toe, sneering even though he clung to the casing as though the wood could keep his frail form from toppling over. Regardless of his sunken, sallow appearance, the old man wore tailored clothing, a hint of expensive cologne attempting to cover the stench of death clinging to his skin. Even nearing his end, he carried an air of authority, like he expected to be heard and obeyed.

"You're a few days too early to lay a claim to my fortune, lad. I haven't yet submitted to the grave's beckoning."

I frowned, already disliking the only family member I'd ever seen in the flesh. "I'm not interested in any inheritance if that's what you're suggesting, Mr. Briggs. I simply wish to know what happened to my mother, Lauren."

"She was an unruly teenager, who refused to be tamed

into a lady." He all but spat the words, making his feelings toward his daughter more than clear. "A complete disgrace to our name and a disappointment to both her mother and I."

She'd been an only child, which meant I was the last of this old man's line. Still, I wanted nothing to do with him, his impending demise, or what he left behind once buried six feet under.

Because he'd felt the same toward an innocent infant thirty-three years earlier.

But I kept my silence and listened to him spew his bitterness because I was that desperate for any information I could get.

"She was the town whore by sixteen and pregnant at seventeen, unable to identify which man impregnated her." He gave me another slow perusal and found me lacking. Whether due to my mother's sins against her father's pride or for the way I looked in my casual clothes, I didn't know. Didn't care. "She removed the stain of her miserable existence from our name days after giving birth to a child no one stepped forward to claim."

Eleven days to be exact, according to the newspapers at the time.

The truth of her death unmentioned in the write-ups I'd read didn't surprise me, nor did it have any effect on my emotions. I'd never known the girl who'd given me life, and she'd chosen selfishness rather than attempting to raise me in a household where she would always be judged and despised.

"Thank you for your time," I murmured, having heard enough to realize they'd seen me as nothing more than another stain to the Briggs's bloodline.

In their eyes, I was as soiled as Lauren—same as the senator's son.

Malcom Briggs didn't have shit to say as I turned my back on him and walked away. The door shut firmly behind me, a sense of finality settling over me that I was more than okay with. Fuck him, his wife, and their money.

My mind settled on Landon.

I climbed into my car and clutched the steering wheel, thoughts of him flashing through my mind. While I'd seen firsthand how he'd been ignored by both of his parents, I had a better understanding of how they must have looked at him after the scandal that ruined his family's name.

The emptiness I'd been attempting to understand in my chest flooded with a swell of emotions I couldn't decipher. Regret? Empathy? Definite longing to hold him and soothe his hurt lay beneath it all along with the need for someone to do the same for me.

Callum.

But fear continued to reign supreme like a selfish bitch, refusing me freedom to accept the love and care both would gladly lavish on me in return.

A therapist would have a field day with my abandonment and trust issues, but I doubted healing from either could be had. Rather than thinking too hard on that truth, I hopped back on the highway toward Boston and called Sean.

"How'd it go?" he asked.

"Worse than I expected, but I can't say I'm surprised," I replied, my tone tired and resigned.

Sean and I had discussed possible outcomes, and since state records clearly showed my lineage, my grandparents could have sought me out if they'd wanted to.

"Suicide?"

I exhaled heavily. "Yeah. Just days after giving birth to me. Could have been postpartum, but considering how much Malcom's bitterness still etched in his face and words all these years later, I expect Lauren couldn't bear the thought of living beneath his roof. I know I wouldn't have wanted to do so if I'd been in her shoes."

"Fuck—man, I'm sorry."

"Don't be. Can you imagine what my life would have been like had I been raised like she'd been? Seen as less than? He called her a fucking stain, for Christ's sake! A disgrace. Disappointment. Whore." I bit each word out, my anger rising in the knowledge Landon's father had done the same to him. "She'd fallen well below his expectations, and I would have reaped the consequences of her supposed sins."

"Well fuck him and his money."

I couldn't have agreed more and didn't even feel guilty about him having one foot in the grave. "He'll be dead in a matter of weeks. Looked sick as fuck."

"Good riddance," Sean added. "So what now?"

"I'm going to go home and crash. Hopefully, clear my head so I can decide what the fuck I should do about the rest of the drama in my head and heart."

"Jamie requested you for next weekend."

"Shit." I huffed an exhale, annoyed with myself and the entire situation that had churned up my life. While I enjoyed every night between the sheets with my favorite client, the idea of sharing my body with him didn't sit right. Even a little blue pill wouldn't have made it as enjoyable as fucking him had been once upon a time.

"I explained you weren't on the menu until further notice," Sean told me before I could decide what to do.

"Thanks, man."

"No problem. Just get your shit figured out and let me know what you want."

"Will do," I agreed.

Landon had shown me how forgiveness could be a simple choice. If only my mind could be swayed as easily.

Chapter 29

Landon

Edits completely buttoned up, I took an entire week off to empty my head of the plotline I'd fucked up but had managed to fix. Cyn had loved the changes, claiming it was my best work to date.

Callum and I had celebrated sending the manuscript off to the formatter only a couple days late with a bottle of wine on our back deck before fucking long into the night. Joy flooded me along with his cum, but a part of me still ached. We'd shared my bed ever since we'd returned from the island, and while we clung to each other at night and loved the growing connection between us, a vital part of our whole was missing.

One we heartily agreed we both longed for desperately, regardless of how much our love for each other deepened with every passing day.

Neither of us had spoken about our desires that final morning Zack had been in bed with us back on the island. Callum and I had lain spent and entwined, watching Zack pull on his clothes as he readied to return to his room to pack. His flight left a few hours before ours, so we hadn't needed to climb from between the soiled sheets until closer to lunch.

There had been no lingering kisses goodbye, no promises to see each other in the future.

Callum told me later that he'd bitten his tongue to keep from asking Zack for more, and I'd admitted to doing the same.

Zack had tucked himself behind his walls after they'd taken me together, and although we'd all gotten off a few more times in the hours that had remained to us on that final day together, he'd lacked emotion while doing so.

He'd made his wants clear, shutting himself off to anything but the physical pleasure we'd gorged on.

While part of me was elated at having Callum's focus in ways I'd never considered once we'd arrived back at home in Rhode Island, the other half of my heart ached, sometimes overshadowing delicious sparks from the newness of our relationship.

I curled on our couch with a throw blanket over my legs, staring out the window splattered by rain that warped the reality beyond as Callum took care of some things in his office. The view was as clear as the jumble of feelings inside me. A complete watery mess, which often caused tear tracks to line my cheeks like the rivulets running down the glass panes.

My chest ached with intense longing I couldn't force away or ignore. Even worse, I knew I wasn't the only one suffering, and I was powerless to lessen Callum's heartache as well.

A shuffle of feet reached my ears seconds before he rounded the couch. More than the usual sadness filled his widened eyes. Face pale, he worked his throat.

I pushed upright so fast my eyesight went dark. My

blood sugar was low—I needed to eat more than I'd been able to since our return. "What?" Blinking twice brought him back into focus.

Without a word, he held his cell out toward me. His hand shook, and my breath left in a rush.

Callum always kept his cool. Fucking *always*.

I clenched my fingers into a fist rather than taking his phone from him. With how badly I suddenly trembled, I would have dropped the phone to the floor.

The image on his screen was one of me in profile, clearly recognizable from a fellow vacationer on the island. And the moment captured in time and posted on social media that had gone viral according to the number of likes and comments?

I held both Zeke and Callum's hands as I'd dragged them toward our hotel intent on experiencing double penetration.

"Oh fuck," I whispered, my past crashing down atop me and making my heart pound in my ears.

"There's speculation about us being together," Callum whispered as though he strained beneath the weight of my so-called mistakes, as Father had called them. "They've yet to identify Zack."

My voracious need of dick has been caught on camera again.

"I'm so sorry, Lan—I shouldn't have booked that vacation. Should have protected you rather than—"

"It's not your fault." I cut Callum off with barely any tone to my voice as my chest caved inward, and every ounce of energy in my body faded.

"But had I not—"

"No, Callum." I shook my head adamantly, refusing to let him take the blame for the firestorm sure to resoil the reputation I'd attempted to tidy up by hiding away from society.

My cell rang, and I didn't need to look at the flashing screen to know Father called me. But, I didn't give him a chance to light into me about more bad choices.

Not that I saw being with two men as such.

I swiped to answer but didn't offer Father a chance to speak. "Did you give Zack money then kick him out?"

"What?"

"That night when you thought he'd attacked me."

"Landon—"

"Answer me!" My voice hovered on the edge of hysterical.

Callum sat beside me, gathering my free hand in his, and I clutched at him with a death grip, barely able to exhale with how harshly my heart pounded.

"Yes," Father replied without a hint of regret in his voice. "I asked that boy to go rather than stirring up a mess that would have tainted my abilities to be reelected."

A muscle in my jaw ticked along with my thundering pulse.

"All this time, I thought Zack abandoned me, and I've lived with underlying fear believing I would do something to make Callum leave me too! Because of what you did, I've had issues with love and acceptance. Both were conditional in my mind, thanks to you." I spewed the truth of my sorry existence. I'd been a selfish brat, and Father's hope to keep our family name as clean as possible had only worsened the consequences.

"About Callum, Landon," Father stated sternly, "the picture running rampant on social media shows you're more than friends as you've led us to believe and that there's another man in the equation." Clear disappointment coated his voice, making me right in assuming why he'd called in the first place. It'd been months since I'd spoken to either of my parents. While he'd never been a physically mean bastard, his silent, judgmental looks and well-barbed words of negativity wounded as deeply as any fists thrown could.

I'd tried for years to gain his affection after the mistakes I'd made during my cum dump days, but now?

Fuck that.

I had the love of one of the best men I knew, and he gave me more than my parents ever had. "Callum and I are together now, and yes, we enjoyed vacationing with another man who also happened to share our bed."

"Landon." Disapproval lay heavy in his tone.

"I've feared letting you down again, but I'm done hiding behind closed doors as though my heart's desires are something to be ashamed of. I'm going to live my truth aloud."

"You're aware of how this will affect my run for local government. My reputation has only begun to be seen in a better light since your regrettable decision that ended up smearing our family's name."

As if I'd had a choice in the making of a video taken behind my back—literally—without my knowledge.

"Quite frankly, I don't give a damn," I snipped, my heart still racing. "It's *my* life I need to focus on. And *my* happiness! Call me selfish, disown me, I don't care. I love Callum and Zack, and nothing and no one is going to make me feel as though these emotions are wrong."

Father didn't speak for a moment as I attempted to regulate my breathing, and I could imagine him pinching the bridge of his nose. Sure enough, an exasperated sigh came through clearly over the line. "That third man was him? Zackary Briggs?"

"Yes."

"It's been fifteen years. How—never mind. I'd rather not know. Perhaps we can work this in my favor to draw in the LGBTQ community though."

I rolled my eyes, shaking my head. Everything was always about him and attaining his goals. He might have found the perfect submissive wife to act as pretty eye candy on his arm while fundraising his attempts to rise to power, but his only son?

I was gay and madly in love with two men.

And I would flaunt my truth for all to see regardless of what they thought. They were free to love, so why shouldn't I have the same right?

"Say what you want, but I refuse to be used to further your agenda with *any* voters, Father. I will *not* support your run, nor will I agree to take any part in your campaign."

I readied myself for more discussion of my failures.

"It's your duty as a Matthews—"

"Sorry, Father," I cut him off to make excuses when I wasn't sorry in the least, "but I've got to go. Tell Mother I've finally found the love I've always longed for—if she ever even cared." I hung up before he could say another word and powered my cell down.

Callum wrapped me up in his arms, pulling me onto his lap.

"Did you hear what he said?" I asked, burrowing into his neck.

"I did, baby." He kissed my forehead, and I gave in to the emotions wrecking me, soaking my faithful lover with my tears.

Chapter 30

Callum

It'd been a week since rumors about the old Soiled Senator's Son had gone semi-viral across social media. The gossip never reached major news outlets, thank fuck, but the emotional damage had broken him down.

Landon was forlorn, and I failed to boost his spirits.

I questioned what I'd done in forcing his and Zack's confrontation, and we both ended up suffering even worse than before that damned vacation. Not that I could actually regret the choice. He and I had found fulfillment there. Unrequited love had been returned. Understanding we'd lacked before now resonated between us and brought us closer together.

We'd been shut up in the condo for seven days, waiting for an explosion of negative media exposure, but that didn't keep us from sating our need for each other often and passionately.

The entire affair never amounted to more than a two-day eruption that quickly fizzled out though.

The shit show that image had stirred on different social sites died down as gossip from real celebrities took precedence, overshadowing Landon's supposed continuance of poor choices.

Good thing, since it kept his father off his back too.

I wondered if Zack had seen any of the chatter. Without having his number, I couldn't check in on him to make sure he was doing all right.

But I knew someone who could.

Stomach in a knot, I pulled up Elite's website on my laptop browser, intending to only retrieve the contact information for Sean Fox. But the longing in my chest controlled the hand on my mouse, and I scrolled through EEMM's menu, hungry for just a peek of his face.

Zack wasn't listed.

My breath left in a rush, and I stared where he used to be in the alphabetical lineup of available escorts. I clicked through the site in search of his name.

He'd been removed entirely. His page. All of the rave reviews that promised satisfaction.

I'd been sick imagining him pleasing other clients, finding release beneath men who paid for the use of his body in ways he hadn't allowed with me. Possessiveness wasn't something I was new to. I felt it daily with Landon. But having Zack thrown into the mix inside my head and heart had only intensified the feelings.

Insecurity, perhaps?

Definitely a desperation I didn't know how to deal with. Landon looked up to me to be the sturdy one, and I struggled on a deep level, same as he did. I just managed to hide my heartache while he owned it. Lounged in it as though unwilling to move on.

Not that I was either.

Fuck, no.

But I tried to lighten Landon's shit mood, hoping Zack would come to his senses and get in touch with us somehow.

Was his no longer being on Elite's website evidence that he was taking some time to figure his heart out?

I jotted down Sean's number, expecting calling him would only lead to a dead end. What employer would give out personal information about their workers?

Needing a glass of wine before attempting to get what I wanted, I ambled into the kitchen.

Landon lay where I'd left him an hour earlier, curled on the couch again and focused on the muted TV. He'd been stuck in waiting mode, sure that his "wild lifestyle" would once more make it onto the major new outlets.

It wasn't Landon's face on screen that pulled me up short and stole my breath with a loud wheeze.

I recognized the blonde woman, even though over a decade had passed since I'd last seen her sitting on the opposite side of a courtroom, bracketed by her haughty, rich parents.

Shannon Taylor.

The young woman my brother had sexually assaulted had overdosed, according to the story's banner beneath the newscaster.

"Turn it up," I rasped, barely recognizing my voice as I perched on the edge of the couch beside Landon's feet.

He clicked the remote, filling the room with what remained of the story.

It was suggested that the news of my brother's early release in the next couple of weeks had reached her, prompting her to take her own life rather than dealing with the truth he would once more be walking the streets. According to her parents, she'd never fully recovered from the attack and had been in and out of mental institutions.

She'd not only been hurt by my brother but by me for not speaking up. For not better holding control over his waywardness. And for not reaching out to the authorities when he had become more than I could handle on my own.

And now two parents suffered the loss of their only child.

Nausea stirred in my stomach.

"Jesus," I choked, leaning forward onto my knees, hands clasped between them to keep from shaking.

"Cal?" Landon stirred, sitting up to wrap his arms around my waist.

I didn't move except for a harsh swallow against the thickening in my throat.

"What's going on? Who was she?"

"A casualty of my greatest mistake," I muttered, my heart breaking.

"You told me not keeping your brother in line was your deepest regret."

"Yeah, this is about him." I heaved an exhale. "I was so ashamed—needed to atone for my mistakes with him. And now this..." I waved a hand at the TV, swallowing hard.

Landon glanced at the screen, his shoulders wilting as though he'd already connected the dots. "Let me be the one to offer comfort for a change."

"The full story's not pretty," I warned in a choked whisper.

"Wrong choices rarely are."

I spilled. Every agonizing word about my mom's death two years after our dad's that had left me responsible for my younger brother when I'd not yet been twenty-one. With every admission, my guilt lessened, Landon listening without a hint of judgment in his eyes.

"He was ten times the handful you claim to have been," I murmured.

"Gay?" Landon asked.

"Bi, I believe. He brought home guys on occasion, but it was mostly girls. I attempted to ban the influx of his fuck buddies, but he never listened. He lashed out at me in his grief over losing first Dad to a heart attack then Mom to breast cancer, and I had to hide my own sorrow. Be the strong, sturdy parental figure I hoped he would eventually cling to.

"He started doing drugs to escape reality rather than letting me help. He drank to excess too. I returned from work a couple nights to find him passed out on the floor, but rather than putting him in some sort of detox, I strove to save him on my own. Prove myself worthy of Mom's trust in me to care for him, exactly as I'd promised to do when she lay on her deathbed. Getting the authorities involved would have been a better choice." I admitted aloud the truth that had haunted me for over a decade.

"What happened?" Landon asked quietly when I'd gone silent for a few long moments.

"He lost his license for driving under the influence. At twenty, he'd escaped sexual assault charges because the supposed victim was known for crying wolf and had lied to the authorities before. But a year later when a second young woman accused him of the same, he wasn't as lucky. My brother's world was reduced to a jail cell, a place he would never have ended up in had I done my job of being a better caretaker. He blamed me. Refused to see me when I attempted to visit him. We wrote each other off, which was for the best."

Landon had been aware my brother was in prison, but

I'd just never gone into the full details of how he'd landed there.

"It wasn't your fault," Landon argued from where he'd landed on my lap, straddling my thighs, his hands on my face. "That idiot made his own choices, same as me. We can blame others all we want, cook up excuses for what we did, but the truth is that we're the ones who decide what we do."

"But had I—"

Landon pressed his fingers to my lips. "No, Cal."

I kept silent, swallowing down how I felt, same as always.

"That woman on the news just now—she was the one he took advantage of, right?"

"Yes."

"You aren't accountable for her death any more than you were your brother's actions," Landon insisted.

Nodding, I wrapped my arms around him and pulled him against my chest, accepting his emotional support.

But I needed more.

Zack. His physical strength that allowed me a different level of vulnerability and comfort. I longed to crawl into his embrace, submit to his ability to empty my mind. Not that he could heal my wounds, but he sure as hell could make me forget them for a while.

I didn't speak about the man we both missed though. Didn't want to have Landon thinking he wasn't enough for me, same as I wasn't for him.

We needed our man.

"We should get out of here. Take another vacation to escape the shit that seems to constantly surround us," Landon murmured, his lips brushing over the skin of my neck where he'd shoved his face.

I glanced around the living room while my hands roamed down his back in soothing assurance. Outside the house, we didn't have much of a life, and while our situation had changed for the better since our five days on the island, it still lacked. We were nothing more than codependent hermits who hid from the world and fucked like rabbits when not missing our third.

"I've always wanted to see Italy." I suggested the one place both Landon and Zack had mentioned they hoped to see someday.

"Let's do it." Landon sat back, a hint of life on his face, the first stir of anything resembling excitement since Zack had left us.

I opened my mouth to agree, but my cell buzzed in my pocket.

Landon climbed off me, allowing me to fish it free.

No name was listed on my screen, but I recognized the number.

"Hello?" I answered cautiously, staring at Landon.

While I didn't know the man's voice, I was very familiar his name. My eyes widened as he stated the reason for his call, my face splitting into a grin at the offer he extended.

It was exactly what Landon and I needed.

Chapter 31

Zack

"You're going to do me a favor."

I snorted at Sean's statement while giving myself some privacy by hiding in the supply closet to take his call. No other volunteers at the shelter knew what I did for a living, and I preferred to keep it that way. "You still owe me for covering you for Valentine's Day when Drake got called to New York." I reminded Sean of what had gone down back in February.

Drake had been booked both nights that weekend, but I'd agreed to fill in for him. Good thing I had. He'd ended up reconnecting with his stepbrother while stuck in a broken elevator, and now the two of them planned on having a white picket fence and a dozen kids.

Crazy, but to each their own.

"This is actually *me* repaying *you*."

I barked a laugh that sounded muffled in the tiny room I'd hidden in. "How the fuck does that work?"

"Trust me just this once?"

My smile faded, and I inhaled the scent of cleaning chemicals deep into my lungs. "Yes."

"Sweet. Got a pen handy?"

"Nope."

"I'll text you the hotel name and room number."

My eyelids slammed shut at what he wanted from me. "Sean…"

"Listen—I know trust doesn't come easy for you, but I've got your back in this one-hundred percent. I would never steer you wrong."

The breakfast sandwich I'd grabbed before heading in to volunteer for the day churned in my guts. But Sean *repaying* me by asking me to hook up with a client…it had to be a positive thing, right?

Maybe he thought meeting with Jamie would be a good idea—

"There aren't any files to look through, no NDAs to sign this time around," Sean informed me, cutting my thoughts on clients off.

"*Okay…*" I drew out the word, waiting for him to fill me in.

"I gotta run, but I'll shoot the info over right away." Sean hung up before I could push for more information.

Lips pursed, I shoved my cell back in my pocket and strode from the closest. A few dozen people lingered at the cafeteria tables, and I forced myself to stop and chat with a handful on my way toward the kitchen to help with cleanup.

I'd taken that time off Sean had insisted on, relieved to have my name removed from Elite's list of available escorts. It had seemed the right thing to do, and I had enough money in the bank to extend my break for months if that's what I decided on.

Volunteering and hanging out at Humanity House still fulfilled me, gave me a sense of purpose I would be lacking otherwise. The gym had become yet another home, when before, it'd been a means to an end of keeping my body in prime condition. I'd challenged myself to lower my walls a bit and be more friendly. Maybe make some friends outside Elite.

I stewed over Sean's text that informed me I had a night of luxury ahead of me. The booked suite lay on the top floor of Boston's most lavish hotel that offered a gorgeous view of both the city and the ocean.

Only a handful of clients over the years had been able to afford similar lodgings.

Regardless of my lack of desire for sex, I thoroughly cleaned myself, trimmed, and shaved areas I'd ignored since my vacation in hell.

Who was I joking?

Being with Landon and Callum had been nothing but heaven. Even the ache over missing them, the desire to seek them out I ignored due to continued fear, was addictive as fuck. Who knew being in love could hurt so good?

A room key had been left at the front desk, but I hesitated before entering the suite.

Trust.

A word that was the bane of my existence. But Sean had my back before. He'd believed me, never once questioned what had taken place with the client who'd tried to extort Elite all those months ago.

Sean had proven himself to me time and again.

I entered the room, a quick glance around the sitting area revealing the absence of a client. Slipping off my shoes, I set the key aside. Rather than voicing a greeting, I made my way farther into the room, a cursory glance noting the buildings beyond the windows backlit by the setting sun.

The bedroom door was left open.

I stepped through, halting at the sight before me that caught my breath. My heart stuttered then raced as adrenaline rushed through my system.

Callum and Landon sat propped against the headboard of the king-sized bed, both in lounge pants and T-shirts. Amber and sea-like gazes both studied me with clear uncertainty, same as when I'd left them in paradise almost two months ago.

And the love...

Jesus *fucking* Christ, the desire spanning the distance between us made my goddamn eyes well up. That flimsy foil I'd clung to as a shield around my heart crumpled as Callum held his hand out in a silent request to join them.

What made me think I could possibly get through the rest of my life without these men beside me? I knew I'd been miserable since returning from that tropical paradise, but I hadn't recognized how truly lonely and heartbroken I'd actually been until I saw them face-to-face.

I might have trust issues and get triggered on occasion, but goddamnit, I wanted to be happy. Loved. Taken care of when I was the needy one.

Still, I instinctively hesitated from openly submitting to Callum's encouragement to simply let go and allow them to give me what I hungered for.

"Lose the clothes," I whispered, my words no more than a rasped command.

Both kept their focus on me while doing as told. With every soft whisper of first shirts then pants to hit the floor, my dick swelled at the sight. Their golden tans hadn't faded, their gorgeously muscled bodies were tensed, their dicks hard.

Muttering a curse, I rubbed over my bulge, devouring

first Landon then Callum with my eyes. The sheets beneath them remained unruffled, evidence they'd waited for me.

Landon's balls were already drawn up tight. Callum's slit leaked, a droplet sliding down along his stiff length making my mouth water.

"Zack—please." Landon was the one to break the heavy silence among us, and my name on his lips caused a shudder to ripple through me, setting my mind on the only course available to me, exactly as my heart yearned for.

I tore my shirt off overhead. Shoved down my slacks.

Climbing onto the mattress, I glanced between the two of them. Who to touch first? Which mouth to delve my tongue into and taste? How to ravage them both, sate my hunger for what I hadn't truly realized I'd missed as desperately as I had?

My hesitation made them reach for me, but Callum had the longer arms, and he grabbed hold of me and yanked me forward. He settled me on my side facing him rather than Landon like I'd expected.

I swallowed hard. "So what—"

Landon slapped his hand over my mouth from behind while getting all up in my space from shoulders to toes. His hard dick poked at my ass even though he wouldn't ever want to penetrate me. His heartbeat thundered against my back. "Sex first because we've missed you too much," he whispered hot against my ear. "Talking can come later."

I eyed Callum and his pupil-blown orbs. "You haven't been taking care of this needy boy?"

"*Our* needy boy," he corrected me, his tone firm.

My chest ached with sweet relief, and that sense of rightness I'd felt with them settled fully into place.

This was where I belonged. These men were the home

I'd never truly experienced before. They were acceptance and love, support and comfort.

"I want you, Callum," I murmured, running a fingertip over his lower lip. "Need you to take care of me. Fill me up. Flood me with your cum."

Landon cursed from behind me, quickly grabbing hold of his dick.

Callum simply stared into my eyes, his own open and vulnerable as fuck. We shared a moment of silence, and I knew beyond a shadow of a doubt he remembered our conversation and me begging him to not ask for more than I could give him.

And here I held my heart out in my hands, willing to submit to the nurturing he craved to lavish on me.

"Nothing between us?" he asked quietly, searching my face.

"I trust you."

He swallowed hard, his eyes growing damp. "Roll over."

I did as told, my heart racing and skin on fire.

My gaze met amber gems as tempting as whiskey to a parched throat.

"This okay with you?" I asked quietly while Callum slid his hands over my back as though worshiping my skin.

"More than." Landon breathed his response, pulling my top leg over his so our dicks pressed tightly together.

"Fuck, baby," I croaked, taking his face in my hands. "You're so damn beautiful."

"No more talking—let us love on you."

I nodded, and we met halfway, our lips hungry yet tender, the same as the palms on my ass cheeks.

Callum kissed over my shoulders, down my spine, and tongued my twin dimples at the base of my back.

I frotted against Landon's stiff length even though I wanted to arch toward Callum's warm mouth.

He spread me wide and lapped over my hole.

Groaning, I fucked my tongue along Landon's. Desperation dictated my actions and stirred my blood into a frenzy. "Callum. Fuck." I gulped a few sips of oxygen and dove into Landon's sweetness in a desperate frenzy to devour his mouth.

He wrapped his hand around my dick, stroking in time with Callum's tongue breaching my hole. All three of us sucked and nibbled on the flesh before us, partaking in a feast that promised fulfillment of our hunger.

"Need your dick, Callum," I begged, the emptiness inside me more than I could bear.

Cool, slick fingers pushed into my hole, and I moaned, pressing toward him, seeking relief.

Landon shifted down on the bed so both men lay nearer to my groin.

Callum finger-fucked my ass, readying me to take him. Landon latched onto my dick like it was a lollipop, his appreciative noises over my taste making my balls firm.

Teeth gritted, I took my pleasure in their combined touch but refused myself release.

"Callum," I grunted his name as he worked a fourth finger into my body. "I'm good—please."

He shifted behind me, the heat of his chest against my back. "You're sure?"

"Yes. Please."

Blunt flesh pressed against my pucker, and I pushed onto his length, hissing as he breached my body. I'd never fucked without protection. Not once. But my first time with Callum felt like the right moment to give myself fully to a man.

He and Landon weren't just a couple of random guys using my dick and hole. They belonged to me, and I to them —but like Landon had said, we could discuss that later. I needed to be one with them, get lost in sensation that would lead to satisfaction. I yearned for that sense of belonging I'd experienced on the island without even truly recognizing it until I'd left them behind.

Callum burrowed fully inside my body and stilled, giving me time to grow accustomed to being stretched open and stuffed full. "Okay?" he murmured against my nape, and I groaned an affirmative as Landon sucked me deep into his throat.

"Not going to last," I muttered through teeth still gritted tightly together. These men...

Callum patted Landon's head, and our lover popped off my dick.

He peered up at us, the golden light of his eyes overrun by black pupils.

"Turn around, baby," Callum said. "Let Zack have your greedy little hole I haven't been able to satisfy on my own."

Landon flipped around quick as fuck, and both of us chuckled.

I tugged him closer as he nestled his fine ass against my spit-soaked cock. "Lube?"

"I'm already stretched and wet for you, Zack. Just hold still and let me fuck myself with your dick."

"Jesus." I gulped as he did just that, filling himself with one backward slam of his hips. "Fuck!" I grabbed hold of his waist, keeping him still, the heat and silkiness of his insides grasping at my bare cock making my eyes roll back into my head.

I'd never fucked without a condom. Hadn't trusted

anyone before these two men. I'd also never been in the middle like this, being loved on from both sides. Had never experienced the pleasure my two lovers gave me. Divine didn't begin to describe how perfect we were, connected not just in body but in soul.

It was one hell of a spiritual high—addictive as fuck. My new favorite place to be.

"Let us make you feel good, Zack," Callum stated, snaking his arms around me.

Landon twisted his torso, reaching out to grasp the back of my head.

I gave him my mouth as Callum's latched onto my shoulder.

We moved in our shared need, eventually finding a rhythm that made pure pleasure tingle up and down my spine. I'd expected to blow my load within seconds, but I fought off my release, desperate to stay in the perfect moment with them.

Lube made a slick mess between us, but we clutched each other close, three bodies attempting to morph into one. That foil had been ripped away, and I no longer wished to hide. I'd never felt as close with someone as in that moment, physically plastered together and yet emotionally attached on a deeper level than I'd ever imagined possible.

A well of happiness and satisfaction rose up inside me, overflowing until I had no choice but to let go.

My cum flooded Landon's ass, his ring clamping on my base a heartbeat later as he spilled onto the sheets, his sweet whimper while coming music to my ears.

"Ah fuck," Callum groaned against my neck, his entire body going tense behind me as his shaft bucked inside my hole. "Zack—Jesus."

Hands grasping sweat-slickened skin, we came together, spurts of seed then aftershocks wracking through us. Too soon, we relaxed, our exhales heavy, and I found myself grinning like a goddamned loon.

Chapter 32

Callum

We spent the night in a cocoon of sex and semen, choosing to immerse ourselves in the physical. Landon and I had agreed to stick with what worked best between the three of us and save any heavy discussions for once we'd left Zack boneless and completely sated.

But he passed out after our fourth or fifth round. I'd lost count, too caught up in the elation of Zack choosing to stay rather than walking out upon finding what his friend had done for him. For all of us, really.

Sean Fox had told me Zack had been nothing but a miserable bitch since returning home from the vacation the three of us had enjoyed together. While he hadn't come out and stated Zack's feelings for the two of us—those were Zack's to share, Sean had said—he felt in his heart that Zack just needed a little push in the right direction toward happiness and fulfillment.

We hadn't spoken many words after Zack's arrival. The appearance of him had caught my breath and made me desperate to touch him again.

Then he'd trusted me to top him, had submitted himself to me emotionally without any hesitation or even fear in his eyes. Because of his actions, I couldn't help but hope for the outcome Landon and I both wanted with him, even if I ought to have protected my heart instead.

If anything, our night together only solidified that we were meant to be together. Our rare triad carved out a three-piece puzzle that created a beautiful whole. Surely Zack would see that now that he'd had another taste of how perfectly we all fit together.

We'd shared morning blow jobs and ordered room service. While waiting for our food, we enjoyed a third shower together, taking turns in caring for one another until we once more emptied our balls, Zack's and my spunk on Landon's tongue, his swirling down the drain.

The three of us sat in robes around the small table, voracious after the sex marathon of the previous ten or so hours.

Landon shifted on the cushioned chair and glanced at Zack with wary eyes, leading me to believe that it was more than a sore ass making him anxious. "Did you, um, see the image of the three of us on social media?" He was the first to pop our bubble with the reality outside the suite's door. "They didn't identify you, but still."

"I'm not on social media much," Zack replied, a forkful of French toast dripping real maple syrup onto his plate as he held it halfway to his mouth. "Is there any need for concern?"

Landon shook his head while scooping up some scrambled eggs. "We weren't doing anything wrong, but considering my past..." He shrugged.

Zack set his bite down untouched and clutched Landon's forearm across the table. "Hey. You all right, baby?"

"Yeah. I expected a huge blowout like the first time I got caught messing around with more than one guy. I freaked out and needed a couple of extra pills to chill the fuck out."

"Nothing became of it though, so there's no need to worry anymore," I interjected, hoping to soothe Landon's unease as I'd been doing on a daily basis. We'd discussed the whole thing to death, and even though he didn't believe we weren't in the wrong, he struggled to move past it, expecting the worst. But even his father hadn't attempted to get in contact with him again about the situation.

"So what's the problem?" Zack asked, glancing between us, still holding Landon's arm.

Landon shrugged again. "There isn't one as long as it stays buried. So, fingers crossed."

"If you're concerned for me and my reputation, I don't give a shit—wait." Zack sat back, hands falling to his lap, his brow furrowed and hazel eyes suddenly wary. "Are you afraid they'll find out who I am? *What* I am and how that will affect you and your family?"

"What? No!" Landon stared at him, aghast. "Of course not! I just don't want *you* dragged down by being involved with the, well, I told you what they called me."

"Fuck the pearl clutchers and homophobes. They don't know how good that stick up their ass can make them feel if they'd only offer it a chance."

Landon snorted a laugh at Zack's snipped declaration, and I relaxed in my chair, not having realized I'd tensed up.

"Need to come over here on my lap and let me comfort you until I'm aching to own your sweet ass again?" Zack asked with a serious face even though his eyes teased.

"Callum needs you more than I do right now," Landon replied.

It was my turn to pause with a fork halfway to my mouth at the sudden change of topic.

Zack once more flitted his gaze between the two of us as though waiting to be filled in.

"You have things you can give him that I can't," Landon went on, "and I don't just mean my dick. His brother... well." Landon bit his lip and glanced at me as though asking permission to spill my shit to Zack. I could guess where he headed and wanted to be the one to share all of me.

"Remember I told you a little about my greatest regret?" I asked quietly, pushing my plate aside.

"Yeah."

"I didn't give you the full story and what has come to pass since then." Swallowing hard, I attempted to set aside my usual guilt.

Zack listened without interruption as I explained about my hesitancy to involve the authorities or another trusted adult in my brother's life all those years ago. He'd paid the consequences of his actions—my *inactions*—but so did the young woman who'd recently committed suicide.

Tears poured down my cheeks as I recounted the tale, and Zack pulled me off my chair beside him and onto his lap. I didn't exactly fit that well, but he hugged me close, his lips against my hair.

I sagged against him, clinging to his robe and the sense of security his arms gave me, trusting him to hold my head above water.

"See?" Landon's quiet voice reached my ears, but I couldn't tear my face from of Zack's warm neck where his pulse beat against my lips. "You comfort him in ways I can't. You're his rock like he is mine. You complete us, and I like to think that we give you what you need as well."

My breath caught and held as I waited for Zack's

response to Landon basically stating exactly what we wanted.

"When did you get so wise, baby?" Zack asked, his voice like honey, sweet and soothing, immediately easing my fear he would once more walk away from us.

"From living and learning the hard way," Landon replied while scooting a little closer, his tone quiet and reflective.

I made myself climb off Zack's lap and sit on the chair he'd forced me to empty. First, I took his hand then Landon's. It looked like I would begin. "Three are stronger than one or two," I murmured, twining our fingers into a beautiful lump that made me feel complete. Understood. "There's nothing we can't face together. I need both of you. *Want* both of you, so this is me baring my heart fully. Asking for more."

I glanced at Landon first, who peered at Zack with love and expectation in his eyes.

Zack stared at where my hand draped atop his. He squeezed our fingers beneath.

"We'll move to Boston if that's what you want." Landon stumbled over his declaration in a rush to fill the sudden silence as though he expected Zack to turn us down. "Or we can start over. I was thinking Tuscany. You always dreamed about traveling the world, right? At the least, we should go there for a few weeks to settle in, you know? Bond—like Callum and I would like to see happen. You want that too, don't you?"

Landon's hopeful tone mirrored the same feeling in my chest. He'd spilled our desires in a rushed lump of words, so all I could do was hold my breath and wait for Zack to make or break us.

Chapter 33

Landon

I might have gotten ahead of myself, allowing complete vulnerability again, going completely off course of how Callum and I had discussed a plan to approach Zack about a possible future together.

All those years ago, I'd made a rash decision to go after what I wanted, and Zack had denied me. Destroyed me. And years of agony lay between then and now where my heart once more threatened to thump through my chest.

But I wasn't going to hurt him this time, and Father wasn't around to stop me from getting what I wanted.

I slid off my chair and crawled between Zack's knees.

"What are you doing?" he questioned me, his voice a low rasp.

"Talking you into giving me what we want," I blurted— then paused to glance up at Zack.

A heavy moment settled over us.

Did Zack remember that night as clearly as I did? I'd been beyond desperate for some sort of intimacy with him that would tie us together. Anything to keep him from leaving me. I'd been hellbent on making him stay.

Shit.

I slumped back onto my haunches, my gaze dropping to the flooring beneath me as the weight of my action settled over my shoulders.

"What's wrong?" Zack asked without a hint of anger in his tone.

Clenching my eyelids shut didn't keep a tear from spilling down my cheek. "I just realized I'm trying to manipulate you again so I can have things how I want them."

Callum's hand settled on my shoulder, and I leaned into his assuring touch on instinct.

"I'm sorry," I whispered, hating the recognition that I hadn't changed, hadn't truly outgrown my selfish ways. So much for that gaining of wisdom BS I'd spouted moments earlier.

Arms yanked me upward, and I gasped as Zack settled me on his lap, straddling his thighs. He peered at me with a tenderness in his hazel eyes I couldn't remember seeing since childhood. My heart raced at the possibilities.

"I've already forgiven you," he murmured, brushing his thumb over my cheek.

His words should have sent my soul soaring, but I couldn't get out of my head. "But I haven't learned my lesson, have I? I'm a greedy brat who will go to any lengths, including sucking you off to get my way."

"And what's that, Landon? Hmm? Spell it out clearly in detail and don't hold anything back." His tone suggested arousal, desire to fulfill my every whim no matter the sexual fantasies I spouted.

Shivers licked down my spine, making the tip of my tongue do the same to my dry lower lip. But what I lusted for more than anything went far above fucking.

"You, Zack. And Callum. With me all the time. I long

for the fantasy come to life. I'm sure things will be shitty sometimes, but what we have…" I took both of their hands and placed them over my heart with mine clasped atop, manifesting exactly what I'd dreamed of. "I've struggled with feeling accepted for so long, but Callum has helped heal that part of me. I have zero desire to fuck up again. I obsessed over my choice that led to you leaving me, and I don't think I can handle you walking away.

"So this time." I inhaled deeply, forcing myself to relax and letting it seep from my lungs until they emptied of selfishness. "I'm going to be honest. I don't hate you like I screamed that night—far from it. I've been in love with you for as long as I can remember. I long for a future with you and you," I said, looking over at Callum. "More than anything."

His soft smile, the promise of forever we'd basically already shared offered me assurance.

"So yeah. That's my truth laid open to both of you, and we can live it out loud. Fuck everyone who thinks we're wrong. I've chosen to cower down beneath others' rules for so damn long, and I just want to be who I am. A horny, poly guy who has finally found satisfaction with his two men."

Zack cradled my cheek in his free palm and tugged me closer, ghosting his mouth over mine. "Not going anywhere, baby. Love you too much to leave you behind." His sweet, maple breath caressed my parted lips, and I thrust forward, intent on licking along his tongue until I swallowed his taste down to a place it became mine.

He humored me, eating at my mouth with the same intensity as bubbles of happiness and life popped inside me, erupting firework-like bursts inside my heart and showering me with glittering colors.

"Love you," I whispered, unable to tear my lips from his

skin, peppering his nose, his cheeks, his jawline between repeating the statement over and over again.

Zack chuckled, turning to face Callum.

"Tell him, Cal," I demanded, planting more kisses against Zack's neck while draping myself over his chest and shoulders, my hands in his hair. "Exactly what you said the other night after Sean called."

"I'm falling for you too, Zack," Callum admitted. "I can't live another day without you between us. Beneath me or in our greedy boy. Want you in our space and sharing our life. Making decisions together, going on vacation, allowing the world to see that a triad is possible and healthy even if there is a little codependency going on behind closed doors."

"It'll take honesty and communication all the time," I tacked on before nipping at Zack's lobe.

He pulled away from my sharp teeth, narrowed his eyes, and pinched my nipple through my robe. "Brat."

I ignored the sting, holding his gaze. Un-fucking-wavering as one last bout of insecurity crashed into me. "Do you want the same?" I asked, my shaky tone proof of my deepest fear.

He chuckled, the lightness of his response bringing a smile to my face and relief to my hitched shoulders. "Yes."

My heart seized in the best way possible—*but*. "So along with your heart, your hole and dick are ours?" I double-checked because that escorting business had to go. Period. Callum and Zack were officially mine, and no way in hell would I be sharing. Ever.

"Is that your way of asking if I'll be your boyfriend?" he teased. "Or that you simply want exclusivity between the three of us?"

"Both. Yes."

"You belong to us." Callum's firm statement held no hint of a question.

Zack gave him his full focus. "I'm falling for you too," he admitted, his tone soft and as sweet as his breath. "Probably faster than is appropriate."

"Fuck that word," I muttered while nosing into Zack's neck again and wrapping myself around him like a koala. My chest swelled as tightly as my throat. How could complete happiness and sadness morph into bittersweetness inside a man's chest?

I didn't hate it. Quite the contrary.

"What I feel for you," Zack continued as though I hadn't spoken, "rivals my emotions toward Landon. But they'll never be in competition, I can promise you that."

"It's the same for me," Callum assured him.

"Oh, thank fuck." I breathed easier now that the cards had been laid out on the table. It appeared as though the three of us had *all* won. "Are we done now? Because this bottom is all kinds of desperate and needs to be in the middle—but spit-roasted, of course."

Callum and Zack chuckled.

"As if we would deny you anything," Zack said, pushing up to his feet, his hands grasping my ass cheeks to keep me in place.

I tightened my hold on him, casting a sly glance at Callum over Zack's shoulder as we headed toward the bedroom.

"He's ours, Cal."

"Yours and mine," Callum agreed.

"And no one else's," Zack tacked on before tossing me onto the bed.

I tore off my robe and spun onto my hands and knees. "Put your dick in my mouth," I told Zack. "And yours in my ass, Cal. Fill me up from both ends, please." I wiggled my backside at Callum, who didn't waste any time in shoving his face between my cheeks. "Fuck yes," I gasped, reaching for Zack who lazily slipped his robe off his broad shoulders as if he wasn't in a rush.

He watched Callum tongue fuck my hole, ignoring my beckoning fingers to stroke along his cock.

"*Need* you," I reminded him, impatience emphasizing my words like a spoiled brat.

"And you can have me. Now. Tomorrow. Forever if that's how long it'll take to fulfill all of your fantasies."

"Yes—that," I agreed, and he gave me what I asked for, crawling onto the bed, swollen dick ready for the warm wetness of my mouth.

Chapter 34

Zack

A few weeks later

Tuscany had proven to be a better paradise than the tropical island where we'd first come together. The villa we'd rented rested in sun-warmed tones of gold and yellow throughout the rooms. Beige marble countertops sat muted beneath dark wooden cabinets in the kitchen, roughened natural stone creating a beautiful backsplash.

We'd fallen into the most pleasant, fulfilling routine while there, one of pure domestic bliss. It helped that Landon was between manuscripts and we waited for his newest release, which meant less hours of work for Callum as well. And I'd officially retired from Elite Escorts, having fully committed myself to Landon and Callum.

Callum had taken on the task of cooking the local Tuscan cuisine, since Landon couldn't boil water, and my skills in a kitchen ended at the grill and a cutting board. He'd put me to work at the chopping block island, more often than not cutting veggies for whatever meal he created.

Outside the bedroom and cuddling, he claimed nothing

pleased him more than feeding his men. Filling our bellies until satisfied.

"I'm going to get another bottle of that white wine," Landon said, sliding off his chair at the island where he sat beside me.

"Will one of you open the French doors to the patio?" Callum asked from where he sweated in front of the stove.

"I got it." The rustic terracotta tile lay cold beneath my bare feet as I traipsed across the kitchen the likes I'd only ever seen in magazines.

I propped both doors outward, and a deliciously sweet breeze wafted over my body.

"We ought to move here," Landon murmured from behind me, his voice dreamy, evidence of his total relaxation.

I was content beyond measure too, the lack of wariness or uncertainty showing in my eyes according to Callum who said they glowed more green than brown beneath the Tuscan sun. I laughed a lot as well. But for some reason, I couldn't find joy in any of the meal-prep tasks assigned to me. That didn't keep me from helping though. Especially when I had a literal kickass view.

Going back to my seat at the table where I'd been cutting carrots, I checked out Callum's fine backside. I would have him later as a reward for submitting to his dominance in the kitchen.

Landon snickered.

I glance over to find a soft smile that curved his lips more often than not these days. He raised an eyebrow, and I shrugged over being caught eyeing our lover's goods. "And you call me the greedy one," he murmured with a chuckle while pouring three glasses of chilled white wine. He handed a drink to me before ambling toward Callum with the another.

"I'm starved."

"Glad to hear it." Callum planted a quick kiss on his lips, but Landon grabbed hold of Callum's nape and held him in place for a long, lazy smooch, the flicks of their tongues showing me yet again how insatiable I was with the two men who'd gifted me a world I'd never dreamed possible.

ℱℱ
MM

Landon had eaten some damned weird cheese for a so-called dessert again, but this time, I couldn't handle the taste on his lips that overpowered his sweetness.

Callum hadn't minded though, and they made out on the outdoor bed, the canopy above them floppy in a breeze scented by jasmine. A headier undertone of cedar from the line of cypress trees beyond the garden we lounged in caressed my nose along with the flowers' sweetness.

I filled my lungs and closed my eyes against the sinking summer sun, basking in its refreshing warmth while I lounged on a bed of my own a few feet from my two lovers.

The sounds of kisses and the rustle of movement eventually quieted, but neither man had sought out release or sexual gratification. They'd simply sighed and gone as still as I was, stuffed after devouring the pasta dish Callum had whipped up for us with authentic Italian groceries from a local mom and pop type store.

Bees buzzed and birds chirped, and even though I wasn't in physical contact with either Landon or Callum, a sense of peace settled over me as though I shared in their embrace, like my spirit rested against one or the other.

Spending time away from reality as Landon had suggested had been a good choice. The best, actually. There was nothing to focus on but building a strong foundation for the relationship we all wanted with each other.

Unfortunately, we couldn't stay away from the pasta, so we would be spending serious time in the gym once we returned to the States, which we would do.

Eventually.

There was no rush, and we didn't have to linger in Italy to avoid drama. The picture of the three of us hadn't ever gained traction, and what could have been ugly, dragging Landon's shit from the past into the present, faded into obscurity.

During our days exploring Tuscany, we'd discussed open communication. Clear boundaries. Promised not to hide our emotions or invalidate other's if they didn't align with our own. If Landon got too caught up in his feels, especially anxiety, Callum's calming hands and soothing words returned him to where he could reason with himself or us.

Callum did the same for me, giving me a safe place to melt and just be without any fear of abandonment. There was no judgment among us either. No questioning or second-guessing each other's intentions, which tended to rise from insecurities. And while trusting still wasn't second nature for me, I'd never felt so loved or cherished in my life.

Callum and Landon put me first, and I, in turn, cared for them as thoroughly as possible, however they wished. If that meant holding one while he slept or taking a walk with the other in comfortable silence or spilling pent-up emotions, our shoulders brushing because we couldn't *not* touch, so be it. But the best? Willingly submitting myself to be their fuck toy, my holes filled, their cum marking me from both ends, which we all enjoyed participating in.

Landon especially thrived on having our undivided attention, but he didn't need manipulation to get his way. Callum and I were happy to let him have it all day, every day.

Arousal slid through my veins as heady and potent as the chianti I'd been sipping with our dinner resting my heavy eyelids.

I peeked one eye open to find my lovers still wrapped embracing. Sudden longing had me on my feet and slinking across sun-kissed cobblestones to join them on a bed meant for two.

The size of a mattress hadn't stopped us from loving each other in the previous week, nor would it in the time left to us while vacationing in Italy.

Our greedy boy lay passed out, lips parted as he breathed heavily with sleep. We'd spent a long day in a convertible, taking in the rolling countryside as the wind whipped our hair. Considering the sizable dinner he'd eaten, I wasn't surprised to see him in a carb coma.

I settled in behind Callum, petting over his warm shoulder, down his waist, to the bare globes of his tanned ass.

One beautiful thing about renting a villa in the Tuscan hills? The private gardens surrounded by cypress and olive trees—and no neighbors close enough to see what went on outdoors in fading daylight.

Callum hummed his appreciation of my touch, stretching in a way that pressed his ass toward me.

"Can I have you?" I murmured against his ear, my cock fully on board with a final fuck of the day.

"Always," Callum murmured his reply with a sleepy

sigh, shifting his upper leg over Landon's, giving me full access to his hole. "I ate too much though," he warned.

"Don't care."

"Mmm. Then use my body for your pleasure."

We'd stashed lube in every corner since arriving a week earlier. We'd also christened each room. The daybed three times, the last being the night before when we'd both made love to Landon, his hole once more stretching to accommodate both of us.

I retrieved the small bottle off the table alongside the daybed and lubed up before penetrating Callum's tight ring with a single finger to find him empty, hot, and silky smooth.

He groaned, his head tipping back.

Lifting onto my elbow, I nuzzled along his ear and neck, breathing in the woodsy scent of his bodywash. My tongue slid over his skin as I probed at his soft insides, salt on my lips and the wetness of lube on my fingertips.

"So delicious," I murmured and nosed over the shell of his ear, exhaling hot breath until he shuddered.

"Please, Zack."

"Love it when you beg, sweetheart."

I worked in a second finger, stretching him enough to take me but not open him fully. He enjoyed the stinging stretch and got off on being overwhelmed by the feeling of being stuffed full.

"Let me in."

Callum hummed and relaxed, allowing the head of my dick to slip inside him.

"Fuck, Callum." I settled onto my side and wrapped my arms around him, pushing into his tight heat with slow, sure strokes until he welcomed all of me. "Your ass was made for my dick. It's like coming home every time I sink into your hole. You're so slick and warm."

"Zack," he moaned my name, bearing down then squeezing his ring around the base of my girth as though attempting to suck me in deeper.

"Jesus," I hissed, reaching for his cock.

He was hard and already leaking for me.

We writhed together, short strokes keeping me buried and rubbing my swollen head over his prostate with every gentle thrust.

"Can't get deep enough," I complained, rubbing my forehead against the back of his head. "Want to burrow clear into your soul."

"You're already there," Callum whispered, reaching to clutch at my hair and keep me close. "Never letting you go."

"Good."

He turned his head, and we shared a sloppy kiss with wet tongues and panted breaths.

"I love you, Zack," he murmured against my mouth, finally giving words to exactly how he felt for me.

I stilled, my groin resting against his ass, my dick aching inside his body. Both of us opened our eyes, our gazes connecting. "Love you too," I whispered what I'd become sure of.

"Oh thank fuck." Landon's giddiness caused both of our faces to break into grins.

I hadn't realized he'd woken up. I pecked Callum's lips and grabbed Landon's hair with a light grip, shoving him downward along Callum's front. "Suck his dick, baby. Gag on his cock until he comes down your throat."

"*Yes*," Landon agreed with a breathless hiss, scrambling to do as told.

Callum grunted as Landon's mouth closed over him. "Lan—oh God, you're so good at that."

"He has a wicked tongue," I agreed, dragging my dick out of Callum's ass until his ring clutched at my glans.

"Zack."

"I know what you need, sweetheart. Just lay there and let me love you."

He did, moaning as I filled him over and over, clutching at his hip bone to keep him still for my dick's plundering. The sounds of Landon sucking on his cock, slurping and moaning his pleasure tightened my balls up against my body.

"I'm gonna come," Callum gasped, and the second his hole clamped around my girth, I unloaded in his ass, endorphins rushing through my blood and pebbling my skin.

Broken words of love and appreciation spilled from my lips with every spurt coating his insides.

Landon coughed and swallowed audibly, drinking Callum down. He whimpered the sweetest noise I'd memorized as him coming, and I realized he'd found release hands-free as he often did when sucking one of us off.

We lay in a tangle of sweaty limbs, unmoving and eventually catching our breath. My softened dick slid from Callum's ass, and he sighed as my spunk slipped from his hole and soaked the mattress beneath us.

"Did we make a mess?" he asked, his tone wrecked.

"Not enough we need to shower right away," I assured him before kissing his hair.

"Good. Don't want to move."

Landon hadn't shifted from the bed's end, nuzzled against Callum's groin, his hand clasping at my calf muscle.

The sweetly scented breeze drifted over our damp skin, but we weren't in a hurry to pull apart. We still had another two weeks at the villa. This vacation compared to our first

one together had been nothing but heaven where vulnerability made connecting that much sweeter.

Chapter 35

Zack

The day after we returned from Italy, we crashed at my place in Boston. We'd discussed our future living arrangements, and while it would have been an easier job moving me to Rhode Island, I wanted nothing to do with the state of my birth and all the pain I'd left behind there. I didn't dig my feet in as an attempt to get my way, but thank fuck for selfless men who agreed without argument to relocate to Massachusetts.

We would eventually require more than a two-bedroom condo, considering Landon's need for an office and all our combined gym equipment, but for now, we would make do. A home farther north would fit us perfectly, far enough from the city for some privacy like they'd had in Rhode Island but close enough to Boston and my volunteer work.

Both men committed to join me at the shelter on a weekly basis, giving us yet another thing to do together outside the house as a triad. They planned on teaching me how to spar, since my gym had a boxing ring, and I would help them both up their weight-lifting game.

The red-eye flight home had left us groggy and struggling to readapt to the time zone, and we had no intentions of rousing ourselves back to reality for at least forty-eight hours.

A local Rhode Island news website Callum browsed over a late breakfast changed our plans.

Malcom Briggs had passed peacefully in his sleep two days ago.

I felt nothing. No sense of loss or hint of grief over a grandfather I hadn't known. Not even anger stirred over the reminder of his bitterness and hatred of my birth mother.

Even still, Landon and Callum both pushed me to attend the burial as a way of seeing that part of my life put to rest. Literally. I wasn't sure if Malcom had ever spoken to his wife about my visit. I had no clue if she was aware of my continued existence or if she even cared.

I had all the family I needed, but I agreed to go and watch from a distance like some shady character in a movie hiding behind a gravestone in the hopes of going unnoticed.

No such luck.

The sun shone, and no long trench coat offered me obscurity. There was no mass of people to lose myself in, no faceless friends or colleagues to wonder over the man standing a few yards away. Malcom's black casket glistened beneath rays from the blue sky as though he'd been blessed by a god I didn't believe in.

Iona Briggs, my grandmother, was a tiny, raven-haired sprite. She appeared untouched by age, even though she had to be in her late seventies at the very least, considering Malcom's eighty-six. Shoulders back and I was sure dry-eyed from what I could tell in the distance between us, she watched as they lowered her late husband's body into the ground.

She stood alone.

And she wore a bright green dress that spoke of the newness of early spring rather than mourning.

As though feeling my stare, she lifted her focus off the box of death before her. Our eyes met and held.

My heart beat a little faster, and I contemplated turning and walking away—until she smiled, her face flooding with happiness. Tears slipped down her cheeks, and she hurried toward me, the lowering casket seemingly forgotten.

I stood rooted in place, unable to move. Not that I wanted to.

She stumbled to a stop less than three feet from me, breathless and taking in the entirety of my face. "It's you!" she whispered the words with a slight Scottish accent, her lips trembling.

"Mrs. Briggs," I greeted her with a nod, not sure what to do with my hands.

"Call me Granny," she demanded with a dazzling smile that made her wet green eyes shine like jewels in the sunlight.

My throat tightened, and I attempted to swallow. How could this lovely creature have been married to that beast of a man who'd been nothing but bitterness and arrogance?

She wound her hand through my arm and tugged me off to the left where a dark-windowed limo sat waiting for her. "Come along, lad. We have our freedom now, don't we?"

I glanced down at the dark head held high, my eyes stinging. She clung to me as though afraid I would abandon *her*.

My only blood relative that I was aware of walked on America's shores.

"I knew I would never be able to change that bastard's mind," she stated, the hint of her brogue like music to my ears. "So I had to bide my time. I kept track of you. Secretly, of course. And being younger than that bastard, I was deter-mined to survive him and finally have a chance to talk to you. Claim the grandson he'd denied me for too long."

A marriage of convenience—for her father, Granny filled me in while I sat in her limo, tongue-tied and still stunned by the turn of events.

She'd insisted on having one of her men drive my vehicle behind the limo. Having gotten her hands on me, she had zero intentions of letting me go.

That declaration resting in my head, I chose to simply listen to the story of a too-young girl who'd been all but sold off into slavery to an emotionally abusive husband she hadn't wanted.

But such were the ways of northern Scotland back in the day, especially when men gambled with more than what was in their pockets.

"I had my wee beauty at sixteen," she told me before sipping a Scotch whisky identical to the one in my white-knuckled grip.

It'd been over a half-hour since I'd set eyes on my grand-mother, and I still couldn't wrap my head around the truths I'd learned in that short amount of time it had taken to arrive at the Briggs' family mansion.

"Sixteen?" I rasped.

"Aye—that bastard owned me two years before that."

Fucking hell. I rubbed a hand over my face, staring at the woman with a spine of iron seated on the chair in front of me.

We'd settled in her sitting room just inside and to the right of the door I'd knocked on weeks earlier. The entryway of the mansion I'd been barred from entering even if I'd wanted to.

The scent of leather and roses had hit me upon crossing

the threshold, and no matter how much I told myself I hated the monstrous house surrounding me, the presence of the sweet, fiery woman sharing a drink with me didn't allow for any negativity in my heart and mind.

"You're...sixty-six?"

"Five." She winked and laughed.

"Malcom was twenty years older than you"

"Yes, the pompous ass." She sniffed, but her eyes twinkled. "I've still got a lot left in me, lad—and I plan on spending the rest of my days exactly how I want and with *who* I want. That would be my only living blood relative. You, Zackary."

I swallowed hard, my thoughts fucking *fucked.*

Her smile softened along with her gaze as though she recognized my inability to process. "I expect you have a life of your own, one you might not want some old, glamorous granny such as myself intruding upon, so I won't push for more than an occasional visit. But I'll never turn my back on you again, nor will I deny you what's rightfully yours." She waved her hand around, the massive emerald on her right hand as vibrant as her eyes.

"I don't want it," I whispered, knowing she spoke about the land, house, and riches.

"Doesn't matter. You're the last Briggs of Malcom's line, and with him finally six feet under and me the sole heiress to his fortune, I can do as I damn well please with it," she stated with her nose in the air.

A huff of laughter rushed past my lips at her haughty declaration. I couldn't begin to imagine the servitude and misery she'd endured the previous fifty-one years. I sobered quickly though.

"I apologize for not being there for you sooner," she said. "For being too fearful to take a stand against the man my father sold me to. For not advocating for our daughter, or loving her enough that she felt it was okay to leave her newborn behind."

"It's not your fault. It was her decision," I said. Same as it'd been Callum's brother's that had landed him in shit. "We make choices and have to live with the consequences."

"You're so much more than a consequence, Zackary—I hope you know that," Granny stated sweetly yet with firm intent. "I hope you'll give me a chance to prove that truth to you."

"I already have the love of two good men, but there's always room for more."

She raised an eyebrow but not in a condescending way. "Two, you say?"

"Yes. I'm in a committed relationship with two men, Landon and Callum." I held still, breath stalled while waiting for her reaction.

A soft smile curved her lips even as sadness filled her eyes. "Your mother had a lot of love to give too, but she wasted it on youngsters who didn't appreciate her heart or her unselfish nature."

Pretty sure I read between the lines. "She was taken advantage of?"

Granny nodded. "Countless times from what she'd told me."

"Do you know who my father is?"

"I'm sorry to say that I don't. No one came forward to claim you, and with Malcom's refusal to let me have you, I had no choice but to give you up. Tell me you were happy, Zack. Help ease my guilt in not fighting harder to keep you."

I wished more than anything that I could.

"I wouldn't change my past," I said instead of making

her feel even worse than she already did. "Being raised in the system led me to Landon and eventually Callum. Without the two of them..." My voice trailed off as my throat thickened. I shrugged, not really sure what to say.

Granny smiled once more. "Well, three grandsons are better than one. I can't wait to meet them. If, that is, you're willing to spend some time with this old lady."

"You're hardly old," I croaked past the tears still clogging my throat, "but yes. I would love to. And I'm sure they would too."

Epilogue - Zack

One Year Later

Micah's daughter perched on his hip, her blonde hair almost white beneath the summer sun. She tugged on his full beard, cooing and babbling all sorts of nonsense that made her daddy melt if his heart-eyes were any indication. We'd gotten together to help celebrate her first birthday.

I stood with him, Kellen, Sean, and Drake, watching our significant others goofing off in the new pool Micah had installed in his massive backyard a few weeks earlier. We hung out close to the water's edge, the occasional splash refreshing, considering the heat of the day.

Kellen and his husband JJ had adopted six-year-old twins, who were the main attraction, both of them rambunctious and thinking they could play with the big boys owning the pool.

"How'd we all get so damned lucky?" Sean asked, grinning as he watched Matteo pick up one of the twins and fling him shrieking with laughter toward the deep end.

None of us had an answer, but he'd nailed the truth. We'd all happened upon men who fit us perfectly. Me, doubly so. I'd been on the end of their teasing quite a bit after resigning as an escort and going public with my relationship but didn't give a shit because my Landon and Callum made life better in every single way.

"So how's Granny and Rhode Island?" Drake asked and sipped his sweating beer.

Laughing over the memory of the last picture Granny had sent me, I shook my head. "She's living it up in Austria —I think. Or maybe Switzerland."

"Still with that gardener boy she dragged along from home?"

I barked a laugh at Sean's prodding.

"She dropped him off somewhere in Spain. Claimed another named Julio? Horace? I can't keep up with her shenanigans."

"Good for her. To Granny!" Sean raised his beer, and we all agreed, clinking our glasses together.

"So what's the plan with that mansion of yours?" Micah asked, switching his little nugget who turned one today to his other hip.

Granny had already signed the Briggs's family home over to me, even though I'd told her countless times I didn't want it, that I hadn't had a single expectation in showing up for my grandfather's burial.

But Landon had fallen in love at first sight with the property and the woman who claimed him as her youngest grandson. She pinched his cheeks and everything. Spoiled him rotten too, much to his delight. And our favorite boy had come up with a great use for the stone monstrosity of a home.

"We've decided to stay," I admitted to what I hadn't been initially been thrilled about.

Eventually, I had agreed to the idea of fostering kids in

need of love and a home until they could stand on their own two feet. Landon had hopped aboard with Callum's suggestion, using all his wiles to get me to agree.

"Are you still planning to fill the thirteen bedrooms?" Kellen asked, watching his own kids and grinning.

"Hell no," I replied, shuddering at the thought, "But we've got our first foster boy arriving next week. Johnny. He's thirteen and has been in the system his whole life. Two others will be here in early September. They're eleven and ten. We'll see how things go from there."

"I'm proud of you," Micah said, grasping my shoulder. His daughter yelled something and tugged at his hair. "Sorry, sweet pea," he cooed. "Daddy will stop ignoring the birthday girl."

Sean snorted and sipped his beer. "You're whipped."

"Wait until you have your own," Micah grumbled at his brother. "She'll melt your heart."

"No female will ever do what only Matteo can," Sean retorted.

Micah snorted a laugh. "I'll remember you said that." He kissed his daughter's forehead. "Let's go find Mommy."

He moved off, and Sean let out a string of curses.

I turned toward what had caught his attention.

His and Micah's parents had arrived.

Their father tottered on his own with a walker, but Sean didn't leave us to greet him or his mom. He ignored them, giving his Teach his full attention even though the light from moments before had dimmed from his eyes.

"Thought shit was a little better between the two of you and your dad," I said, keeping my voice low.

"Meh." He shrugged and sipped his beer. "It's not nearly as bad as it used to be, but things aren't exactly good. No biggie though. Matteo is everything I need."

Sean's Teach blew him a kiss before one of Kellen and JJ's boys attempted to dunk him.

Landon pulled himself from the pool, water rushing down his body as he stood beside me. He'd put on some muscle and had a gorgeous tan from our recent vacation in Tuscany, which we'd agreed would continue to be a family tradition no matter how many kids we ended up fostering.

"You're drooling," Drake teased, elbowing me and making Landon flush.

"Can you blame me?" I couldn't tear my gaze off the rivulets running over the muscles my man had packed on thanks to his new coach—me—pushing him at the gym for almost a year.

"I like mine a little more on the lithe side," Drake said.

Drake's husband, Preston, was indeed that, his red hair a beacon beneath the sun, his eyes like emeralds and set on Drake from where he treaded water a few feet away. They'd gotten married one year to the day they'd spent stuck in an elevator for four hours. It'd been there that they'd reconnected and had given into the love they'd felt for each other since childhood. They'd also recently begun the process of adopting their first child, something they'd both been dreaming about for years.

"We're *all* whipped," Kellen stated—and not a one of us argued.

"Sean."

We all turned at Mr. Fox's greeting. The old man had approached on his own, the wheels of his walker clattering over the cobblestone patio. He held out his hand.

Sean stared for a few uncomfortable seconds of silence before accepting his dad's greeting.

"I'm happy for you, son."

A hush seemed to settle over Micah's backyard at the

old man's off the wall and completely unexpected declaration.

"Mom put you up to this?" Sean croaked, wariness like a shield over his face regardless of welling tears.

"No." Mr. Fox shook his head. "I just had a come to Jesus minute last night. Thought my heart was giving out and realized I needed to set things right before I meet my maker."

"You're too stubborn to give up the ghost just yet, old man," Sean argued, his tone jovial regardless of underlying shakiness and the lingering wetness in his eyes.

"Goddamn right, I am," Mr. Fox grumbled. "The wife told me I'm not allowed to go first. Said she can't live without me. Don't know what I ever did to deserve that woman's love."

"She's the best," Sean agreed, his tone still broken.

Mr. Fox nodded and glanced around our small circle. "I'm happy for *all* you boys finding your soul mates. Hang on tight because life is short. You never know when your time will be up."

A warm, damp hand slid into mine as Sean ambled off with his dad toward Micah and the rest of their small family.

My heart ached in the best way possible having gotten to hear in person the one reconciliation I'd never expected.

Gave me hope that Landon's father might eventually see the light too.

Speaking of...

"Hey." I turned and kissed Landon's temple as he tucked against me, soaking my hip with his wet swim shorts. "How was the water?"

"Cooling. You ought to come in."

"Maybe later." I glanced over to find one of Kellen's

sons on Callum's shoulders, playing chicken with his twin atop JJ. Their laughter, smiles, and shrieks filled me with happiness, and I hugged Landon tight.

"Sure you guys are ready for a houseful of kids?" Drake asked, turning to better take in the ruckus and spray of water occasionally reaching us.

"Can't wait," Landon replied for both of us, his amber eyes glinting in the sunlight, full of contentment and happiness.

Another late arrival drew attention—Mason and Jasper. They approached and greeted us with handshakes before settling in all cozy against each other, Mason doing the leaning, Jasper while smaller in height and weight, acting as his oak.

Pink flushed Mason's cheeks as he glanced at the men in the pool.

Preston gave him and Jasper a little wave, his face just as red as Mason's.

Drake snorted. "How the hell you were an escort," he said to Mason, "I have no fucking clue, but you seriously need to get over this embarrassment every time you're face-to-face with your old favorite client."

Everyone but Mason laughed, and Kellen clasped his shoulder as though feeling the silver fox's pain.

"For the record *again*, I don't care about my husband's past any more than he does mine," Drake assured both men who'd had a taste of his stepbrother prior to their finally getting together.

It was a few minutes before Mason relaxed, same as always whenever the Elite found family got together to celebrate someone's milestone. The last time had been Drake and Preston's small wedding.

Callum eventually dragged his ass from the pool and

leaned against me as though exhausted from entertaining the younger boys. I wrapped my free arm around his waist to hold him upright as Kellen dove into the deep end to take his place keeping his sons amused.

"You okay?" I murmured against Callum's wet hair.

"Yeah, but beat. Maybe we need to rethink this fostering thing," he said, his voice full of shit.

"Nope!" Landon argued from my other side. "It was your idea, and now my heart is set on it. No take backs. We're going to get right what my parents failed at."

He and his parents were on speaking terms, but there'd been no full reconciliation over the fallout of the potential second shitstorm and his loving two men. While he claimed he was over them, both Callum and I expected a part of him would always hope for understanding and acceptance. We'd made it our task in life to ensure he got every bit of the love and attention he needed from both of us.

I turned to kiss *his* hair, loving that no one looked at us strangely, no one cared about my being in a poly relationship. Even after a year, we were a seamless fit. Sure, we had spats here and there, but it'd been nothing but paradise to be with these two men.

That whole vow to always be honest made shit easier, that was for damned sure.

"They didn't fail," I argued what I'd said before. "And I'm not angry with them. Consequences aren't all bad."

"Yeah, I know," he said with a sigh.

We'd all learned that lesson.

Landon's poor choices had led to his meeting Callum then getting caught up in a whirlwind romance with two men he'd only thought attainable in fairytales like those he continued to write.

Callum had become more peaceful and had found acceptance of not being at fault for the ruination of the brother he was still estranged from. Even though he walked free, we were fine with continued distance, considering his record.

Granny had a shit ton of money to blow through and traveled the world without the old ball and chain, as she called her late husband.

And me?

Hell—I was rich beyond measure in every way possible. There was nothing I would change about my life. And there was one man deserving of my thanks.

"You're the glue, you know," I told Callum, pulling his soft smile off Landon, who leaned his head against my left shoulder.

"How do you figure?" He smirked, rubbing his thumb over my lower lip.

"You brought us together on the best vacation ever."

"I thought you said Tuscany last month was your favorite?"

I pursed my lips and pretended to think hard on what I *had* said after purchasing a second home in the hills of central Italy that was surrounded by cypress trees and olive groves. "Pretty much any getaway with the two of you can't be beat. Doesn't matter where we go."

Landon released his hold on me and shoved his way in between Callum and I until we both wrapped our arms around him as we did dozens of times every day.

"Feeling left out, greedy boy?" I asked, snickering at how he rubbed his cheek all over Callum's hard chest.

"Nope. Never. Just needy."

"No big surprise there," I murmured before leaning around his head to kiss Callum.

Someone catcalled, so Landon got in on the action for a quick three-way smooch.

"This right here," I whispered, our foreheads still pressed together, my arms full of warm, wet flesh I'd long since memorized every inch of. "You're all I'll ever need. Love you both so goddamn much it hurts."

"I'm sure we can find a way to take care of that," Landon teased, rubbing his ass against my groin.

"Promise?"

Someone shoved us from behind, and as one, we tumbled straight into the pool, hitting the surface in a tangle of limbs. Cool water washed over my head, and I stood, sputtering, wiping wetness from my face, chest-deep in salt water that was definitely *cooling* as Landon had said.

Drake smirked down at us.

"Asshole," I muttered.

He lifted his beer and started away, but I swung out an arm over the surface of the water and drenched him.

He pulled up and turned, eyebrow raised, mischief in his vivid blue eyes.

"Oh," Preston snickered from behind me as Drake set his beer bottle on the grass. "You're in for it now."

Callum and Landon dove away from me, but I held my ground.

"Bring it," I challenged with beckoning fingers.

Drake let out a caveman-like yell and cannon-balled fully clothed, creating a wave that washed over my head.

I was blessed with two lovers, found family, and friends who cared about me.

Life definitely couldn't get any better.

THE END

About the Author

USA Today bestselling author Lynn Burke is a CrossFit and coffee addict. Her three spawn dictate how often she can be found hunched over her Mac, typing as fast as her fickle muse cooks up hot stories.

You can find more about Lynn at her website: www. authorlynnburke.com

Also By Lynn Burke

Abel's Obsession

Divulging Secrets

Healing Storms

In Between

Reluctant Lumberjack

Resisting his Mate

Billion Dollar Love Anthology

Blood Born Series

Bonds of Worship Series

Dark Leopards MC

Darkest Desires Series

Devil's Outlaws MC

Elite Escort Series

Elite Escorts MM Series

Fallen Gliders MC

Forbidden Obsession Duet

Found by Fate Series

Midnight Sun Series

Missing Link Series

Risso Family Series

Sandy Ridge Series

Sinful Nature Series

Vicious Vipers MC

9 781955 635523